American
Sextet

by Warren Adler

For Lissa and Jonathan

ISBN: 1-59006-010-5

Inquiries: www.WarrenAdler.com

STONEHOUSE PRESS

I

Fiona's heels sank into the soft earth as she moved across the marsh to the edge of the creek. Her thin raincoat offered little comfort against the persistent drizzle that threw a gloomy chill over the gray morning. She heard Cates's shoes making squishing sounds as he followed close behind her toward the two policemen in shiny slickers. Above her loomed the great brownish arches of the Calvert Street Bridge, recently renamed the Duke Ellington Bridge, over which stretched a symmetrical string of lighted globes.

The body rested precariously on the creek's rim against a rocky outcrop that kept it from slipping into the rushing water.

The early April rain had churned up the ground, stripping away the last vestiges of winter and releasing the earth's pungent odors. After being with Clinton, everything seemed good again—colors deeper, odors richer, sounds clearer. He had crept beside her earlier than usual this morning, but she was instantly awake at his touch. She still tingled with the afterglow of having been with him.

Now, beneath the bridge, she slipped and fell on the damp soil, her nostrils tickled by the manurey smell.

"You okay?" Cates asked, offering his hand. She grabbed it, allowing him to lift her. Struggling upward, she felt a tear in her raincoat, covered now with a coat of mud. Her pantyhose had been ripped along the knees. One thing about being a cop, she thought. It was hard as hell on pantyhose.

She let Cates go ahead of her now, guiding the way along the slippery ground to where the body had landed. As they arrived, the policemen pointed their flashlight beams on the sprawled lifeless heap that was once a young woman. They kneeled beside her, studying the body in the play of light. She was blonde, mid-twenties, Fiona guessed.

1

"Makes a mess," one of the policemen muttered as Fiona touched the body, lifting an arm. It wriggled, then, when released, fell like a length of heavy rope. On impact, a jumper became crushed bones in a blubbery bag of bruised flesh. Fiona sniffed as her nostrils picked up the body's odor, the stench of death strong enough to mask any natural competition. One of the policemen handed her an alligator purse.

"I didn't open it," he said. She wondered briefly if he had rifled the wallet. The woman's driver license identified her as Dorothy Curtis, born December 8, 1958. The shock of similarity made her wince. Fiona was also born on December 8, six years earlier. The photo on the license showed a remarkably pretty woman. Fiona bent down again to confirm her identity. Except for the mouth, set irrevocably in a tight-lipped smile, it wasn't easy. The body had hit face first.

Cates stood nearby writing in his notebook. The sound of sirens pierced the air until an ambulance pulled up, not far from where they'd parked. A pair of medic technicians quickly unloaded their gear and started towards them.

"Always seems stupid this way," Cates said, shaking his head, his light brown complexion looking deceptively like a deep tan over caucasian features. His speech was clipped and sounded slightly British: Trinidadian parents, he'd explained to Fiona on their first assignment together. He was resented for that as well. Like her, he was a misfit in their tightly circumscribed MPD world. As the ultimate misfit—the only female in homicide—she was always partnered with those considered out of the mainstream; freaks. Poor Cates. He had the right appendage for getting ahead at MPD, but the color wasn't quite right. The majority of the department was black and the percentage was rising fast. Cates unfortunately didn't precisely fit quite into the prevailing tone. Luther Greene, commander of the Homicide division, who they called the eggplant, had mated them with a special glee verging on malevolence—two square pegs in his gameboard of round holes.

She fingered the handbag's contents: a thin shiny alligator wallet, edged in gold, two fives, three singles, a ring of keys, a compact, lipstick, a perfume vial, a stub from a paycheck. The woman apparently had worked at Saks.

"No note?" Cates asked.

"None."

"Lover's quarrel?"

"Maybe." Fiona noted the woman's alligator shoes. Her white cocktail dress, gooey with mud, still properly covered her body. Peeling the dress upward from the hem, she noticed the policeman's light beam hesitate near the thighs. She motioned his arm upward and the beam followed, showing satin panties that covered a sculpted triangle of jet black hair. There was always a message there, Fiona thought, but what? The medics arrived and she stepped back to let them bag the body and lift it to the stretcher.

"How do you see it?" Cates asked. Because she was his senior he routinely deferred to her, but sometimes his wide-eyed eagerness grated on her. Like Fiona, he was trying hard to make it—and like her, the odds were stacked against him. They had been together only a month, but in that time Fiona had assumed the role of teacher—she felt she had to take the lead if they were going to get anything done. He was also five years her junior, which didn't help. Perhaps that was why her age was beginning to matter. Thirty-two. The child-bearing years left were narrowing. She had made the observation to Clint, whose only response had been stony silence. It was, of course, a stupid thing to suggest to a man who already had a wife and family.

"All the signs of a jumper," she muttered, forcing Clint into the background again.

"If there was a note," Cates said.

Fiona looked at him and shrugged; she hadn't found a note pinned to the woman's dress or any other sign of a personal motive.

Cates's features were smooth and delicate, the skin taut on prominent bones, the eyes set deep with flecks of green in the light brown, the hair like a tight curly cap against his skull.

"They do that," she said. "Sometimes the act itself is a note."

"Aren't people who die like this nearly always suicides?"

"Depends."

"Probably some trouble over a man."

"How would you know?" Fiona said harshly. This was the wrong case for her, she thought, I'm overreacting. Trouble over a man? Again, the image of Clint returned, the man she shared.

Fiona still clutched the alligator handbag, fingering the reptile mosaic as she watched the technicians start back across the marsh. She turned her eyes away when she saw one of them slip, dropping the body into the soggy muck. The dead deserved more dignity than that, she thought. Could love really have caused this? Don't empathize, she warned herself. It's not professional.

The drizzle had turned to fine mist as she and Cates started back to the parkway. She was more cautious now, making sure of each step.

Once in the car, she used a half box of tissues to blot the moisture on her clothes and skin and rub the mud off her shoes and raincoat.

"She sure got dressed up for it," Cates said, starting the car.

"They always do. Sometimes they even fold their overclothes. Or line up their shoes."

"Shiny new panties," Cates muttered, shaking his head. "A dead giveaway."

"So you noticed. You're all prurient."

He laughed appreciatively.

"Keep an open mind. Nothing is as it seems," she said.

"You think she was thrown?"

"Never think with your guts," she said irritably. The eggplant was always putting down her intuition, and along with it, her sex. The eggplant had earned the nickname from the dumb looking vegetable that, like the chief, could be cooked in a thousand ways. Little did he know that detection was an art as well as a science, she'd argued privately. She didn't need to compound the persecution.

"I had a buddy did that," Cates said, "Jumped from the sixteenth floor."

"Trouble over a woman?" she asked innocently.

"A woman?" Again he laughed, and she immediately understood why. Men never committed suicide over a woman. They died in fights over them, but they never deliberately destroyed themselves. Not for a woman.

The thought increased her agitation as Clint surfaced again. Love hurt—it blunted judgment, destroyed instincts.

Forcing concentration, she guessed the time of death at between midnight and five, the horror hours, the time when anxiety replaced reality. They weren't exactly her happiest hours either. She caught Cates glancing at her.

"You okay?" he asked. She quickly looked away, determined to shake her annoyance.

"Rough night?" he persisted. It was harmless small talk, but it was hitting the mark.

"Turn here," Fiona snapped. Cates turned the wheel abruptly, forcing her to sway against the window. In the absence of anything else that could make her feel better, she took comfort in his obedience. They had turned into a side street of townhouses, and Fiona held the woman's license in front of her, comparing addresses.

"That one," she said, pointing to a townhouse situated in the middle of the block.

They looked at each other in a mutual double take as they entered Dorothy Curtis's apartment, struck by the unexpected image—a flash of white, temporarily blinding. The living room was like a cloud bank, with puffs of white everywhere. The over-stuffed furniture, covered with a velvety white material, resembled rows of huge marshmallows. Heavy drapes of white hung from the windows. On the wall was a painting of a field of daffodils breeze-bent against a backdrop of cottony clouds. There was a white artificial fireplace with white birch logs in one corner, before which was a white bear skin.

In the bedroom, also white, were more marshmallow pillows and a platform bed under a mirrored ceiling, surrounded by white stuffed animals: rabbits, teddys, a lion, a Cheshire cat. The bathroom was carpeted and papered in white. There was a shower curtain of what seemed like plastic lace. Even the hardware was antiqued white.

"Looks like a white freak," Fiona said. The woman's white dress tarnished with mudstains troubled her now. It seemed so out of character. This woman should have died of an overdose in a white nightgown, lying on her platform bed with arms crossed over white lilies. The image made her wince.

"What is it?" Cates asked.

She ignored him, resenting his minute inspection. His dependence was too cloying. Looking through drawers and closets, she confirmed her expectations. More white.

"More like Hollywood than Washington," Cates said, moving out of the bedroom.

Once he had gone, she stood motionless, soaking in the room's silence, listening. The broken body in the ravine was totally foreign to this setting. Looking around, her own frazzled image in the overhead mirror caught her attention. There it was, the white room, reversed, and herself, out of place, incongruous, floating upside down.

She longed suddenly to run from the room, return to her own nest and the cluttered familiarity of her bedroom, with its mismatched furniture and its flash of colors, the candy-striped sheets and pillowcases, the jumble of clothes, the throw rugs and straight-backed wooden chair. Clint would be rising now. He always catnapped at her place until it was time for him to go to his office; it was part of their thrice weekly routine. He would leave his wife's warm bed in Cleveland Park, proceed to hers on Connecticut Avenue, let himself in with his own key, and slide in beside her, ready to make love. She was always as eager herself. Sometimes, like tonight, they would have dinner in her apartment, another ritual of their affair.

Tonight, she thought, it could not go on like this. To her surprise the thought soothed her, penetrating the contrived whiteness and flogging her mind back to the job at hand.

"I found this," Cates said, returning to the bedroom.

He held a photograph in a cardboard frame. The woman smiled back at her from a craggy promontory with a blue sky in the background. She wore a small bikini, white, of course, fully revealing a voluptuous figure.

"A knockout," Cates muttered.

"And she knew it," Fiona said. It was a model's pose, blonde hair rippling shoulder length, the cleavage imposing, a flat belly, thighs well turned on slender legs.

"What a waste, to deliberately toss it all away."

"Maybe it wasn't deliberate."

"Maybe," he responded, without conviction. "You really think she got some help?"

Fiona didn't answer, but began rummaging through drawers, looking for traces of a male presence, a telephone book, notes, names. The scent was there but not the source.

"Find anything?" she asked Cates, who was rifling through living room drawers.

"No," he said, looking around the room. "But this place is obviously subsidized."

"Obviously." The feeling of maleness clung to the place like a layer of dust.

"It's around here somewhere," she said. Dorothy Curtis died because of a man. And Fiona FitzGerald was determined to find out why.

They were ordered back to headquarters by noon. Captain Green, a.k.a. the eggplant, had called a meeting of the entire squad and, as usual, he was fuming. Three black teenage girls had been strangled within three weeks, all on Wednesdays, their bodies chucked into trash cans awaiting the sanitation trucks. The press had already dubbed them the "can murders." All three girls were mothers of illegitimate children.

"This ain't Atlanta," he ranted. The *Post* and TV reporters were already pointing up the comparison. The eggplant dreaded being second-guessed by the experts, pushed aside by the FBI or any other enforcement agency. They were always trying to muscle in on his business; he seemed to be fighting constantly for his professional life. It was a sure sign of his incompetence, Fiona thought, all this strident posturing.

Assigning more men to the can murders meant more pressure on her and Cates, whose assignment that week was "routines," which meant checking out all deaths, natural or otherwise, that occurred in the District of Columbia. It was an assignment that rotated within the squad and was, occasionally, the eggplant's method of punishing offenders, real or imagined.

The question that was in everyone's mind was, was the killer white or black? In the MPD such thoughts always came first. The department was very sensitive about its competence. Whenever a murder wave hit, the eggplant became the pressure point of the MPD brass.

"We're missing things," he shouted, banging his fist into his palm. Behind him was a blackboard with a short list of clues. The air in the room was smoke-filled, stifling, and Fiona felt exhausted from her early morning bout with Clint. Her eyelids were like small weights and she fought to keep them opened.

Suddenly Cates jabbed her thigh and she looked up to see the eggplant, his dark face shiny with sweat, glaring at her.

"You see me later, FitzGerald," the eggplant shouted. As always, he needed a scapegoat. Although the rebuke awakened her, it did nothing to help her concentration and she struggled to look attentive. Again the jumper surfaced in her thoughts. Trouble over a man, Cates had said. Was such trouble worth dying for? She shivered, recalling her relationship with Clint.

After the meeting the eggplant, who hadn't forgotten, summoned Fiona into his office. As always, several ashtrays on his desk overflowed with cigarette butts. His black hands gripped the desk's edge, and she was sure his smoldering anger was magnified by her white female face. Office gossip had it that his wife mistreated him. Pussy-whipping, they called it, not that the eggplant could do anything about it—his wife was related to the MPD chief's wife. When under the gun, the poor bastard got it from all sides. But when he dished it out, his victims were carefully chosen. Taking flak from the eggplant had become an accepted part of the job, like leave, pension rights and coffee breaks.

"This case may not be a big deal to you, FitzGerald," he began in a low voice. For appearance's sake, his barbs had to be muted. She was, after all, a double minority, which meant double protection—another source of irritation to the son of a bitch.

"I'm sorry," Fiona said, determined to disarm him. "I was absorbed with the jumper." She felt stupid for being caught drowsing, but she had enough of her own personal pressure and didn't want to deal with the eggplant's problems—not now. The look of smoldering anger didn't subside, and instinctively she knew that any effort to placate him would have little effect.

"No white-assed twat is going to bust morale around here. You don't know what's comin' down. We have an Atlanta here and we've all bought it. They're just looking for a chance to show up us dumb nigger cops."

There it was. "They." The ubiquitous white enemy.

"Why don't you put me on it?" she said brightly, ignoring his mood. Instantly, she knew it was a mistake, like throwing a match on dry tinder.

"Sheet," he said, lifting a cigarette from a pack and shoving it in his mouth. "You like puttin' us down, white princess." The cigarette stuck and bobbed on his lower lip as he spoke.

"No need to get racial," she mumbled, feeling the Irish temperament rise like an expanding bubble in her chest. Cool it, mama, she ordered herself, thankful that he took time out to light his cigarette. Inhaling deeply, he exhaled the smoke through his nostrils, like a black dragon. Her comment was gratuitous—she knew that everything around them was racial by definition.

"I'm gonna bust this fuckin' case before it gets out of hand and I don't need no shit from you." He appeared to have already forgotten her transgression.

"I'm sorry," she said.

Seeing it from his point of view softened her—it was no more personal than usual. Her brief drowse had simply ruffled his dignity.

"This jumper . . ." she said, trying to keep his anger deflected. There were times when he could be quite rational about police business. She avoided his eyes and took out her notebook, using it more as a prop than an aid.

"There may be more to it."

She rattled off details, the absence of a note, or some other tangible sign, the uncommonly neat apartment, her youth, her beauty, her pretty clothes, the lack of any male evidence. His disinterest was obvious.

"I don't need this," he muttered, inhaling again, the cigarette burned down to a nub. Removing it from his lips, he squashed it into the butt pile in his ashtray.

"I know about female jumpers," she said quickly. "It just feels different." Was she fishing for his commitment to further the investigation? He turned away, looking out of his window at the rain-slicked street.

"I'll know more when I get the medical examiner's report." Somehow she was unable to put the matter to rest. The dead woman seemed to be goading her, flaunting her death. Trouble over a man. Clint, you bastard, she cried out to herself. None of them was worth it. She remembered how she had broken up with Bruce Rosen, the congressman. A triumph of will over emotion. Had Dorothy, too, been put to that test and failed?

"Gimme a break lady," the eggplant said.

He was right, of course. Suicidal motivation was for the psychiatrists, not cops. Besides, there was a backlog of naturals. He couldn't spare the manpower for something so inconsequential, having already diverted most of the squad to the can murders. His back was to her now, his shoulders hunched over in frustration. The hell with it, she decided. Who needs this?

When she finally left him she noted that the office was deserted, except for Cates.

"Don't ask . . ." she said.

"I got a make on the jumper."

She shrugged with disinterest. Returning to her own desk, she sat making doodles on a notepad.

"Personnel office at Saks, where she worked. The woman was from a place called Hiram, Pennsylvania. Probably coal country. I called there."

She tried to ignore him.

"I got a next of kin, a second cousin in Hiram, with a real pollack name. Zcarkowiz." He read it aloud and spelled it. "That's her real name as well. Her parents are dead. Apparently all the brothers split. The cousin's an old lady. Won't claim the body."

From the way he hesitated, she could tell there was more. She wanted it to end.

"About a year ago, a newspaperman came through Hiram. Did a piece about unemployment in the mines. *Washington Post*. She left town with him." He hesitated, perhaps noting her indifference. "The cousin still had the clipping. The reporter's name was Martin."

The name meant nothing and she stood up and slapped her notebook shut.

"Don't you see," he said. "I found the man in the woodpile."

She was thinking instead about the man in her own woodpile. The fate of Dorothy what's-her-name had certainly called him to her attention.

Picking up the phone, she dialed Clint's number.

II

Below them, the Potomac slowly flowed eastward, its surface glinting in the high noon sun. The front windows of Jason's Cutlass were open on both sides, catching sparse midsummer breezes.

"Wrong," Nolan said for what seemed like the hundredth time.

Jason Martin continued to press him, his reporter's pad ominously perched on the windshield shelf. He had put it there deliberately, a symbol of his power. Occasionally Nolan held it in his gaze, a rattlesnake he was determined to avoid.

It was a test of wills. A simple question lay at the heart of it. Did someone on the vice-president's staff leak the China grain deal to favored commodity dealers, thereby shooting up the price? No matter how he asked it, backtracked, broke his field, tried every psychological investigative reporter's ploy, Nolan's answer was always some version of "no."

"Speculation doesn't always require information," Nolan said coolly. He was tough and good at capping his exasperation. "Sometimes it's only instinct, wishful thinking."

"Sooner or later, I'll find out," Jason replied. By then, all pretense and subtlety had evaporated.

"It won't wash. The only reason I'm here is to categorically deny it."

"Then why all the secrecy? You could have told me on the phone."

"The meeting was your idea, remember," Nolan said. "I would have said it in my office."

Jason had picked up the vice-president's man three blocks from the Executive Office Building and driven across Memorial Bridge to the George Washington Parkway, where they had pulled onto a promontory. It was all for an orchestrated cloak and dagger effect. It had worked before. He had expected Nolan to suggest that they

13

do their talking outside the car, not that he couldn't bug that conversation as well. It annoyed him that Nolan didn't show a lick of fear.

"We're all clean, Jason," Nolan said.

"Millions were made by the speculators—surely you don't expect me to believe it was a stroke of luck."

"Nothing is ever airtight, Jason. Washington is one big ear. Maybe the Chinese said something."

He wondered if Nolan was softening. His gaze drifted across the Potomac where the great gothic spires of Georgetown University rose in the distance. Without the glass and concrete slabs of buildings around them, the view might have seemed old world, perhaps a hill beside the Rhine.

"The issue," Nolan said, "is whether someone in the vice-president's office profited from the deal. That's the dirt. Without that, there is no story and you know it."

"I'll find it if there is one."

"Good luck."

Jason gunned the motor and swung the car back onto the parkway, barely hiding his annoyance.

He'd been working on it for a month. Up to now, Webster, his editor, had been cooperative, but hadn't let him write a "fishing" story.

"What I'd really like to do is put out the bait," he'd said. "Someone will come forward. It never fails."

"That's assassination by implication," Webster had countered. He'd made it sound as if Jason were bending ethics. They were very touchy about that at the *Post* these days, now that they didn't have any competition to worry about. His instincts told him they were soft-pedaling the real investigative stories. When he had broken the FDA scandal, they'd let him go the distance without any obstacles. But that was four years ago and now he needed this story, needed it badly. Heroes had a short shelf life in this town.

* * *

"Dammit, Nolan, it's another cover-up and you know it," Jason said, knowing that his own exasperation had broken through first. It was going badly.

"You're off the wall, Jason. The guy is sitting pretty for the next election. He doesn't need the headache. Besides, money isn't real power around here."

He's putting me down, Jason thought, wondering why Nolan wasn't the least bit unnerved. Was the *Post* losing its power or was he losing his grip? Or his credibility? They were supposed to shit when the *Post* came smelling around like this. Had he been misled? Earlier, when he had picked Nolan up at the street corner near the F Street Club, he was dead certain he'd found his inside man. It was a gut reaction that hadn't failed him . . . yet.

"This is the eighties, Jason," Nolan said, sighing. "It's different now." Nolan had once been a reporter for the now defunct *Star*. They had covered stories together, but any evidence of the earlier comradeship had now been lost.

"You've really gone over to the other side," Jason said, pulling up in front of the Executive Office Building.

"Good try, Jason," Nolan said as he stepped out of the Cutlass. "But you can't bake bread with horseshit."

The man had played with him. Jason was too unnerved to go to the office. Instead, he drove back to Capitol Hill and mooned about his cluttered apartment, missing Jane and Trey and the old glory. He finished half a bottle of Scotch.

Maybe he had been out to lunch while the rest of the world rolled by, he thought, tossing restlessly on cold, rumpled sheets. Indignation over government corruption was on hold. These days investigative reporters looked for the big story with one eye on book publishing and movie rights and talk show hype instead of concen-

trating on the simple act of going for the jugular. He could have par-
layed his FDA stories in that direction, but had eschewed all offers.

"You're stupid," Jane had told him. More than once.

"I'm an investigative reporter. A newspaperman." When it came
to other writing, he planned to do a big book. *The* novel. But he had
to remain pure as a reporter; it sustained him.

Twisting and turning, he got up finally, finished the bottle of
Scotch and went outside to get the *Post's* bulldog, which he spread
out in front of him at an all night coffee shop. His eye caught a bold
headline just below the fold.

"What's this garbage," he said to no one in particular.

"More coffee?" the man behind the counter asked.

Ignoring him, he read the headline. "Agency Change Suggested.
SEC to SEX." The secretary to the chairman of the SEC was coming
clean—cross-country trips, jets hustling her around the country so
that she could be with her boss, a married man with five kids, a
Catholic. Sexual peccadillos and conflict of interest, the story
implied, citing sexual acts in the SEC private dining room, the
chairman's office, the boardroom table.

It was prurient scandal, pure and simple. The *Post* had bought
the girl's story hook, line and sinker. The poor bastard never had
a chance.

"My God," he whispered, his stomach congealing in a knot, anger
and disgust rising above the alcoholic buzz. He pushed the paper
away from him, paid the check and walked out.

"This is what the eighties are all about," Nolan had told him. And
who would know better than he?

Webster sat behind his desk with both legs curled under him, a
characteristic stance meant to soften the sting of authority. Jason
Martin stood at the opposite side of the desk. Inside the glass wall
he felt he was on exhibit to the entire city room, although the staff
worked busily around them.

Didn't the bastards know he was being heroic? He was standing up for real journalism, not that entertainment pap that was passing for reporting nowadays.

"I'm onto something, Paul," he said, his fingers spread on the polished desk.

"It's only a hunch," Webster said. "We can't commit to hunches."

"What about Watergate? Woodward and Bernstein?"

"It paid off," Webster acknowledged. Not that again. Jason saw the flicker of forced tolerance.

"I need time. More people to work on it. It goes all the way up to the vice-president. Someone is covering up a tips-for-profit scam in his own shop."

"It's a fine line thing. Not a deliberate cover-up."

"Someone in the vice-president's office leaked advance word on the grain deal with China. The commodities market goes bananas and . . ."

"Coincidence. Hunches. Commodities people speculate. You can't pin it on anyone."

"You can if you dig."

"And what will that accomplish? Bring down a vice-president? He can't be responsible."

Jason sucked in his breath, carefully watching Webster's tanned face. The man was into sailing now, investments, trendy company, a new wife.

"Are we losing our balls?" Jason had quickly edited the second person pronoun to the first. "We used to go for the inside story no matter who got it."

"He's innocent," Webster said, shifting in his chair, his pose of tolerance cracking. "I spoke to him."

"You spoke to him?" Jason shot back angrily. He should have guessed—the old school tie. Both same year Yalies. "I thought they were supposed to be our adversaries. Now we're all in bed together."

"I know the man forty years. You use things like that, Jason. I have gut reactions, too. And they've been damned solid all these years. They haven't forgotten Watergate either."

He had him on the defensive. Jason liked that. A man reveals his vulnerability on the defensive.

"This used to be a great newspaper. Now look at us." He pointed to the front page. "Some broad screws the chairman of the SEC and it makes page one."

"It's news whether you think so or not and it sells," Webster said, still tolerant. "The headline was a corker, don't you think?"

"It's not substantive." He had wanted to say "crock of shit," but he'd held back, trying to formulate a more subtle response. "And what if the vice-president were caught with his pants down? Would you print that?"

Webster rubbed his arm. "No question."

"Even if it destroyed him?" Jason pressed.

"Of course. Corruption is corruption. If not us, who?" the editor said, obviously losing patience.

Yeah, Jason thought, whip us with self-righteousness.

"This sex stuff stinks and you know it," Jason countered.

"Sexual corruption is a category, Jason. A man who used his political clout for that is dangerous."

"It's also cost effective. The broad comes in, confesses and it's confirmed. Then she writes a book, shows her box to *Playboy* and sells the movie rights."

"My concern is what makes news, not books and movies. If the mighty fall that's news, especially when they get caught with their pen in the inkwell."

"We never used to cover that shit."

"Where've you been? Maybe twenty-five years ago we didn't, but it's a whole new angle now. Women's rights. The woman cries exploitation. Hell, the big boys know the score. Every time they whip it out, they're playing Russian roulette."

"I think it sucks."

Webster laughed at the inadvertent pun.

"It's not my kind of journalism. I'm an investigative reporter, Paul. That's the way we built this damned rag."

"You're a hunter, Jason. Problem is we've given you big guns to play with. When you carry one on a hunt you look for prey. But it's my job to dole out the bullets. If it was up to you guys, you'd shoot up anyone in sight." Jason looked up at Webster, who blinked first, turning his eyes away.

Webster had changed, Jason thought. Grown soft. He had a point, though. The paper *was* overweight with reporters who itched to topple the guy on top, like himself. Wasn't that what Washington journalism was all about?

"Look, Jason. Cool it for a while. We don't manufacture these scandals. They happen and we report them. You're right about one thing, though. The other kind is expensive. Requires too much checking. That phony Pulitzer thing hurt us more than you think." He paused, studying Jason for a moment. "Look, on the V-P thing I think you're wrong. Call it gut reaction, judgment. Still," he said, pressing his chest, "it's mine to make. I suggest you let that anger run on idle for a while.

"I can't," Jason muttered, thinking of Jane, who had said the same thing three months before. Then she went back home to Indiana, taking Trey.

"It'll destroy you," Webster warned him. Jason wondered if he knew about him and Jane.

"We're just a glorified *National Enquirer* these days, Paul. And I'm not the only one who thinks that."

"Take it easy, Jason," Webster said, obviously wanting to end the conversation on a high note. "You've earned your stripes around here. You shook up those buggers in the FDA. It's just that this one won't fly. That doesn't mean there won't be others. Let it sit for a while. Remember, there's a financial angle to this as well. We're still a business and I've got to juggle a lot of balls."

"It's a fucking sellout just because you know the man. It clouds objectivity." It was absolutely the worst accusation one newspaperman could make against another.

Webster untangled his feet and stood up, lifting his hands palms forward. A flush of anger rose in his cheeks.

"That's it, Jason. You're pushing."

Looking into the city room, Jason saw a few faces turn towards them. Sweat began to roll down his side.

"I'm sorry. It's just . . ."

"I do understand, Jason."

It was maddening not to control one's destiny. Contrition seemed his only choice. Or he could walk. Hell, the *Post* was still the only game in town. Webster loosened up, sat down again and handed Jason a memo.

"We've budgeted a piece on the Pennsylvania coal situation. Big guys gobbling up the little guys. Forcing unemployment until things shake-out. Venal big business stuff."

"But away from town." He was being patronized now and it galled him.

"You got it, Jason. No one can do it up brown like you. Worth two in a series. Anyway, you can still be angry."

"Coal," Jason said, looking over the memo. "Most of the mines are owned by the oil companies. They advertise. Suppose I offend them?"

"Fug 'em. The more we shit on them, the more they love it. Besides, they have no place else to go."

Neither have I, Jason thought, turning to leave. "Who knows," he said sarcastically, "maybe I'll find a juicy sex angle."

"So much the better."

The meeting over, Jason walked quickly through the city room, speaking to no one. What he needed now was a goddamned drink.

Alone in Art Smart's motel on route 63 on the outskirts of Hiram, Jason pounded out his story on his Coronamatic. Beside him, amid the clutter of cigarette butts, was a spiral notebook filled with scribbled notes which he checked periodically for correct spellings. Goddamned oil companies. They really were buying up the mines. An elite few controlling everything. Bastards, he muttered, pulling out the last page of copy. They had no right. After he'd revised and polished it, he lay on the bed and tried to calm himself. Jane came to mind, only making it worse.

"You Martins," she'd once remarked, "are one breed of angry, frustrated men. When are you going to realize you can't remake the world, Jason?" It had started out as a mere lover's quarrel when they were at Columbia together, sharing a room above a fish store on Columbus Avenue. Big Jake, his father, was a burnt-out case working on the copy rim of the *New York Daily News*. He wrote catchy headlines, mostly to cop the ten dollar prizes for booze money since his paycheck was sent directly to his wife.

"Why is he so angry?" Jane would ask.

"They screwed him over."

Her confusion later gave way to exasperation. Jane never did understand the chemistry of pride mixed with indignation. Worse for her, it was evident in their son, Jason III, who they called Trey. Luckily, the boy was old enough to handle himself and proved a source of pride for Jason, despair for his mother. She actually thought that by separating father and son, she would be able to change that difficult mixture. Time and patience, he knew, would give him his revenge—one could never escape from the genes.

"Just be sure to keep an eye on the boys upstairs," Big Jake had always warned him. "You're just chattel to them."

Someday, Big Jake told everybody, he would write "the" book, a novel, one of great truth. He had died with the promise on his lips.

"Your old man's brilliant," people told Jason, "a genius," although no one could explain in what way, except that under the influence he was remarkably articulate, a barroom performer. His tongue never slurred. Eloquence would pour out in a barrage of eclectic quotations, bits of esoteric knowledge on every conceivable subject from mathematics to botany to poetry.

"Impotence. That's what it is," Jane had concluded finally. She had meant the whole spectrum of his father's psychology, not just his sexuality, which she could not have known. Yet in the way his parents lived in their cluttered Jackson Heights apartment there was a nagging thread of truth in what she'd said. His mother had dried up early and swollen-bellied Big Jake rarely got to bed sober.

"It's not going to happen to me," Jason had promised her. "I'm really going to write that book."

"Sure, Jason. Sure."

Jane never tired of analyzing him, basing her insights on undergraduate psychology courses. It grew more relentless over the years until, near the end, it became a constant barrage.

"You're just trying to get even," she would say. "That's what it's all about."

"For what?" By then, the conversation had become a painful ritual that repeated itself over and over again.

"For Big Jake, for his failure, for the injustices in the world, for everything."

Even Jason's success in ferreting out corruption in the FDA met with Jane's stony praise.

"Feel better?"

"I feel great."

She was surprisingly gentle when they finally parted, knowing that setting him adrift after a dozen years of nesting, leaving him no place to fly home to, no body to be near, no child to love, would unsettle him more than her. She had been right. Without the family anchor he drifted, just like his father. He bled for mankind, not for men. It was a journalist's minefield. Life was unjust. Power corrupted. Big people hurt little people. He knew that deep inside of him, he had the capacity to love. The problem was drawing it out of himself, showing it to others. Knowing that only made him more angry.

"I'll change," he'd promised, another part of the ritual, knowing it lacked conviction. Secretly, he had tried. He had stretched the fuse as far as it would go. Even analysis, which she had suggested, wouldn't have saved them. He knew his own ingredients, his chemistry. He *did* want to get even and he could make up a thousand reasons why. Still, he reasoned, how would it have made a difference?

Once she was gone, it was losing Trey that had hurt the most. His son! God, had he been happy to hear the doctor's announcement. A son. A lifetime of hope and aspirations had been invested in that boy from the moment of birth. All those dreams of immortality that went through his mind . . . Conception and pregnancy weren't only a woman's game, he thought bitterly. And fatherhood. How could she have taken that away as well?

He got up and reread his copy, annoyed that his professionalism demanded that he tell both sides. The fact was that the oil companies would actually make it better for the miners, whose occupation was grim at best. Their work was, quite literally, the pits—an exercise in self-flagellation. Even the towns that grew up beside the shafts reflected the bleak, joyless gloom of the underground caverns. Rows of dreary houses, bars covered with imitation stone and cheerless orange neon; the inevitable church steeples, some with odd Byzantine touches that reflected Eastern Europe's remembered influence. At least at night you couldn't see the slag heaps.

He phoned in his story, took a cold shower, dressed in jeans and T-shirt, the local uniform of summer night life, and walked along the highway toward the flashing neon of "Johnny's Roadhouse Go-Go Bar." Like all things in Hiram, it was an anachronism, maybe fifteen years behind the times.

Squinting into the smoke, the smell of stale beer in the air, he went in. A jukebox blared a noisy rock tune. In the South, the clientele would be considered redneck. Here the necks seemed more than figuratively coated with black grime. Every male along the bar had nails filled with black half moons. He made fists to hide his odd cleanliness and ordered a brew, served up straight in cold bottles. It seemed a badge of male dishonor to drink from a glass. Even the few women present drank from bottles.

Above the bar, standing on a precarious wooden platform, a go-go dancer in a tiny beaded skirt and bra bounced her tits and hips in time with the music, her face as bored as the customers were eager. It was late, nearly one, and the alcoholic level of the blood was high, reflected in the cacophony of high-pitched voices.

He ordered a couple of rounds of rye doubles to go with the beer, which came in over-sized shot glasses. He rarely drank rye, but Scotch seemed almost effeminate in this atmosphere.

As the crowd thinned, the music grew louder. The booze drew him deeper into himself, into that recessive pool of anger and self-pity.

By two A.M. the dwindling crowd seemed to develop a strange air of expectation. He noted that the neon light had been turned off and heavy canvas coverings had been pulled over the windows. He noted, too, that those who were left bellied up to the bar, a mixed bag of all ages, including a grizzled toothless gent who could barely keep his head up.

"Twenty bucks to stay," the bartender said. He was built like a slab of stone with bulging neck muscles and an ample belly that hung over tight-belted pants.

Without curiosity he took a twenty from a roll of bills in his hip pocket and pushed it forward.

Suddenly music exploded in the room and the lights went low except for one above the rickety little stage, on which a young blonde woman in a white bikini stood, feet astride. Ruffling her hair, she twitched her tight smooth full rump, swaying to the music with uncommon grace, obviously different from the girls before her.

Bending forward, thrusting out her buttocks, she rolled down her panties, showing tight perfect globes. There seemed to be a simultaneous swallow in the crowd, the sound of a gulp, louder than the music. Naked from the waist down, the woman unloosed her bra then straightened, showing the proud posture of youth.

When she finally turned, the men applauded. He did the same, less out of lust than admiration. The woman had the face and carriage of a junior league hostess. Her hair cascaded in a perfect ruffled line. Even her cheap makeup couldn't hide the strangely patrician aura about her. Her mouth was set in a painted smile above an upward thrust cleft chin over her long, swanlike neck.

In the icy white light, her body had no edges. High tipped nipples jutted upward from the rosy centers of her full breasts. Her belly was flat with a button that seemed to wink like an eye in step with her gyrations. Below was a dark curly bush, the upper part of which had been shaved into a heart's shape.

"My little valentine," he chuckled.

The men were uncommonly silent, lost in private fantasies.

"Makes a dead man hard," a hoarse voice said beside him. Jason agreed completely, feeling his own tumescence begin.

The girl performed an exhibit more than a dance, but that seemed okay with the crew that watched, in fact anything would have been okay with them; she was like an angel that had simply descended from outer space. He wondered if he were fantasizing himself, embellishing the woman's charms with his own overheated imagination. He had been womanless for quite awhile now. Even before she'd left, Jane had withdrawn herself and occasionally he experienced a "nocturnal emission," something that hadn't happened since he was an adolescent. It always disgusted him, reminding him of his joyless existence and stimulating his self-pity.

Watching the girl in his drunken state, he became convinced she was throwing out a special scent, sending him a personal message. He ordered two more rye doubles in quick succession.

He watched in awe, inspired by the awakening desire in himself. Still, his reporter's instinct nagged at him. How had this lovely woman come to this place? Was he investing her with a mystique that didn't exist, something dredged up from his own intense yearning? He persisted in questioning his reaction to the woman—it was the curse of the journalist. He had to hack it to the bone.

His excitement grew and he wondered if the others felt as he did. Even the old man had ceased his nodding, a thin smile lighting up his unkempt whiskered face.

Not only me, he told himself, his journalist's mind quickly flipping the coin of logic. The men were ready for it, conditioned. How many would rush home and finish it with their blubbery, protesting wives?

The music's end was a signal to the bartender, who flicked the light, darkening the stage and the woman disappeared. The spectators settled up, emptied their glasses, and filed out into the night.

"One for the road." He signaled the bartender, who hurried over and poured.

Jason caressed the glass as the bartender mopped the bar clean. He felt his stomach tighten as he mustered the courage to say what had to be said. Emptying his glass, he felt the spur of sudden inner heat and the drunken illusion of courage.

"She do private performances?"

The man scowled, looked up for a moment, then went back about his mopping.

"That's her business," he said. He looked at Jason's empty glass, an unmistakable gesture of termination.

"I'll lay a hundred on you."

"On me?"

"You know what I mean," Jason said. For him, it was totally off the track, as if he was suddenly not in charge of himself. What the hell am I doing?

"And a hundred for her." He seemed to be saying it in another language, another voice. He took out his roll and put it on the bar. Like in the movies, he thought. Choreographed machismo.

"Hey Dot," the bartender called out in a booming voice. There was silence, then a rustle behind the walls of bottles. She came out from a doorway in tight jeans and T-shirt.

"He wants to give you a C," the bartender said, not mentioning his own stake in the enterprise. She came closer. Such close proximity did not shatter the illusion. She inspected Jason and smiled, seeming childlike, innocent. If there was a hardness in her, it didn't show.

"I'm Jason Martin," he said awkwardly, clearing his throat.

"I told him it wasn't my business," the bartender said quickly, suggesting to Jason that there was nothing more between them. Jason was thankful for that.

"My boyfriend's in the mines 'till five," she said hesitantly, betraying her interest. A part of himself was disgusted. She looked toward the bartender.

"What's your business is your business," he said, clearly anxious to close.

"I'm just down the road at Smart's," Jason pressed. "Leaving tomorrow. Just passing through."

Surely it's not her first time, he told himself, but she seemed so guileless. Was she that good an actress? Or was it natural? That was too much to hope for.

"I have to pick him up at five," she said, apologetically. A battered clock on the wall read 3 A.M. Fifty bucks an hour, he thought. More than I make. She seemed to be watching him closely.

"Where you from?" It was the first slight crack in the illusion, the first hint that her junior league facade wasn't real. He shook off the thought. He needed her. Needed her now. But why? He was following a lead, he told himself.

"Washington, D.C.," he said.

"Gosh."

This had to be the real thing, he told himself. He couldn't remember the last time he'd heard "gosh," especially from a woman.

"You ever met the President?"

He couldn't believe it, nodding finally.

"Gosh," she said again.

He slapped the bar and gathered his bills in a fist. Pausing in his mopping, the bartender winked at him.

"I'll be a minute," she said, hurrying off. He watched her move away in her tight jeans.

"He's a jealous bastard, her boyfriend. Better be careful."

Jason peeled off two fifties, putting them in the man's hammy hand. His stubby fingers closed quickly and he slipped them into a side pocket.

"I don't know from nothin'. I'm supposed to be watching out for her."

"I won't hurt her," he muttered. Man's greed could not be overestimated, he thought. And his ability to corrupt.

She came back looking neat and freshly scrubbed, a tiny hint of lipstick, like a kid ready for her first date.

"I walked," Jason said.

"I'll take Jim's pickup."

"You crazy, Dot," the bartender said.

"Better not," she replied, after a hesitant frown.

On the road, he walked beside her, listening to the sounds their shoes made on the gravel. Her high heels gave her walk an uncommon stiffness. They seemed like ordinary lovers on a warm summer night.

"You do this much?" he asked.

"Do what?"

She hadn't even broken stride. It was a novice's inevitable question, as if he had to be genuinely attracted in order to make the transaction palatable. He let it pass.

A canopy of stars was overhead, the road deserted, the air heavy with the scent of wild honeysuckle. He was thankful that Art Smart's neon was turned off. Silently she walked beside him, like a trained puppy. He reached out and took her hand; her fingers returned the pressure. He felt wanted. The tide of anger receded as he unlocked the door and let her into the room.

"Don't," he said as she flicked on the overhead light revealing the disarray. The bed was mussed and dirty underwear was strewn on the floor. A chair in the corner was piled with sweat-stained shirts and stray socks. He felt embarrassed by his untidiness until she turned off the light.

"You a writer?" she asked, having noticed his typewriter.

"Newspaperman."

The "gosh" again.

He lit a cigarette and sat cross-legged on the bed, kicking off his shoes.

"I write for the *Washington Post*. Doing a story on the mines."

"The mines? That's boring."

She started to undress, unzipping the fly of her jeans and stepping out of them. The tumescence was instantly triggered again. She lifted her T-shirt.

"You're a remarkable beautiful woman," he said, feeling the pulse in his throat.

"You want to see me dance?" she asked.

"I saw that."

"It's fun," she said. "Feels good, too."

"You like showing . . . yourself?"

"Sure. Men like to look at me," she said proudly, rolling down her panties and turning to exhibit herself.

"Come here." He could barely speak; his breath was short in his excitement.

She moved forward, standing close to the bed, until he was a hairsbreadth away from her breasts. Reaching with his tongue, he licked her nipples, first one, then the other. They hardened instantly.

"I wish I could gobble you up." He had never said that to anyone before. Against his cheek, as he caressed her, he felt her heart beating rapidly. At least she wasn't indifferent, he thought.

"Undress me," he said. He was surprised at his tone. It was a command. She obeyed, tugging at his pants. When he was free of them, she bent over him, caressing his throbbing erection with her breasts.

"You feel good?" she asked.

He nodded his head appreciatively.

"What about you?" It would simply be too much to ask for.

"Love it," she said. "The best . . ."

Is this what joy means? He was sure it was.

She was tucked in the crook of his arm, fitted there as if her body were clay. Along with his explosive pleasure his anger had dissipated, leaving him tranquil. It was an uncommon sensation for him and he felt transformed—almost happy. He breathed in the sweetness of her flesh while his fingers caressed her smooth haunches.

"6.7 on the Richter scale," he told her when they lay quietly together. Her passion had surprised him as well. Jane hadn't given him much mutuality, especially not after the first few years. Before Jane, other women had offered quick pit-stops. But this was different.

"Who?" she responded, confused.

He let it pass.

"What do you want?" he said suddenly. It had been there all along, the quintessential question. It bothered him to want to know.

"Want?"

She was alert, not drowsing. During their lovemaking, a rim of perspiration had burst on her skin. It had cooled now, a delicious cool. Against his flesh, hers was like a compress to a bruise.

"I mean what do you want to do with your life?"

"Gosh."

"You always say that," he teased. It was not meant to hurt, nor did it. She seemed awed by life. Was she a true innocent or an outstanding dissimulator? This wasn't just a woman. She was like a dream materialized.

"Dress up. Look pretty. Be happy. Make other people happy," she said. She was silent for awhile, then lovingly patted his sex again. Why was he asking "big" questions, expecting "big" answers. She was just a pretty wildflower growing in the slag heaps. Why was he romanticizing her?

"All in white," she said. "I want everything to be white. Clean." He could understand that.

"And money," she whispered. The stereotyped dream injected a slice of reality he didn't appreciate and he tried to ignore it.

"You live with . . . what was his name?"

"You mean Jim? Yeah."

"Why don't you marry him?" It was, he realized, a ridiculous question. Pay your money and take your pleasure. Stop trying to give this toy a life.

"Marry Jim? He got a wife. Five kids."

"Why do you stay with him?"

"He's good to me. That's the most important thing."

"You don't have a family?"

"Over in Hiram. An aunt. My parents died. Three brothers in the Navy. I never see them." She sighed, thinking of the early misery.

"That it?"

She shrugged her body against his. That's a history? he thought. So dry and empty.

"What do you do with your days?" He supported himself on one elbow, looking down at her face, a perfect oval, her hair mussed as if by design.

"I used to work in a store. Then a beauty parlor." She thought about it some more. "Do up my hair. Watch TV. Jim and me. We both work nights." She looked up at him and smiled. "We do this a lot."

"Just like this?" It was a deliberate injection of reality. He had begun to believe the illusion of her caring.

"I'm going to buy him a birthday present with the money."

His money! Used for another man. The idea destroyed the illusion completely.

"Would you have done it without that?" he asked stupidly.

She looked up at him, her eyes shining, like great saucers.

"Might," she said, stroking his cheek. "But Jim takes care of me, and I make him happy."

Her convoluted reason defied logic.

"Well, I'm getting my money's worth," he said, kissing her deeply, sucking her soft smooth tongue. Reaching out, she caressed him and he hardened swiftly. She moved under him until he was inside her again, her eyes closed in concentrated pleasure. She lifted her knees, digging her insteps into his sides, grasping his buttocks, pushing him deeper. She emitted a low moan, like a kitten meowing. Soon his body erupted in excruciating joy. This, he knew, was ecstasy.

"You happy?" she whispered later.

Beyond imagination! But he said nothing, afraid he was only dreaming.

When he awoke, he was surprised to discover that he had drowsed and was still connected to her. Her breathing was so shallow, he had put his ear against her mouth to hear it, reassured by the tiny cool wafts. In the darkness, the air-conditioner purred. Something, he knew, had awakened him and he listened for a break in the night sounds. Slivers of light had begun to poke through the drawn blinds.

It was too late when he realized what it was. The door crashed open and grimy rough hands were pummeling him. Fighting off the attacker, he jumped and tripped. Then he felt an overbearing pressure, a sweaty malignant human form, pinning him to the floor, heavy blows sinking into his face and body.

"Stop, Jim!"

She hadn't screamed, nor panicked. The sweaty miner now had Jason's arm in a pretzel twist and was pulling it upward. The pain was agony. Turning, he saw a fist fly out and swat her back to the bed like an annoying fly. Undaunted, she came back again, pulling at the arm that was inflicting his punishment.

Loosening his grip, the man slipped off of him to concentrate on the girl, punching her in the midsection and the face.

"Are you crazy? You'll kill her," he shouted in disbelief. He got up unsteadily, somehow finding the strength to pull him off her. Apparently, his anger was spent. Lowering his fists, he watched the girl slowly move her arms, raised in self-protection. A blue nob was rising on her cheekbones and blood trickled down her nose.

Grimy with coal dust and unshaven, the man turned and inspected Jason's nakedness. His face broke into a sardonic smile. Oozing sweat, he filled the room with his sour, unwashed odor.

"Cunt." he hissed, looking at her, but his animal anger was drained.

"He gave me a hundred, Jimbo," she said softly. Her voice was clear, without a whimper or a trace of judgment. "I was going to get you a present."

"You didin ask," he said harshly, showing the true core of his discontent. "And you didin pick me up."

"I fell asleep."

"Sheet," he said, clearing his throat and spitting on the floor.

Jason hadn't yet given her the money. And now his reactions were confused—the trip from paradise to hell had been too abrupt.

"You let him beat you like that?" he asked quietly. The man turned to him and sneered.

"He didn't mean any harm," she said, standing up now. In the quickening daylight, he could see the redness of her flesh where he'd pummelled her.

"I tole you," the man said, pointing a finger at her nose.

She lowered her head like a punished child. This is incredible, Jason thought, like the ritual of some foreign tribe.

"I ain't takin' you back no more," he said, waving a finger, the nail topped with its black half moon symbol. Then, as quickly as he came he left, leaving them staring after him, frozen, naked figures. They heard him gun the motor of the pickup angrily. Tires squealed and the truck sped off.

After he'd gone, the girl slipped into the bathroom, leaving the door ajar. He saw her clean up her puffed face, then step into the shower.

Sitting on the edge of the bed, he tried to understand this new spectrum of emotions. Her docility blunted his compassion. Was it some kind of environmental aberration? The area itself had a burned out feel about it, a sense of futility and resignation. Not at all like Washington, with its frantic striving, its ambitious arrogance, its self-serving subterfuge. There was something about this place that was raw and basic.

She came out of the shower wrapped in a towel, her hair moist and glistening, wearing her wounds with disinterest. She seemed devoid of pride or vanity and he viewed her like some new anthropological discovery.

"Did he ever do that before?" Jason asked.

"Never." She paused thoughtfully and shrugged. "Maybe he's telling me it's time to split."

"Isn't that a strange way of saying it?"

"I guess," she said.

She curled up on the bed and fell into a deep sleep, her face immobile as if all memory of the past few minutes had been obliterated.

Sometime later the telephone rang, jarring him out of his own deep sleep.

"You up?" the voice said. It was Barrows, an assistant editor.

"Up now," he groaned. The girl beside him didn't stir. He shook his head, remembering. His pained shoulder told him it definitely was not a dream.

"Your piece," Barrows said. He wasn't one for small talk. "Too unbalanced. You say there's money up there now that oil companies are taking over." He waited in silence, refusing to fill the gap. "So why the absence of hope?"

"Hope." He blinked and looked at the mouthpiece.

"You said there's more dough coming in. Then why is it so bleak and hopeless?"

"It's the work. The darkness. The pits." He realized he was incoherent.

"King Coal is coming back. Where's the dancing in the streets?"

"I called it like I saw it," he said defensively, the old anger returning. When you're out of favor, the vultures like to pick at the carcass. He took refuge in the thought. They were edging him out, he decided, culling the ranks of the disgruntled.

"Don't get paranoid. I'm trying to be constructive. We're rewriting. I'm the salvage team."

He felt the blood beat in his head. Barrows was an editor on the national desk, a company man. "You? Don't touch a goddamned word. You'll mangle it."

"Watch it, Martin, your hotshot days are long gone."

"Shove it up your ass."

"Listen, wise guy." He could hear Barrows's heavy breathing and wished it would stop. "The word's out on you. If you got a complaint, take it up with Webster. Hell, I'll do it for you."

"You do that." The mention of Webster inflamed him even more. "And don't touch one word of that copy or my name comes off the by-line."

"Big deal. Your name on a story doesn't mean shit anyhow," Barrows said, clicking off. Prima donna! The insult rang in his ears, knowing that Barrows would indeed tell Webster. It was all changing anyhow, he told himself. He lay back, watching the ceiling, seeing its flaws and flakes. The focus had changed. They were into other things now, trivia. Who boffed whom? That wasn't reporting. Remembering, he looked at the girl, curled like a fetus, oblivious to his rage.

"They want that kind of trivia," he hissed, considering her sensuous form, "bet you could give them a snootful." He patted her bare arm, the idea slowly taking shape, growing inside him. She didn't stir.

III

Fiona drew the draperies, then lit the double candles in their creamy Irish glass holders, a gift from her mother years ago. Being Irish, according to her, required the possession of Irish things and this glass was one of them. She had made a pâté from a recipe in a French cookbook and bought a loaf of French bread and a good Bordeaux for the steak au poivre. Asparagus with hollandaise sauce was boiling in a plastic bag. The table was set in her two place Irish china bought piece by piece, placed carefully on the tablecloth of Irish lace, still faintly camphory from its long slumber in a bottom drawer. Lord knows there was little enough romance in this life, she told herself, composing an image of Clint in her mind, a face pink and smile-crinkled under a cascade of prematurely gray, curly hair. She was beyond guilt now, eschewing sorrows and self-pity, taut with expectation. Nor did she care what subterfuge he used to free his Monday night. That wasn't her business. The memory of Dorothy Curtis had prodded her. Tonight was high noon.

The mind computed its own rationalizations. She had never considered herself a mistress in a technical sense. Not as she was now, the lover of a married man, Clinton Chase. Gather ye rosebuds while ye may, she had concluded finally, when it became evident that she was, all protestations notwithstanding, hooked.

She met him as she had met all her men in the last few years, through an investigation. The reverse twist was that he had been investigating her investigation. He had worked then for the *Detroit News*, Washington bureau. To make matters more steamy, she detested having to do her work under the scrutiny of media people, unless she was passing information for a specific purpose. It inhibited her. Besides, all media dealings were covetously usurped by the eggplant. Because it was a Detroit paper, she decided to go along with it. Anyway, she had learned, it was one of his last assignments. He was about to accept an appointment as undersecretary of transportation, in charge of public information.

The case involved a young man, son of a prominent Detroit lawyer, who had run over a prostitute with whom he had just had sexual relations in his car. He was drunk as well. It was purely accidental, but it made a juicy story for Detroit. To make matters worse, a legal curtain had descended, engineered by Daddy's money and, as she knew, her report constituted the only real unvarnished truth. The girl was a teenage prostitute who was also a drug addict.

Clinton had dogged the eggplant for two days and he had ducked the man with equal persistence. Drugs and prostitution did not reflect proudly on the police force. Nor was there a mystery to be solved or glory to be had. When Clinton put pressure on the Chief, the Chief put pressure on the eggplant, who put pressure on Fiona.

"You go," he ordered her.

"Me?"

"Yeah. Only watch your mouth."

She met him at the Regency Hyatt, her first mistake. She would have been better off meeting him in the ugly anteroom that served as an interrogation spot for suspects. Windowless and stinking of stale smoke and fear, the room itself always gave her the upper hand. But the hotel cocktail lounge, dark and cool with its lush ambience, designed for salesmanship and seduction, caught her off guard, softening her up for what she would later refer to as the romantic kill.

Not that he was consciously seducing her. He was professional to a fault.

"His father is up for a federal judgeship."

"It's the son, not the father."

"I know," he said. "I have two myself."

The remark further disarmed her. Or was it the chemistry of the man himself, that shock of curly gray hair? Almost from the beginning, she wanted to shove her fingers through it. He reminded her of Bruce. Was she destined always to be attracted to the same type of man?

"The kid got drunk. He picked up a floozy then ran her over. Pure accident. What has that got to do with the father?" She was oddly defensive.

"I spoke to the man. He blames himself."

"Then he's a fool."

"He blames himself anyway."

"Only because it hurts his chances. Bad publicity. I know the disease."

"Hey," he said. "I know the guy. He really loves the boy."

"I thought newspapermen are supposed to be neutral."

He shrugged and emptied his glass. "There's no law against compassion." Behind the words, she caught his vulnerability, drawing her interest. She saw, too, that he hadn't bargained for the intimacy.

"I've never been a parent," she said, sipping her martini.

"I owe it to the guy not to make it seem lurid. We all give our kids too much. He had a car, too much pocket money."

"Are you talking about him . . . or yourself?"

"Generally. As a father."

He'd made her uncomfortable. Maybe she was getting too hard, too indifferent. As if to compensate, she spelled out the facts again.

"Now who's to blame?" she said when she had finished. By that time, too, her martini had disappeared. "The girl had thrown away her life, walking a treadmill to hell. All the boy was looking for was a thrill." Her anger was disturbing—something about the man had touched her, shaken her.

"Will it really hurt his chances?" she asked.

"Yes."

"But that's unfair."

"What's that got to do with it?"

He had put away his notebook and ordered them another round.

There was a long silence as she felt his gaze, like a warm tide, lap over her. The feeling, although long dormant, was a familiar one. Her business was finished. She knew she could get up and leave, refuse the second martini, run like a bunny. She stayed, although she made an attempt to blunt the onslaught.

"Aren't you going to ask?" she said in an attempt to ungrapple their greedy mutual stares.

"Ask what?"

"Why a cop."

"Is that what I was going to ask?"

"They all do."

Her guard was down by then. She felt foolish and afraid, open and vulnerable. Does it happen like this sometimes? She hadn't the will to unlock her eyes from his. Her heart was pumping furiously. Watching him, she sensed the mystery of attraction.

Her mind told her to be clinical. Was he a widower, divorced? At her age, she could confront that kind of second choice. I won't ask, she decided. By then it was too late.

A few days later, he invited her for dinner. They went to a restaurant in Prince George's County, far off the beaten track. He's married, she realized, noting the restaurant's darkness and his nervous glances as they entered. But she was too far gone, even then.

His knees were pressed against hers and they held hands under the table.

"This is utterly absurd," she told him.

"You're telling me."

They had lots of wine and talked a great deal about their childhoods. Everything they told each other seemed important. She discussed her parents.

"I am my father's child," she told him, explaining how for three generations the FitzGeralds were in the "farces." "Wrong sex. Wrong town. But right occupation."

"And your old man? Is he proud of you?"

"He'd never admit that. But he doesn't have to. I can tell how his eyes light up when he sees me."

"So do mine."

He was from the Upper Peninsula of Michigan, a country boy. He had started on a weekly paper.

"Will you be happy in your new job?" she asked.

"Happy?" he mused. "What's that?"

He drove her back to her apartment in his car and they grappled with their first kiss in the front seat.

"You're not coming up," she said firmly. His kisses had sobered her.

What followed was a kind of trench warfare. As soon as she had gained one trench, she crawled out of it to another.

"I will not have an affair with a married man," she told him, although she couldn't resist meeting him for drinks or an occasional dinner.

"And I don't want to subject you to that."

"So there. It's settled."

"But I love you."

"Don't say that. Save it for your wife."

"I don't love her."

"Then why do you stay with her?"

"Because I'm responsible."

"Well, so am I. I'm responsible to myself."

"How do these things get started?" he had asked.

"You started this one."

"I was only doing my job."

"What do you think I was doing?"

The questioning stimulated their excitement. He called her at odd hours and they went over it again, protesting their involvement, until finally she had let him come up for a final parlay.

"For a cop, this is very undignified," she said, when within seconds of entering her apartment, he was undressing her in the foyer.

When he felt her gun he stopped momentarily, and without a word, she undid it herself.

Later, nestled against his naked body, she told him: "This doesn't mean we're involved." It was a refrain that was to last the first few weeks.

Under the circumstances, the logic was convoluted. At first, she chalked it up to a powerful sexual attraction between them. The uncontrollable force that transcended logic and caution. They were certain it would burn out quickly. It didn't.

"I wish I were a courageous man," he told her. By then, he had outlined his life. He was a Midwesterner in outlook and spirit. The simple verities were programmed into him. "Home. Hearth. Church. Family. That's me."

"And girlfriend on the side," she pointed out.

"I'd never done this before."

"That's supposed to be my line."

The morning trysts were his idea—it left him free of suspicion. At least he was honest, she assured herself, going along with the arrangement.

They settled into an odd-hour affair, discreet, passionate and anguished, contrary to all rules she had set up to protect herself. She was now part of a peculiar Washington subculture, the other woman. It was a debilitating, painful, masochistic role. It doomed her to lonely nights, a flood of tears on an icy pillow, unbearable longings. Days were lived by rote on the edge of anger and despair, her concentration spoiled, her sense of individuality and achievement sullied.

But nature's compensation was bountiful. Their moments together overflowed with joy, psychic and sexual, with an intense mutuality that, she was certain, came rarely in anyone's lifetime. This was the real thing, transcending words and reason.

"Why you?" she asked aloud, or to herself a thousand times.

"Why you?" was his inevitable response.

During those moments of practicality and lucidity between their lovemaking, they would broach "the subject," their sword of Damocles. Ann Chase, Clint's wife, worked as an AA, administrative assistant, for a Colorado senator, Charles Hurley. When Clint spoke of her, it was always with regret. Whenever Fiona called that to his attention, he would look at her in disbelief.

"Maybe," he finally agreed. Between frantic encounters they would lay in each other's arms, wallowing in self-analysis. "She was a devoted, loving housewife for fifteen years. Then she became a super-achiever and our marriage came second, or third." He stole a glance at her and winked. "I wouldn't be here if she hadn't changed."

Why is he risking it all, Fiona wondered.

"Have you ever discussed it?"

"As an exercise. Not a final exam."

"I don't understand," she pouted, just this side of pressuring him. She had her own risks to run.

"Neither of us wants to torpedo the ship," he said. "The kids . . . they still need the family concept." His hesitation when this came up was always pronounced. "Then there's this new job."

He had explained earlier that his wife's employment by a powerful senator had gotten him the appointment.

"I took it. We needed the money. It's nearly ten grand more than the newspaper job."

"So you're a vassal," Fiona had said, cruelly. She was angry and wanted it to hurt.

"Not a vassal. A hostage."

"And if she finds out about us?"

"Let's not think about it." Obviously, he thought about it all the time. Also, he admitted he liked the new job and all its perks. Where is love in all this, she wondered?

Nowhere. He was frightened, stealing happiness.

"And what about the future?" she would ask. It had become her most persistent theme.

"Not now," he would beg off, just as persistently.

"When then?"

Was this Fiona, who could look convention in the eye and spit at it? It was appalling to her to be reduced to such a whimpering fool.

The low point of their relationship was the weekends, which he always spent with his family. She dreaded those weekends when she was off-duty; they became a sentence of abject loneliness. Mooning around the apartment, she seemed to spend most of her time staring at the telephone, waiting for it to ring when he had found a safe moment.

The last weekend had been the worst. The rainy gloom seemed to permeate her bones, prompting her resolution to end this servitude immediately, a resolve that, predictably, lost its energy on Monday morning when he came to her.

The jumper lying there in the mud at the bottom of the bridge had a sobering effect on her paralyzed will. There but for the grace of God, she thought dramatically, remembering the sight of the broken remains. Was it possible that she, too, could find all other exits locked?

Inexplicably the experience had motivated her, and although she had no set plan, she knew that the time had come for a change. She'd had it with being a closet mistress.

He arrived unsuspecting, carrying flowers, and embraced her. He was surprised when she pried herself out of his arms, a massive act of will and self-denial on her part.

"In a good meal, timing is everything," she whispered, hurrying to the kitchen, mostly to gather her strength.

"What are we celebrating?" he called after her.

Celebrating? From the urgency of her phone call, he must have known something was up.

"I must talk to you," she had said on the phone. "Tonight come for dinner."

"Tonight?"

She brought in the chilled pâté and put it on the plates, sitting opposite him.

"Pour the wine, please," she said.

"What is it?" he asked, bottle poised.

"Just pour it, please."

He obeyed, watching her eyes. A few scarlet drops fell on the lace cloth.

"Sorry."

Just before he'd arrived, she was at the peak of her resolve, a condition that was quickly receding. I'm sorry, darling, she said silently. Sipping her wine, she picked at her pâté, put some in her mouth, but couldn't swallow. He saw it and started to push himself from his chair.

"Don't . . ."

He sat back, throwing his napkin on the table.

"What have you done to me?" she whispered. "I'm not even in control of myself anymore."

"Hey," he said. "You're not exactly an innocent. I'm as hooked as you are."

"That doesn't change anything."

She watched as a confused frown etched itself on his forehead.

"What set it off? Things were wonderful this morning."

The memory of the broken, doll-like figure at the bottom of the ravine popped into her mind like a photographic slide. Lowering her eyes, she looked at her pâté, her stomach lurching.

"I just can't go on, Clint. Not this way."

"Inevitable, I guess. It all boils down to a tacky little scene."

It was not that he was being deliberately cruel. She had noted it before, the journalist's objectively trained mind, looking from the outside in. She knew his pain was as acute as her own. "Forget it, Fi," he added quickly as if editing his copy. "I don't know how to react. I've never been through this before."

"Marry me. Divorce her," she blurted. The words had come out in a whoosh, almost taking her breath away. Marriage? In the end that's what they all wanted.

"Haven't we been through that?" he said, standing up, pacing now.

"No," she said, her eyes brimming. "You've been through it. Not me."

"I'm just not ready." In the candlelight, his eyes had misted as well. "Not yet."

"Well, I am. Overdone."

"Breaking up a family is a tough step," he said. His pacing had brought him closer to her.

"I know," she nodded, thinking suddenly of her own family. In that cabbage-smelling Irish Catholic nest, such things were unthinkable.

"I need time," he said softly. She had expected the retort, searching her mind for an apt response. Take all the time you need, she wanted to say. It was the way she dealt with suspected murderers when she had whipped them down to the edge of confession. To deliver what had to be said next would take all the courage she could muster.

"You've had time."

He paced away again, shoulders drooping. She fought her compassion, bludgeoned herself to reason.

"I just can't live this way, Clint. It hurts too much." How could this have happened to her? Fiona FitzGerald, self-reliant, controlled, wary, street-smart Fiona. She had learned to deal with almost anything.

Suddenly the steak was burning, sending waves of smoke from the broiler. She ran to the kitchen, and without thinking grabbed the glowing metal, screaming in pain. Clint rushed in, grabbed a dishcloth and threw the charred meat, pan and all, into the sink. A douse of cold water made it sizzle and smoke. Reaching for her burnt hand, he put it under the tap.

When it cooled, he brought her fingers to his lips and kissed them. She made a half-hearted effort to remove them from his grasp, but her resolution had dissolved and she fell against him, embracing him tightly.

"Give me more time," he pleaded, leading her out of the kitchen. She went, docile, and expectant. Defeated. Trapped. Like the *jumper?* Like *Dorothy?*

Later, in the calm of his arms, wedged against his cool flesh, she tried vainly to put the scene in perspective. The room was pitch black, but she refused to look at the radial dial of her bedside clock. That was his problem, she told herself defiantly, dreading the moment when he would rise and squint toward it. His stomach growled and she fingered the line of hair on his belly.

"You're hungry," she whispered.

"Not any more."

The memory of their encounter made her smile and she dug her knuckles into his belly.

"It must have been the jumper that set me off," she said.

"Blue Monday," he said. She felt for his eyes which were open. "Jumper?"

"A suicide. At least, that's what it looks like. A beautiful young woman. Good for maybe a half century more of living." Saying it aloud sparked her caution. She wondered if she was deliberately inserting the equation, injecting fear like a threat. She could only hear his soft breathing in the long silence that followed.

"I'm going to tell her, Fi. Tell Ann."

The thump in her chest prevented a response.

"It's against the grain. I'm a lousy liar."

She had tried not to imagine his life at home, the ordinary pursuit of family business, other concerns, other worries. That took place on another planet. Except that she knew that he and Ann shared a bed, touched. It was an image getting exceedingly difficult to block out of her mind.

"You're not the only one living alone," he said.

"Does she notice?" Fi asked. There she was, empathizing again. The portrait he had painted was of a woman obsessed with achievement, someone who had grudgingly taken time out for the sake of her children, then thrown herself back into the fray with an awesome resolve.

"She's too involved with her job. And I don't give her reason not to be. Hell, she thinks I go to work early, a real eager beaver. And I'm home every night, almost." The thought triggered his anxiety and he looked at the radial clock.

"My God. It's nearly three." Rolling over her, he got out of bed and started to dress. Reaching out, she touched his thigh, as if it were necessary to leave a last mark on his body.

"I don't believe you," she said calmly. "I believe you want to, but you won't. It's too comfortable this way."

He stopped dressing and looked down at her, bending to brush his hand over her forehead.

"See, you're scared. Then you'd be stuck with me."

Love, however complex, seemed a charted course compared to reading the future. At thirty-two, she was still young enough for kids. There were moments when that seemed almost idyllic. Moments, too, when it seemed like penal servitude. Tell him to get lost, she begged herself.

Always, when he prepared to leave—perhaps the act of dressing was erotic for her—she felt the pull of sexual longing. It was when she needed him most. Needed! When had it become need, she cried silently, knowing that for him anxiety had already taken hold and the extra time spent would only make it worse.

There was nothing to do but close her eyes, shut him out until he bent over her for that last sweet kiss. It was an act she let happen, although it hurt rather than consoled her. The thing, this monster inside, had reduced her to a simpering slave.

"Wednesday?"

"Like always," she sighed.

She listened for the click of his key rolling the chamber of the double lock, caging her once again. Again, she thought of the girl, the jumper, the broken body, the half smile. The image stuck to her like paste.

Trained as she was for odd hours and catnaps, she was always too energized for sleep after Clint had gone. Getting out of bed, she gobbled up the remainders of both portions of pâté and washed it down with red wine, directly from the bottle. To fight the first surge of loss, she called Benton in his office. He seemed always to be there at these odd hours.

A relationship, personal and professional, had grown up between them ever since the Remington case. It leaped over whatever barriers of race, age and gender that existed between them. Reluctantly, even with some embarrassment, he accepted her confidences, offering only the wisdom of his years. Essentially a moral man, he was by experience, if not by instinct, conservative and cautious. A darker skin—two grandparents were quadroons—had taught him that survival was still the first priority. Because of that, he had chosen a role in the bureaucracy where he had risen more by skill than ambition. His dead wife had been his only love, but he seemed to know a great deal about women. Many of them gave away their secrets on his autopsy table.

His voice on the telephone, deep and resonant with its cajun cadence, soothed and comforted her.

"The young woman," she said, after the amenities. "The jumper. Caucasian."

"A skeletal grab-bag."

"Death instantaneous?"

He hesitated. "She dropped from 300 feet. I could give you the technical data."

"Was she dead before the fall?"

"You suspect that, Fiona?"

She ignored the question.

"Did you take a vaginal swab?" she asked.

"It wasn't requested," Dr. Benton said, the bureaucrat's caution showing. It was, they both knew, a detective's option in a suicide.

"I forgot."

"All orifices?"

"Might as well," she said. "I know it's extra work, Dr. Benton."

"Nothing lost in going with your instincts, Fiona."

"At least we'll have the information, just in case." Not wanting to ring off just yet, she volunteered information. "Next of kin probably won't claim the body. It looks like she's a candidate for burning."

"Sad," he said.

"Cheaper, too," she said coldly.

He seemed to detect her depression, despite her efforts to remain professional. The conversation was quickly ended when she couldn't think of anything more to say.

Feeling alone again, she threw herself on the bed. The sheets were cold, even where his indentation had been made.

"Fool," she cried. "Dying for a man . . ."

At least Dorothy was safe from them forever.

IV

Jason Martin sat in his parked car on Cathedral Avenue across the street from the townhouse in which he had rented the ground floor apartment. The upper floors were deserted. The house was owned by a foreign service officer on temporary duty in Malaysia, a stroke of luck.

He had looked very carefully for the apartment, which had to satisfy a variety of conditions: total privacy, centrally located on a quiet off street, roomy and attractive. Above all, it had to appear "safe."

"But why do we need another place?" Dorothy asked. He still had his old apartment on Capitol Hill.

"You'll see."

"Gosh. It's pretty. Like a hideaway."

"You got it. A place to hide. Just trust me, baby. You've got to trust me. It's all for us. You'll see."

"I love it," she said. "And we'll fix it up all in white. Real pretty."

"Do whatever you want. It's your place," he said, looking out the rear window. The narrow yard stretched out to a chain-link fence, beyond which was a deep ravine which fell sharply to Rock Creek Parkway. They were a stone's throw from Calvert Street and the high stone bridge.

"Look how high," she said, crouching beside him at the kitchen window. She pressed her cheek against the pane.

"They call it suicide bridge. Lots have gone over. I did a story on it once."

"Gosh." She shivered and he put an arm around her shoulders.

Perfect, he'd decided. He had Dorothy call the agent and pay three months rent in advance.

Glancing at his watch, he sipped beer from a can. Anxiety had dried his throat. It had begun to happen.

51

Had the idea come to him like a light going on in one of those balloons of comic character expressions, or had it seethed and festered like garbage creating methane gas? He would never be certain.

He was not even sure whether or not he had asked her to come with him to Washington. Had it simply occurred, a natural event like sunrise or rain? There she was, crunched close beside him in his car heading east on the Pennsylvania Turnpike, her hand on his inner thigh.

"We'll have one hell of a time, Dot," he had said.

"Great."

Nor did he have any clear idea how she would fit into his life, barren now, shorn of family and self-respect. Half-woman, half-child, she might be a surrogate family for him, a comfort without the pressure of Jane's probing and intellectualizing, a mere child to be stroked and petted.

He was ashamed at showing her the untidiness of his apartment, such an obvious reflection of his inner life, but she went to work without a word and by the time they were ready for bed, she had made it cleaner and more orderly than Jane had ever done.

"Do you like it here?" he asked after they made love that first night in the apartment together. Where Jane had been indifferent and sometimes hostile to their sex life, Dorothy was eager, deliciously wanton.

"I love this," she told him.

"And me?"

"I think you're the greatest, Jason."

The greatest? It was certainly coincidental that she had dropped into his life at the moment of his most profound anguish. A heavenly gift, he decided, toying with thoughts of fate and the cosmos.

His altercation with Barrows, so utterly unnecessary in retrospect, had further eroded his position with Webster. He had considered an apology, but it was too late. A hotshot's fall from grace was something to be cheered in this nest of bloated egos fighting for space and by-lines. Webster enjoyed watching his stars collide, disintegrate and reform into new stars in his whirling solar system.

When Webster called him into his office on his first day back, he'd expected to get worse news. To be fired for "insubordination" was a favorite management ploy, but it did require a Newspaper Guild hearing, a process that had a flavor of humiliation about it. Having a committee rule on the issue of holding one's job didn't do much for one's pride. Besides, hadn't he already earned his journalist's stripes?

"How could you do this to me?" he asked Webster after he'd announced that henceforth Jason would be covering the Fairfax County Council, a kind of Siberia for someone of his experience. Worse, he would have to take orders from another young hotshot working his way up the ladder.

"This paper's a machine, Jason," Webster told him blandly. "You got a faulty cog, the whole thing rattles." His arm swept over the city room. "I got a thousand egos to placate. You're just one." Keep cool, Jason warned himself.

"You're cutting off my cojones, Paul," he told the editor, forcing a pose of contrition. At all costs, he'd decided, he needed this job now. Avoiding Webster's eyes, he looked downward and saw a proof of tomorrow's page one sprawled across Webster's desk. A headline read: "SEC Commissioner Resigns."

"I had no choice, Jason. It's all I can give you now," Webster said.

"It used to be different."

"Things change." Jason's eyes shifted again to the page proof.

"So I see." He was being deliberately cryptic. At one time he'd practically worshipped Webster.

"Do you good to go back to straight journalism, Jason," Webster said, winking inexplicably, as if there were a conspiracy between them.

"The Fairfax County Council. I'm overqualified for that and you know it."

"The opening is there," Webster snapped, showing his sense of command. "I don't have to justify it." He became absorbed in the page proof, an obvious dismissal.

"Still playing that on one?" Jason asked.

"They eat it up," Webster muttered, ignoring the obvious malice. Jason stood rooted before the desk. Webster looked up again. "Just do the job," he said, his tone placating now. Jason knew what was coming. The editor's system was the carrot and the stick. "We'll watch you, kid. Keep it straight for awhile." Webster studied him calmly. "Put the flame on low—it'll do you good." His eyes drifted slowly back to the page proofs.

"And if I come up with a really big one? I've still got contacts . . ." There was a note of desperation in his voice now. Leave it alone, he told himself simultaneously, knowing it was Big Jake's voice prodding him.

"Sure, kid."

Webster said it like offering a useless trifle. It was an unmistakable dismissal. Hypocrite, Jason had screamed within himself as the offensive headline caught his eye once again. You wait, he jeered silently, I'll come up with something that will blow your mind.

The taste of bile flooded the back of his throat as he strode out of the city room under Barrows's triumphant gaze. Screw you, he mimed to him as the elevator door closed.

"I'm unfit for human consumption," he'd told Dorothy later. She had tried everything to dispel the gloom. For brief periods, her lovemaking comforted him, then he sank again into depression and sleeplessness. When she came at him again in the early hours he pushed her away roughly, although he apologized quickly for it.

"All I want is for you to be happy," she'd said.

"I know, baby."

He had wanted to explain what had happened to him, but the thought of everything else it involved was discouraging—his childhood, his failed father, the fear of genetic emulation, the ego-bruising life with Jane, the loss of his son—a litany of outrageous self-pity. His earlier success at the paper had made the pain recede, and he had hoped he could put those thoughts out of his mind forever.

But things had changed around him. There was no more oxygen for the pure blue flame of indignation that he thrived on. They were getting into trivia, sex as substantive newsworthiness, scandal-mongering. How could he explain to this flower of the slag heap what it all meant?

"You've been good to me, Jason."

"That's it? That's the criterion?" He corrected himself, knowing that she wouldn't comprehend. "Am I the missing father?"

"What?"

She had told him that she had only known her father briefly, a miner crushed in a cave-in when she was three. Psychological implications were Jane's bag. Raking up those coals wouldn't help here.

"Never mind."

"I'll do anything to help." She traced his lips with her fingers. "To get a little smile."

Miraculously, he'd actually smiled.

"I'd like to show that bastard," he muttered. Webster, he knew, was at the heart of the problem—he alone was setting the tone of the paper, approving every story down to the last word. "I'll come up with something that'll blow his mind."

She giggled suddenly, her implication clear.

"I said his mind."

He slapped her playfully on a bare buttock, and the idea had come fully formed, screaming into his consciousness. Hadn't it been there all along?

"Suppose it was important to me. To us . . ." He paused, watching her calm face, assessing her, sensing the living idea as it sculpted itself in his mind, wondering how deep an explanation would be required.

Her eyelids flickered, long dark lashes brushing her cheeks, as if in consent.

"You're my man now," she assured him, patting him possessively.

". . . you know," he stammered, hating the empty words, the flotsam of the inarticulate. "It's a lot to ask."

She shrugged. Perhaps she already knew what was coming. Her face was placid, unalarmed.

"Like having relations with other men," he said, averting his eyes, but adding quickly, "Not for money." Too late, he realized his error. She would have understood money.

Her expression when he turned to watch her again seemed confused. But he didn't find panic there. He felt self-righteous about not saying "make love," certain that those words would profane the thing between them.

"Would you do that?" he pressed. "For me?"

He held his breath as she retreated inside herself, her eyes glazed with deep inner thoughts. He did not deny to himself his own shame in making the demand, nor the violation to all his past ethics. But circumstances were forcing him to chart new ground, find new rules, explore a new landscape of morality.

"It wouldn't turn out like with Jimbo?" she whispered tentatively, revealing her consent. He wondered if it were out of loyalty or survival or even love.

"Of course not," he said with exaggerated indignation, the plan emerging now clearly shaped.

"I wouldn't want anything to come between us, Jason," she said firmly, as if to recapture her dignity.

"Between us?" He kissed her deeply. "Never." He searched his mind for some disarming illustration. "It will be like play-acting. That's all."

"Acting?" She shook her head. "I don't know, Jason. I'm a bad liar. I always get found out."

"Acting isn't lying. It's a game. And it could do great things for us. For what I've got in mind." He checked himself, unsure about how far he could explain it. "Trust me, baby. It could be very important."

"Important?"

"I mean the men would be important. Powerful."

"Powerful?"

He was sure he was only confusing her now. This was not within the parameters of her understanding. Men were men in physical terms only. Old and young, big and small. Gradations of power seemed out of her frame of reference.

"And you wouldn't get mad or jealous?"

"Not if you were true to me in your heart."

In the half-light, her body was as smooth as alabaster, her features soft.

"You're a beautiful girl, Dot," he said with feeling. Bending over her, he kissed her again. As always, she tasted sweet and he thought of candy.

"You're the perfect gift," he whispered. "Those lucky guys."

She seemed so innocent. Virginal. Yet something eluded him. There seemed more to her than her tantalizing physicality. Something deep inside of her, something hidden.

"I won't hurt you," he said with feeling. "Never."

She turned toward him and embraced him and he felt his whole being rise to meet her. She would be his vindication.

Poor Arthur Fellows, he thought with sarcasm, his first victim, lured into the Machiavellian web by simple uncomplicated lust. It couldn't happen to a greedier guy. Jason had known him for ten years, ever since he did his FDA stories, for which the ambitious young lawyer had been the principal source. The publicity had paid off and Arthur had clawed his way up the greasy pole to be named a counselor to the President, one of two gatekeepers. In Washington, that was prime power. Arthur Fellows had made it. As such, he was a perfect potential victim.

Arthur arrived at the townhouse door, briefcase in hand, as if he were just another hustling government lawyer. From his car, Jason had watched him approach. There was a hawklike look about him, a sense of alert caution. The horny bastard knew the risks. He'd gotten away with it for years. He didn't take many chances. And he trusted Jason. Dumb bastard, Jason thought.

Jason had discovered Arthur's propensity to womanize ten years ago when he was sleeping with his secretary at FDA. It wasn't an uncommon development for a rising government lawyer who had just graduated to an office with a couch. Sexual harassment as an issue was not yet in vogue. Arthur was married to a very conventional woman, had two achieving children and a house in McLean. They had exchanged family dinners with the Martins in the days when Jason was being helpful. Later, of course, when Arthur's career skyrocketed, the Martins were no longer social equals. It was the Washington way, although Jason retained Arthur as a "contact," calling him periodically to keep in touch.

Arthur was easy. He had a lascivious streak which he cleverly masked by humor. Even in the old FDA days, he was always suggestive when he and Jason would get together.

"I'll trade one of mine for one of yours."

Jason would kid him along. He was, after all, a prime source.

"Hell, I'd be bringing coal to Newcastle."

"Even when it's bad, it's good. The important thing is to get it. Hell, what's all this power for anyway but more and more pussy."

The line, of course, was familiar. Arthur jumped to the bait like a hungry fish.

"I thought of you immediately," Jason said. He had managed to get Arthur out for a quick drink at the Press Club. At first they had talked politics, issues, gossip. Both knew it was a keeping-in-touch situation. Jason was not lunch material in Washington power terms. Arthur was simply throwing him a bone.

"I can set it up," Jason said, after Arthur dropped the facade. He looked about him to be sure no one was listening.

"All she has to be is ready, good looking and safe." Arthur cleared his throat. "Above all, safe."

"Above all," Jason assured him. It was an accepted fact that men who wielded power accepted such perks. For a newspaperman, the unwritten trade-off was that one day Arthur could again be a "source."

Thinking about Arthur did not summon up any pangs of conscience. Behind his thin veneer of probity, Arthur was a grasping climber like the rest. He was also clever and knew how to survive in the jungle. Besides, the horny bastard would wind up making ten times his salary as a parasitical Washington lawyer. Jason would be doing him a favor.

An hour later Arthur came out of the townhouse, wearing the look of the self-absorbed Washington lawyer. Who could possibly guess what he had just done?

Jason's explanations about Arthur to Dorothy had been deliberately vague. She would never have understood his real motives.

"We live on favors in this town, baby." He had reiterated the point to be sure she hadn't changed her mind.

"I understand, Jason."

He refused to question her own value system—he didn't need any extra baggage for his conscience.

He'd let her decorate the apartment in her special way, an expression of her own fantasies.

"But why don't we live here, Jason?" They still stayed at his Capitol Hill apartment.

"Some day. If you do exactly as I say."

"Of course, Jason." She thought for a moment. "I'll make sure he returns the favor."

"Oh he will, baby. That's been settled."

"Better be."

"It'll all be perfect in the end. You'll see."

"Sure, Jason. Anything you say."

When Arthur had disappeared around the corner, Jason crossed the street to the townhouse. The outside door worked on a buzzer system, but he let himself in with his own key. Dorothy was in the shower. Getting out of the sooty coal area had increased her passion for cleanliness. She had shined and primped the apartment until its floors and furniture were honed to a fine gloss. Everything was tucked neatly in place.

Dorothy came out of the shower, scrubbed and sweet smelling, wearing a flouncy white negligee. Seeing him sitting on the couch, she smiled brightly. He forced his expression to match hers, surprised at the brief stab of jealousy. Watching her now, fresh from another man's arms, oblivious in her innocence, made him feel uneasy.

"He was very nice," she said, insinuating herself next to him, locking her fingers in his.

"Didn't I tell you," he said hoarsely.

"And you're not jealous?"

"Not a bit."

"As long as he helps you, Jason, it's okay with me."

Her nearness made his concentration falter. He had the sudden urge to explain it further to her, to justify it, but gazing at her perfect face, it didn't seem to matter anymore. Her malleability was a phenomenon.

From his pocket he took his small tape recorder and locked in a blank cassette. Standing it upright on the cocktail table between them, he tested it, checking its range and pitch. She watched him with childish curiosity, emitting the inevitable "gosh." He had toyed with the idea of wiring the place, but that would have required bringing another person in to do the job. Debriefing was second best, but far safer. The type of "visitors" he had in mind would all be paranoid about security. As it was, he would have to have Dorothy offer them elaborate assurances. The slightest hint of a "setup" would scatter them like frightened geese.

"Remember. It's like a game," he explained.

"Okay."

"Everyone to his own aberration," he said, caressing her shoulders.

"Aber what?" she asked, laughing, her eyes fixed on the running recorder.

"Never mind."

He'd already assumed that the first time would be the most difficult. "Just tell me how it was." Her eyes narrowed in confusion.

"Tell you? I don't understand."

"It excites me," he whispered, biting at her earlobe. He wondered if it really would.

"It does? But I thought . . ." He observed her mulling it over in her tortuous plodding way. It was contrary to her experience. She looked at the recorder and frowned.

"I'm not sure, Jason."

"Just trust me," he whispered. "It's important to us."

"To us?"

"Go ahead," he coaxed.

"What?"

"Just tell me what happened. What he said. What you felt."

"He smelled nice," she giggled.

"What else?" He kissed her forehead. "How did he do it?"

"You want to know that?"

"Yes."

"Just like he was starving to death." She smiled and turned to face him. He chuckled benignly, and it gave her courage to proceed. What he wanted was facts, bits and pieces, the juicy stuff. He continued to coax her.

"He liked to talk dirty when he was doing it. Usually like dogs do."

It came out like an instruction sheet for elaborate sexual exercises, boiled down to their ultimate simplicity. Wanting to please him, she relayed each movement with as much detail as could be hoped for. And then he did this and then that. It became more clinical than pornographic.

"It felt good," she said. Knowing her reactions, it was always an obvious conclusion. To her, it always felt good. As she talked, staring at the recorder, obediently offering the mechanics of Arthur's technique and reactions, she reached out to caress him, stopping finally when she discovered no response.

"It doesn't do what you said," she said, turning away from the recorder.

"It will when I replay it," he said.

"Did he talk about his job?" he asked. Where he worked?"

"He said it wasn't far. A big southern mansion not far."

A good line, Jason thought. Meant to ridicule. He felt better about what he was doing now. The bastard had played on her naiveté. He was tempted to tell her what Arthur had meant but held off. She mistook his long silence for disapproval.

"You're not sorry?" she asked. "I did it because you wanted me to."

"I know, baby," he said, patting her shoulders.

"He was very nice."

"Yes, he's very nice. Did he ask to see you again?"

"Next week. I gave him the new number." He had already hooked up an answering machine.

"Should I?" she asked.

"Of course."

"As long as it will help you, Jason. I wouldn't do it if you minded. I would never do it on my own."

"I know that."

He turned off the recorder and put it back in his pocket. The apartment was beginning to stifle him. He took a five dollar bill from his wallet and handed it to her.

"Take a cab home tonight," he said abruptly. "I'll be late. Another zoning meeting in Fairfax County."

He had worked it out very carefully, both the rationale and the plan. Simple justice was too tame for today's new world.

Lasciviousness was the bitch goddess now, a paradox since the sexual revolution was supposed to have made a simple exercise of the genitalia uninteresting as news. The irony was that a few years back when sex was merely a dirty little secret, reporters looked the other way. Deviates could ply their persuasions without fear, provided they didn't violate other norms.

Now, he knew, the peccadillo brought to light could send up a national leader like a Roman candle. People cluck-clucked and said it was too bad, but an aggressive woman with a good body and a photogenic face could turn a good buck out of sexually exploiting someone with even the remotest shred of power. There was a hot market out there for that—books, serial rights, foreign translations, photos in the flesh slicks, movies, television. A well placed fuck could bring notoriety, fame. That kind of spectacle sold. It was disgusting, Jason thought. America had become vulgarized.

What was needed was one good overdose of it. Enough to revolt even the most prurient. It would smash the taste for it in the public mind. And it amazed him that he, Jason Martin, had stumbled upon the instrument to do it. Dorothy. All that was needed now was a manipulative intelligence, the right targets and the courage to act. The former was already in his possession, the latter took a bit of research, and the guts to put the honeypot near the flies.

Money alone was not his motivation, he assured himself, although an up-front investment was already straining his finances. He had begun to fall behind on his payments to Jane for Trey's support. Decorating the apartment had been expensive.

As for Dorothy . . .

She was the perfect weapon, an innocent with an uncanny talent. She had easily transferred her dependency from Jim to himself. It was almost *too* easy, Jason had thought. Yet he was comforted by the knowledge that what he was doing would benefit her as well, at least in monetary terms. Hadn't she once told him that money was also one of her goals?

He had already calculated the split, giving her the lion's share of all proceeds. Such gestures assuaged any pangs of guilt. The tapes would be his principal documentation. Maybe he'd even take the chance on video or, at the least, photo stills. He'd have to be extremely cautious. None of his potential victims had reached these heady precincts without developing antennae for this kind of scam. He looked upon them as adversaries, an appropriately journalistic posture.

Naturally, they would all cry entrapment. It would be their principal defense. More raw meat for the media mill. Even if they chose confession, which was the latest strategic vogue, it would only increase the after-play, making the titillation even more valuable.

After their moment in the lurid glare of scandal, after the anguished breast-beating, the protestations and confessions, they would all land on their feet. Some would also write books themselves. Maybe sell the rights to a movie. Hell, it was a great growth industry. One or two might even take refuge in religion. Ambition, he was certain, also had its genetic base. The kind of boys he had in mind would make out anywhere. For most, it would be a good excuse to change direction, find a new track. Some would even use it to dump their wives. They would all have to be lusty boys with heavy appetites. That sort should be easy to find, he reasoned. Sexual discipline wasn't much of a virtue in today's world.

To do it right, though, it had to be massive, not just a single isolated exposure, not just Arthur Fellows. It had to be bigger in scope, touch the untouchables, the high and mighty of government and society. By God, he wanted to bring them all to their knees. He would become the P. T. Barnum of sexual scandal, a three-ring virtuoso, touching every point on the American power compass. The White House, the Senate, the House, the Military, the Diplomatic Corps, and, if he could pull it off, the Supreme Court. An American Sextet. With Dorothy as his instrument, he'd singlehandedly send up the entire checks and balances system.

V

The tension in the office had the tautness of a violin string. They had brought in a suspect in the teenage murders. The man was a Marine sergeant stationed at the barracks on Sixth Street. Worse, he was white, and had been observed trying to pull a young black woman into his car.

Picked up swiftly, he had been booked and hustled into the interrogation room under tight security. Grim-faced media people hung out in the corridors. The newspaper and television reporters were having a field day over the murders, focusing on the lurid sob stuff. A fund had been started for the illegitimate children of the victims.

After a round-the-clock grilling, the man continued to maintain his innocence. He insisted that he'd accosted the young woman because he was certain it was she who had stolen his wallet two weeks previously.

"The chief's chewing carpets," Lieutenant Brooks, the number two said. Known, not without affection, as one of the eggplant's stooges, Brooks was the eggplant's huge but gentle sidekick who was always happy to fob off both authority and blame on someone else. Like many policemen, he had a side trade, house painter, which he plied in his spare time. Since he was making more off the books than he could hope to draw from the public payroll, he wasn't up for rocking the boat.

"Muvva had to be a honky," he groaned. "Set the juices going. Bad for the boss. They're really pushin' upstairs . . ." His manner was furtive; his eyes darted from side to side.

". . . and he's got orders to crack the bastard or it's his ass."

Despite her own feelings about the eggplant, stories like that triggered compassion. Somebody was always about to have the man's ass.

"He could be the wrong man," Cates stage whispered. Brooks heard him and smiled.

"If he has to, he'll make it right."

"What the hell is that supposed to mean?" Cates asked Fiona on the way to their car.

"Police bravado. The myth that everybody's guilty of something. Sometimes a false confession with good circumstantial evidence can provide a good breather."

"You mean a deliberate frame-up?"

"Tsk. Tsk. We're being quite a boy scout this morning."

She knew immediately she'd made a mistake. His skin cast turned slightly yellow. Was it the "boy" reference? Or had she gratuitously flaunted her knowledge of the way things worked?

"It happens sometimes," she said. She'd noted that in him before, the taut sensitivity, the smoldering inner life.

"I suppose I'll find out when I'm older," he said.

"Touché!"

Even later, as they investigated the "naturals," all of which were routine, something was still awry between them. Part of it was her own uneasiness. She hadn't told him about her conversation with Dr. Benton, a violation of the partnership code. That was police business, not secret thoughts. It nagged at her all morning. It wasn't until they were having a cup of coffee in Sherry's, a staticy radio crackling between them, that she found the courage to broach the subject.

"I asked Dr. Benton to take a vaginal smear of the jumper," she said.

"You did? I thought you had lost interest." Sipping his coffee, he squinted at her over the rim of his cup.

"Whatever gave you that idea?"

"I figured you told the eggplant and he put you down for it."

"You think that would stop me?"

"It had to be something. You had been so turned on."

"I still am," she said flatly.

"Good." He reached into his pocket and threw a metal object on the table. She looked at it, then back at him. The object was a tiny pin, less than an inch long, four silver stars on a silver bar. After inspecting it, she put it back on the table.

"For me?" she asked facetiously.

"For someone."

"Are we playing games?"

He seemed to enjoy her confusion, then wiped away his grin, and looking around him, spoke in a whisper.

"I went to her place again. I found this pinned to a panty. In an odd place. Right at the Y." His throat caught and he cleared it. "I wasn't sure what the hell it was at first. Anyway, there it is."

"Sly little bastard," she mocked.

"You were making such a big deal about it."

She fingered the object.

"A general," he said.

"I don't know what it means," she admitted.

"Sure you do. She had a general for a boyfriend. Four stars."

"That's no crime," she said, watching him. Finally, she asked, "Why did you go back?"

"Pissed off," he said, making it sound like a genuine confession. "You were blowing hot and cold. I thought you put me down for what I'd found out . . . the man in the woodpile. I thought that was pretty damn good detecting."

It was, she supposed, fingering the pin. She hadn't found it, although she had looked in the drawers, not thinking to disturb the neat pile of panties. It told her something about male curiosity, but he had plowed fertile ground.

She held the pin up to the light, inspecting it. Taking it as a signal to proceed further, Cates took a notebook from his pocket.

"The lease was in her own name," he said, referring to his notes. "The rent was $575, and she paid three months in advance. Her take home from Saks was $800 a month. Figure that out. They said she was good when she worked. Sporadic attendance, but they liked her. No close friends with employees. Very close-mouthed. A little slow on the uptake, but good with the customers. One of her co-workers thought her job seemed like a hobby."

He rattled on, his handsome, light chocolate features infused with an excitement she found distressing. The implications, of course, were obvious. They had been obvious from the beginning. The girl had been someone's mistress, just like herself. The coffee became acidy in her stomach and she was suddenly nauseated.

"The basic question is still foul play," she said, gulping air. "We're not the Moral Majority."

"No," he said. "The basic question is you."

"I don't understand."

Was she that transparent? she wondered. Had he investigated her personal life as well? She had studiously avoided discussing with him any private references to her life. But he hadn't volunteered much about himself either, as if their lives began and ended with their work.

"Frankly," he admitted, "I couldn't see why you were so interested at the beginning. Then I decided you must have had a theory in mind, something I'd missed. So I went to see for myself. I wasn't going to tell you. Then you told me about the smear."

Once she had gone rafting in white waters at Harper's Ferry. She recalled the sense of powerlessness when the raft was caught in a downward surge, bobbing in the unpredictable eddies. Listening to him replicated the same sensation.

Maybe he was trying to foreclose on it before it got out of hand. It happened sometimes. A case comes up that pushes a detective beyond logic. It becomes an obsession, crowding out all other considerations. A theory becomes faith. Like being sure beyond doubt about the existence of God.

"She was kept by some married cat. He wanted to end the deal. She balked, threatened to blow the cover. He flung her over the bridge."

She wanted to protest. Would Clint do that to her? She looked at Cates, surveyed his chiseled features, imagined his tall muscular lithe body. He reminded her of Harry Belafonte.

"You think that's my theory?" she asked.

"Or a variation thereof."

"And what do you think?"

"I think it was the other way around. He gave her the boot. She couldn't take it, saw all exits closed, then jumped."

"You know that much about women in love?" she asked. It was a challenge more than a question.

"Enough," he said, sipping his coffee.

"Machoman," she said tartly.

"I've made you mad."

Agitated, she wanted to say. He had indeed stirred her up. To avoid his eyes, she again looked at the little pin, forcing her concentration.

"Your man in the woodpile?"

"A reporter," he said. "For the *Post*."

"That makes two men in the woodpile."

When she looked at him he was frowning, searching the dregs of his cup for a response.

"A triangle," he said.

"Which blows your theory about my theory." It was getting out of hand now and she hadn't the power to stop it.

"We could find out," he said, after a long silence.

"Why not?"

She wondered who was goading whom.

Jason Martin was easy to find, a dry throat at the other end of the telephone line. It was nearly noon. Apparently, her call had awakened him.

"I'm terribly sorry," she said politely.

"One of those late County Council meetings. They were arguing about where to put the new dog pound."

She imagined he was expecting her to laugh, which she politely did.

"Routine police business," she explained, waiting for a reaction, a subtle breathing ripple. There was the barest hint of hesitation.

"A story?" he asked, emitting a distinctive yawn.

"Could be."

His apartment was not far from Sherry's, from where she was making the call. They were there in fifteen minutes.

"It's a mess," he apologized.

It was an apartment in a still unrenovated townhouse, the halls of which stank of stale pizza. For a newspaperman, he seemed to be living in penury. A glance into his bedroom told her he'd made a half-hearted attempt to make his bed, but the telltale lumps under a stained comforter belied the attempt.

Although his brown stringy hair was still damp from the shower, his bodily cleanliness seemed negated by a torn, stained seersucker robe under which two hairy legs protruded like stilts. Cool brown eyes shifted in their almond-shaped sockets, peering over an aquiline nose with flared nostrils and thin tight lips. His chin was cleft, square and strong, investing him with an overall look of quick-tempered pugnaciousness. The caged animal image clung to him like body odor. The predatory, repressed anger was palpable, the air of casual cynicism contrived. He was a relic of the rebellious sixties, Fiona decided. It was one of her dead certain instant judgments, but she wasn't condemning the man for it; it had been her era as well.

Clearing a battered couch, he offered them seats, taking a place opposite them on an upholstered chair that had seen better days.

"You were a friend of Dorothy Curtis, formerly Zcarkowiz," Fiona began, watching his face.

"Were?" he snapped, a bit too quickly. Then he corrected her pronounciation, shaking his head, and let out a long gasp of breath, more like a deep sigh. "She in trouble?"

Fiona ignored his question. "You brought her to Washington from Hiram, Pennsylvania?"

"Hey," he said. "I know the game plan. Just tell me what's come down."

"We know you did. Her aunt told us," Fiona said.

"I'm not denying that." He withdrew a long leg from across the chair's arm, showing a swath of white jockey shorts. "Do me a favor, guys. Don't go by the book. Just tell me what's happened to her."

"Why are you assuming that anything has happened to her?" Cates interceded.

"Amateur night," Martin muttered. "I'm also trained to interrogate."

Surely, Fiona thought, surveying the man, Dorothy hadn't died for him.

"We found her in the creek under the Duke Ellington Bridge."

She watched him carefully. His lips trembled.

"Found her . . ." He turned his face away.

"She was not a pretty sight." Fiona was deliberately harsh. Sometimes shock value could be very useful.

"Christ," he muttered, standing up. From the litter of his dresser, he found a cigarette and lit it with a Zippo lighter. For a moment, he looked at himself in the mirror and, after a deep inhale, blew smoke into his image. He seemed shaken, but was holding himself together.

"What the hell did she do that for?" he said, turning to face them, showing a burst of anger. The veins in his neck stood out.

"We've classified her death as undetermined," Fiona said.

"What the hell does that mean?"

"It's just routine, Mr. Martin."

"Routine?" he said with raised eyebrows. "I used to cover the police beat. You think someone threw her over?"

"Have you any reason to think that?" Fiona asked. "Since you mentioned it first . . ."

Puffing deeply, he paced the room. When he finally sat on the chair again he rested his elbows on his knees, still in deep thought. "She gave me a lot of happy moments."

"And you?" Fiona asked. "What did you give her?" To cover her embarrassment, she took out her notebook.

"When did you last see her?" Cates asked.

"A couple of months ago, maybe." Martin shrugged. "We lived together for awhile. Apples and pears. She wasn't exactly an intellectual giant. We shared our bodies." He looked at Fiona, almost as if he were searching for understanding. You've come to the wrong pew, buddy, she told herself, thinking of Clint. This must be depersonalized, she admonished herself silently.

Thankfully, the recall set him off and he rambled on. She wanted to get out of Pennsylvania, find a new life in the big city. Her dreams smacked of typical media myths.

"She was an innocent, without guile. She wouldn't hurt a fly," he concluded.

"Not even herself?" Fiona asked.

"Who knows?" For the first time he appeared genuinely confused. "Something must have set her off. Frankly, I can't believe it."

There was a long pause as Martin sucked the end of his cigarette down to a glowing butt, finally smashing it in an ashtray on the floor. "What makes you think it was something other than suicide?" he said without looking up.

"Did you know any of her other male friends?" Fiona asked. He looked up suddenly, laughing.

"Not in the last few months." He paused. "You saw her. That was the only thing she'd have no trouble finding."

"She was hardly appealing when we got to her," Cates said, with what seemed like unnecessary malice.

"You should have seen her when I did," he said, ignoring the barb. For the first time since they had arrived his expression softened. "She was wonderful."

"Without guile," Fiona pressed. Something odd seemed embedded in the phrase and she detected a slight stiffening as he heard it thrown back at him.

"Yeah," he mumbled. "Nobody can survive in this town without that. No one."

"We couldn't find any names in her apartment. Nothing. Everything in its proper place." Fiona looked around his apartment. "Not like this. She was a fanatic about white and being neat."

"Yeah."

"How did she support it? The apartment?"

"Don't ask me."

"Somebody paid three month's rent up front in cash," Fiona said. "She didn't make that kind of money."

"So?"

"How could she have done that on a take-home salary of $800 a month?" Fiona asked, aware of her pressure. Something about the man was aggravating. Had they any business being here, wasting the taxpayer's money?

"What are you trying to say?" His eyes moved nervously between her and Cates. Without answering, she pressed on, unable to stop herself.

"All I want is the truth." The statement was premature, unprofessional.

"About what?" Martin snapped. She caught Cates's glare of caution but decided to ignore it.

"You know what."

Martin looked at Cates.

"She's mad as a hatter. Are you accusing me of throwing her over the bridge, murdering her?"

The word hung in the air like an unbearable stench. She knew she was going too far.

"You brought her to D.C. Why?"

"That's my business," he said, on the edge of exasperation. "I don't have to take this shit. You're harassing me." He stood up, then sat down again. "I adored her. You're profaning our relationship."

"Why did you split up?"

"That's also my business."

"I think you're full of crap," Fiona said vehemently. She was pushing it now, skirting caution. It was, she knew, professionally dangerous. Verging on harassment.

"You're insulting her memory," he said sharply. "She was my friend. We were lovers once. If that's a crime, then you can arrest half of this town."

"Show him the pin," Fiona ordered. Cates hesitated. She could see he was very unhappy with her behavior. Reluctantly, Cates drew the pin from his pocket and gave it to her. Holding it up, she glared at him.

"Ever see this?"

Martin looked at it curiously, while she studied his reaction.

"No." Was something awry in his expression?

"General's insignia. Four stars. Tell him where you found it, Cates."

Cates appeared to force his concentration as he explained where he'd found it.

"So?"

"Means nothing to you?"

"I'm no general."

He got up and turned away. When he faced her again, his eyes were moist and his Adam's apple was sliding up and down in his throat.

"Get the hell out of here," he said, his lips trembling.

She pointed a finger in front of his nose. "I'm going to watch you, Martin," she warned, seeing Clint's face. This was no damn interrogation, she realized. She'd been conducting an inquisition. But against whom?

"Just get out," Martin said.

She moved toward the door and Cates followed her.

Something about the man gnawed at her. Was it because he reminded her of Clint? It annoyed her to connect them.

"You were rough on him," Cates said cautiously when they were in the car again.

"On myself," she mumbled, ashamed. Why couldn't Dorothy leave her alone.

VI

Jason had always been contemptuous of the Washington social scene, an endless round of parties faithfully reported in the newspapers and recorded by the Capital's social chronicle, the *Washington Dossier.*

Like most Washington media types, he loudly proclaimed the exercise an orgy of back-scratching and hors d'oeuvre munching; nothing more than a chance to dress up and exchange trivia. When not officially invited for press coverage, media people publicly criticized these events, as if the act of putting them down was, in itself, a badge of superiority. Privately, they thirsted for invitations, knowing that they provided easy social access to people who wielded power. For that reason, Jason knew that the party circuit would be the principal channel of accessibility to the types he wanted to cast in his sexual extravaganza.

The cocktail and buffet arena was a cornucopia of potential victims. What good was fame or success if you couldn't receive the plaudits of your peers? Egos required stroking. Power as a rule was so splintered that even those who exercised it needed the validation of their fellows to appreciate the joys of having a piece of it.

Since he was not on any favored lists, he had to pursue a program of research that would give him the access he needed. It was easier than he'd imagined. Meeting places were everywhere, in the hotels, the private and government office buildings, the restaurants, association headquarters and, of course, the private homes of Washington's social elite whose status was determined by who attended their receptions and dinner parties. Celebrities gloried in being with each other, and because these events were a spotlight for media coverage they came; and because they came, others came. And what good was being a celebrity if there wasn't a claque of inferiors present to further insure their superiority?

Crashing these parties, Jason discovered, was simple. Except when the President or vice-president attended and all guests had to be carefully screened, it was considered bad form to make a fuss about invitations. At some events, guests did present their invitations, but most of these looked alike. Usually, those charged with responsibility at the door merely nodded appropriately-dressed guests through without recourse to a minute inspection of the invitations.

If a sit-down dinner was planned, guests were assigned places with name cards alphabetized and assembled on long tables for easy access. But that didn't stop anyone who looked the part from attending the obligatory cocktail mixer before the dinner, which was, for many, the main event. Once seated, there would be obvious limitations to social contact.

Still there were risks. Dorothy would inevitably attract attention, no matter how demurely she dressed. Flirtations did not go unnoticed, especially by the wives of important men. And the camera lens, despite all caution, was ubiquitous. An attractive woman was a photographic magnet. Notoriety and media exposure could strike a death knell to his plan. For his chosen victims, Dorothy had to be the forbidden fruit, reasonably anonymous, absolutely discreet. Excessive risk in public would scare them off, however appealing the honeypot.

He had already calculated that Dorothy's ingenuousness would pass for poise and her patrician good looks for sophistication. A beautiful, well-groomed woman did not need intellectual assets in such a social setting. Besides, Dorothy was not awed by any man, regardless of his title or so-called power. They were all merely men to her. In these terms, she had all the assets she needed to approach them. A gamble, yes, but one that he knew he had to take.

He pursued his investigation with scientific zeal, determined to find the one event that might net a number of candidates in one swoop. To help finance the operation and provide her with a credible occupation, he encouraged Dorothy to get a job. She quickly found one in the makeup department of one of Washington's fanciest stores, a branch of Saks Fifth Avenue.

Using her discount at the store, he bought her a spectacular evening gown. She looked good in every one she'd tried on, but he knew she truly wanted the one that was all white, that clung to her hips and offered just the right promise of her cleavage. It cost him twelve hundred dollars and got him further behind on his support payments. He bought himself a tuxedo at a second-hand clothing store.

"Nobody has ever been this good to me."

They lay in his rumpled double bed. She had thanked him in the only way she knew.

"You're good to me, too, baby."

"I am?"

She was beyond mere docility, she was loyal and obedient to a fault.

"Will you always take care of me, Jason?" It was, for her, at the root of everything.

"Of course."

"And never leave me?"

"Never."

"Just be good to me, Jason."

"Haven't I been?"

"You've been great."

"You just trust me, baby," he told her. "Whatever I do is for the both of us."

"Of course I trust you, Jason."

She embraced him again.

"You're my man," she said. Had he detected a bit of uncertainty?

"You're sure you don't mind?"

She looked at him, puzzled at first, then her face brightened.

"If it's important to you, Jason."

He wondered about that look. He would have to watch her very carefully.

Arthur Fellows had become a weekly event, and their debriefings had already filled a number of cassettes.

"He thinks the President doesn't like him." She was a slow learner, but once she found the track, she chugged along in a straight line.

"He told you that?"

"He says that somebody is bad-mouthing him."

"Who?"

"I can't remember."

"It's important, baby."

"I'll try to listen harder next time."

Paranoia in the precincts of power was a common Washington ailment. It added spice to any story.

"You did fine, baby," he assured her whenever a note of despondency crept into her voice. Reassurance was always her best medicine.

A benefit for the National Symphony, to be thrown at the Corcoran Gallery of Art, provided what he considered his best shot. The guest list, easily obtainable, included some of Washington's most prominent people, among whom were some likely candidates for his purposes. The inevitable cocktail hour would provide the perfect opportunity to mingle. To simplify any potential follow-up, he had her name and the telephone number of the apartment printed on little cards.

Dorothy looked spectacular in her white evening gown. She had taken great care with her makeup, adding a few extra touches she'd learned at her job.

"You're beautiful," he said.

"You really think so, Jason?"

"Of course, baby."

He was, he knew, betting on the instinctive egomania of men who wielded power, the Achilles heel that breached their invulnerability. Because they lived exclusively within their own exalted orbit, these men knew the aphrodisia inspired by their aura, sensed its special attraction to women. The few exceptions were those who were absorbed so deeply in power's pursuits that all sexuality was blunted.

At the other extreme were those who considered themselves objects of phallic pride, encouraging the image, sometimes overtly, accepting any sexual favors offered if the circumstances were reasonably safe. Still others covertly lusted, quietly hiding behind their facades of propriety, anxiously waiting for some outside force to answer their need.

Perhaps, he thought, he was exaggerating Dorothy's own power to touch the chord of male sexuality. It would not do for her to seem overly aggressive. Nor was it in her character. She was guileless and whatever social poise she had was more apparent in her carriage and passivity; in the innocent arrangement of her near perfect features and the wonderful roundness of her body, shown to marvelous advantage in her new clothes.

Was it naive to think he could point her like a missile and find an instant mark? No! But Dorothy, he was dead certain, was double-barreled buckshot. If there were a likely target within shooting distance, a piece of shot would find its victim.

"I'll point out the people I want you to talk with."

"But what will I say to them?"

"Tell them," he said, "that you are the goddess of the forbidden fruit, one bite of which will send them soaring to a sublime paradise."

Because he was nervous, he had overly fortified himself with Scotch. His giddy facetiousness confused her and he forced his seriousness.

"Tell them how much you admire them. Tell them how handsome and wonderful they are and how you've wanted to meet them. Offer them the unspoken promise."

"The what?"

"Dammit. Just be yourself. If there's no sexual energy between you, forget it. They just have to respond to the calibration. Their own egoism will do the rest. If you see a connection, hand them the card. It's a very tangible message."

"Wouldn't it be easier if you just made the arrangements? This way seems so . . . so unnatural."

"You trying to make a pimp out of me?" he snapped, immediately feeling the flush of his own stupidity. "What I meant was . . ." She hadn't really grasped the full implication of his outburst. ". . . you really don't need any help from me." Even as he spoke the words he felt an unexpected pang of jealousy.

They walked into the large main gallery without incident. Eyes turned as they spotted Dorothy, easily the most attractive woman in the room. They moved to one of the many bars. He ordered her a Scotch and water.

"But I want a beer," she protested.

"You don't drink beer here."

"You don't?"

Standing in a corner, sipping their drinks, he surveyed the crowd. He'd made a list of potential targets, about twenty-five newsworthy gentlemen of varying degrees of importance. Not far from them, he spotted Senator Charles Hurley, a tall well-nourished jovial fellow, recently elected majority leader of the Senate.

"Him," Jason told her. "The big fellow with the pink face."

Watching her, he waited until she registered recognition.

"He's cute," she said.

They moved over to where a knot of people surrounded the senator, who was telling a story. As he finished, they all laughed politely. He prodded Dorothy to move forward.

He saw the senator's peacock response, a stiffening of shoulders, a sucking in of gut, a little flush on his cheeks that hadn't been there before.

The tight circle around him dwindled, and Dorothy was left alone with him for a moment.

A tall woman beside him stirred, poised for protection. She was obviously the senator's wife or companion.

"I'm Jason Martin," he said pleasantly, deflecting her. "*Washington Post.*" He knew such an identification had an intimidating effect.

"I'm Ann Chase, the senator's AA." She seemed uncomfortable. "Mrs. Hurley is out of town. Got to be on call for these things." Her air of defensiveness was embarrassingly transparent.

"Know what you mean," he said, noting peripherally that Dorothy had engaged the senator. She was smiling, listening, occasionally nodding as the senator postured. It was a special talent, he knew. She was a natural magnet, and, best of all, she wasn't acting. Everybody's dream girl.

He soon noted that the senator's AA was more interested in the senator's conversation than in her own with Jason, and she managed to shoot him a stony glance when he momentarily looked away. The senator's eyes became furtive and he shifted his weight uncomfortably. As she had been instructed, Dorothy palmed him the card which he put into his jacket pocket.

"He was very funny," Dorothy said when they had moved away.

"You were wonderful," Jason said, embracing her shoulder.

"This is fun, Jason."

He spotted other possibilities, pointing them out.

"Sprinkle your rosebuds," he said. He was elated. She had met the challenge. As they moved about, the possibilities seemed endless. It was like a hunting expedition.

At one point he lost her in the crowd. It was an odd sensation that inexplicably frightened him. Suddenly she seemed beyond his control, on her own. The idea twisted his stomach into knots. He stood at the bar and ordered a double Scotch, suddenly feeling out of place and uncomfortable. He was confronted, too, with a sense of inadequacy in himself he did not wish to face. Was he using her to compensate for all his lifetime failures and frustrations? He had never been able to mix, to make human contact without anguish, a quality that he felt doomed him forever to loneliness and disconnection. Perhaps he could only satisfy his craving for human contact by manipulating others. As his gaze drifted through the crowd, he imagined he saw kindred souls, standing aloof, acting out the charade of participation, desperately wanting to be somewhere else where the confrontation with themselves would be less painful. Where was she? he fumed. He had not given her permission to desert him. Not yet. Not now.

Fifteen minutes passed before he spotted her gliding toward him, head high, wearing a smile like sunshine.

"You scared me, baby. I thought I'd lost you."

"Lost me? I was doing what you told me to."

"I didn't tell you to get carried away," he said, his irritation and frustration suddenly surfacing.

"What's wrong?" she pleaded, the smile fading.

"We have to be selective. You can't just flirt with anybody." He moved to the bar where he ordered another double Scotch.

"But I thought . . ." She didn't finish the sentence, but instead stood near him, pouting.

How could she understand, he thought. He could not control his irritation.

Ignoring her while the bartender poured, he took his drink and moved nearby to a deserted corner. The cocktail crowd was thinning as the guests made their way to designated tables. She followed him.

"I did what you told me, Jason," she repeated, her voice small and remorseful.

He started to move toward the doorway, assuming she'd again follow. When he arrived there, he noted that she'd been waylaid by a tall man with a colorful decoration pinned to his lapel. From the corner of her eye, she looked at him, hesitating. He signaled approval with a nod, the smile bloomed, and the brief moment of contact continued. Dutifully, she slipped the tall man the card which he looked at briefly before sliding it into a pocket. Jason recognized him. He was Edward Templeton, Army Chief of Staff, slated to be the next chairman of the joint chiefs.

Passing through the doorway he stood waiting on the stairs, ignoring the questioning eyes of those who still manned the entrance. He breathed deeply, trying to control the strange inner eruption as she approached him.

"Are you mad at me?" she asked, confused. He was as confused as she about his strange reaction. They walked down the wide stone steps. Attempting to keep up, she held the hem of her gown to free the movement of her legs. Her high heels made pocking sounds along the pavement.

"But I thought . . ."

"Don't think."

He had parked near the Ellipse, a lawn setting behind the White House, across Seventeenth Street. An early fall chill had come in with the darkness, chasing the Indian summer's day. A three-quarter moon cast an eerie light from the cloudless sky. The Ellipse was deserted, although the twinkling lights of the White House and the old State Department Building gave the illusion of activity. Occasionally a car drove past.

"What did I do?" she asked, facing him.

He said nothing, lit a cigarette and puffed smoke between them as if to obliterate her. Why was he so annoyed? It was all his doing. Dammit, he thought, am I jealous?

Watching his eyes, she seemed to be trying to penetrate his and her own confusion. Maybe, he thought, he hadn't the courage to go through with this. He returned her stare, softening. Her eyes had the look of a hurt puppy. Just be good to me, she'd said. That was always her one condition.

"Maybe we should stop now," she said. Tears had begun to spill onto her cheeks. "I'm afraid, Jason."

"Of what?"

"You promised it was all right. That you wouldn't get upset."

"No. It's fine." His sudden hesitation sobered him.

"If it comes between us, it's not good."

"It won't. I promise."

They stood near the trunk of a tree. A stone's throw away was the booth of the White House guard at the south entrance. He could see the man's vague outline in the lighted booth.

Was it time to seek some validation? He looked at Dorothy, her face shadowed, its expression distraught, as if all she needed for her happiness was his approval. Was what he needed now a test of his surety? Something to thwart his hesitation about the project? And hers? Reaching out, he drew her toward him, enveloping her in his arms. He was leaning against the tree, watching the guard's booth while he breathed in the sweet smell of her. He unfastened the top of her gown freeing her breasts, which caught the glint of the faint light.

"Here?" she asked.

"Yes."

Without hesitation, she responded. It was a test, he told himself. Right here in the shadow of the White House. In the face of danger. This would be the validation, he decided, a flaunting as well.

Lifting her, he felt her naked legs entwine themselves about his torso as his organ speared her and her tongue reached inside of him. He continued to watch the guardhouse as her body undulated, the novelty priming her pleasure while his own waited, testing his omnipotence, challenging his vulnerability.

He felt her orgasmic contractions and heard soft moans, wondering what would happen if she screamed out, alerting the guards. All would be over then. In his heart, did he want it to be over, leaving just the two of them . . . under the stars in the soft night?

When his own release came he lifted himself on his toes, stretching himself taut, his head turned upward like a wolf baying at the moon.

"Are you happy, Jason?" she whispered.

"Yes."

"And not angry?"

For what, he wondered. He had never been angry with her. Only himself.

For a moment, nothing stirred. Life seemed suddenly suspended. No cars moved through the park. He had heard no horn sounds in the distance nor the roar of jets taking off and landing from National Airport across the river.

"In there," he said. "You were wonderful. For a moment I didn't feel worthy." He stroked her hair. He wondered if she would be able to face what was to come. Run, he urged her silently, as fast as you can. If he had shouted it out, would she have obeyed? He didn't want to know the answer.

They got into the car. She moved close to him, like an insect to a flame.

"You know something, Jason?"

His mind had drifted as he maneuvered the car out of the parking place. Finally, he responded.

"What?"

"It was easy," she said. "The men liked me. I mean, they were just like ordinary people."

"Didn't I tell you?" he said, smiling easily as he swung the car onto Pennsylvania Avenue.

VII

Fiona sat on the upholstered white chair, her hands caressing the satiny arms. The room faced west, but the setting sun's last rays had already disappeared behind the houses that lined the street. Logic, she knew, had not brought her here. Why couldn't she let the poor lady rest in peace?

She had let her own frustration get out of hand. She had, indeed, stepped beyond the bounds of police protocol, grilling Martin for no reason, superimposing morbid fantasies in which he was the villain. Her target, she knew, was Clint. It was the damnedest thing how thoughts of him stuck to the surface of her mind, tinging every thought.

She closed her eyes, probing the hushed silence, wondering if this was the place where the dead girl waited. Waited for whom? Had it become, like her own place, a cage?

Thinking of Clint, following his day's routine, she wondered if images of her surfaced in his mind, confusing him. Did it prompt longing? Emptiness? Or was he able to isolate the idea of her, their love, and put it away until he saw her again? She cursed her vulnerability. It was impossible to exorcise him. Her longing was acute, pervasive, uncontrollable.

Was the doomed Dorothy also the victim of this impossible terror? Had the loneliness become unbearable? Did she really bring on her own death?

Tell Ann, Clint, she begged in her heart. And come to me. Was this the whimpering plea of valiant, plucky Fiona FitzGerald, a woman who had stormed the male ramparts of the most macho organization in our society? It sickened her to see herself so helpless.

She got up and began to search the apartment again, peering into closets and drawers. They were not as neat as they had been earlier. She attributed this to Cates, who had poked around and found the little silver pin. Although he had obviously tried to put things back in order, he had not been as fastidious as the former occupant. It offended her to know that a man had disturbed this very private woman's world. She opened Dorothy's underwear drawer, where white satin panties had once been filed like index cards. It was a mess now.

Determined to right this male violation, she began to refold the garments in that special way that only women know. For some reason, she could not get it right. Something was wrong with the uniformity of the pile. It took her some time to discover that three of the satin panties were of different sizes from the rest. Removing them from the drawer, she stretched them, noting that they were at least three sizes larger than the others. There was also one bra much bigger than the others.

She began to rummage through the rest of the drawers. One, which she had assumed was filled with pantyhose, contained as well a collection of garter belts and, also neatly folded, a pile of stockings, the kind that only sheathed the legs up to the thighs. It was the kind her mother used to wear. A number of them were a larger size than the others, longer both in the length and the foot.

Was it possible that *two* women lived in this place? The excitement of discovery seemed to clock off her anguish. She felt professional again, like a bloodhound locked into the scent. Poking in the closets, she opened shoe boxes. The woman was a size six. After going through twenty boxes, she discovered, as she now suspected she would, a pair of white high-heeled shoes with open backs that were much larger. There were no others that size.

A thorough search of the closets failed to turn up any outsized dresses. An explanation eluded her. Perhaps the woman had an occasional visitor, a larger female, who had simply left some of her things around. She contemplated the collection, which she had lined up on the dresser: panties, bra, stockings, and one pair of high-heeled shoes. After a while, she put them back where she'd found them.

It had grown dark by then and she lit the bedroom lamps. Suddenly the sound of the telephone's ring pierced the silence.

The phone was persistent. When it had rung five or six times, she finally picked it up.

"Hello."

She heard the click simultaneously. Replacing the receiver in its cradle, she looked at it for a long time. So somebody still thinks she's alive. Fiona had been in the apartment for hours and the phone had never rung before. What did it mean? Again she thought of Clint—a single love, a single source of agony.

A tinkle of metal alerted her. Someone seemed to be picking the lock. As a reflex, she quickly doused the lights. A key was turning in the lock. Flattening herself against the bedroom door, instinctively unbuttoning her holster and slipping out her gun, she waited. The door squeaked open. Footsteps moved into the apartment. The movement was cautious, tentative. A burst of light illumined the corridor. The intruder moved forward, less cautious. Through the crack in the doorjamb, she saw the figure of a man. A light flashed on overhead and she stepped into his path, sliding her piece back into its holster.

"Goddamn," she hissed. It was Cates, his startled eyes round as saucers.

"You scared the shit out of me," he said, obviously glad to see her.

"I hope so."

For a moment, they glared at each other.

"I was sure you'd be here," he said haltingly. "The key was missing from the files. Besides, you were acting strangely." After the interrogation of Martin, they had investigated two naturals. She had been unusually distant, tight-lipped and morose. Cates had done most of the talking. She remembered leaving the office in a fog, heading straight to Dorothy's apartment.

"I called your place first," he said, regarding her. "Are you all right?"

"I'm not sure. I made an ass of myself with Martin. If he's smart, he'll complain. He has good grounds."

"This thing bugs you," he said flatly. "I saw it from the beginning."

"Look who's talking. Who found that pin?" But it was a lame sortie. Leave it alone, she begged herself. It was time to bow out.

"I explained that," he said. "I was just trying to see what I missed and you saw. I mean," he stammered, "to me, it was a simple case of suicide. I came back last night to understand it . . . why you were still uncertain."

"I'm not anymore."

"Now I'm totally confused." He paused. "I may not have your experienced instincts, but . . ."

"The hell with it."

He scratched his head, more as a symbol than an itch.

"I don't understand."

"Let's just shelve it. Too many naturals. Haven't had a good murder mystery for a long time. I guess I tried to manufacture one."

"Then you're satisfied?"

"Yes."

"I'm not," he said tentatively.

"Shit." It was out of control. All her fault. And Clint's.

Cates drew in his breath. "In the kitchen," he said, leading her there. He opened the refrigerator, which was empty except for a few beer cans. Reaching behind the beer, he brought out three small cans and held them up. She inspected the labels.

"Foreign," she said.

"Beluga caviar. Russian."

"What's so strange about that?"

He pointed to the label.

"Written in Czech."

She looked at the labels, not comprehending.

"I wrote down the words," he said. "It bothered me all day. I didn't want to raise . . . Hell, we had enough going down. After I did the naturals, I called around to all the gourmet shops. They sell Beluga, but not this. This is Czech. Direct. Sold only in Czechoslovakia. They change the labels."

"So?" She was determined to be noncommittal.

"So she got these as a gift from a Czech national. Maybe a diplomat." He squinted at her. "Come on, Fiona. You see what I mean?" He showed a brief annoyance, then became diffident. She knew exactly what he was driving at.

"Look what we got. A miniature silver bar, studded with the rank of four star general. Cans of Beluga caviar sold only in Czechoslovakia. Rent paid three months in advance. A suspicious reaction from a newspaperman. Martin, you know, used to be a top investigative reporter . . ." And oversized clothes, she silently added to the list. And a single telephone call.

"All right," she said, leaning against the refrigerator.

"Am I fantasizing?" he asked.

"That's your job," she snapped. He lowered his eyes and fingered the small cans.

"I was all set to drop it after this afternoon," he said. "I felt funny after this Martin bit. You were acting . . ."

"Stupid."

"Maybe." He paused. "Then this other thing occurred to me."

"Now we're both in the manufacturing business."

"Why be different?" he smiled, slyly. She felt her resolve breaking down. "What did you find?"

Was she that transparent? She filled him in about the oversized underwear and the phone call.

"But where is there evidence of murder?" she asked. "We first need a victim. It's the usual chronology."

"At least it's on our own time and we're not costing anybody anything."

They closed the apartment door behind them and walked out into the quiet, darkened street.

"Lift?"

"Sure." She slipped into his car beside him.

"You don't think we're going bananas."

"An occupational hazard."

"I think she's trying to tell us things."

"Let's not get ahead of ourselves," Fiona cautioned. It was uncanny the way he was picking up her own thoughts.

He stopped the car in front of her apartment house. Before she could open the door, he reached out and offered his hand.

"Partners?" he said.

Her hesitation was brief. It was something she needed as well. "Partners," she said, grasping his hand, returning his grateful pressure.

She could hear the phone ringing inside the apartment. Fumbling with the key, panicked that it would stop, she finally made it to the phone, slightly breathless.

"I was worried," Clint said.

"Worried?"

"I tried the apartment all night."

Her heart lurched. Had he told Ann? But the joy quickly dissipated when she heard party noises in the background.

"I had to go with Ann to the senator's reception. I'm here now." She held the phone away from her ear and took a deep breath. All the earlier anguish rushed back.

"You?" he asked.

"Just the usual."

"Miss me?"

"Of course."

"I love you," he said. The three magic words, she snickered. She wanted to scream out her anger. Tell her, goddammit.

"I ache for you, baby," he sighed. "Leave the chain off the hook."

It was a signal between them. It meant he would be in her bed before seven. Fresh from his and Ann's.

"I will, Clint."

Her eyes filled with helpless tears.

"I'll count the minutes. Got to go. Love you."

No one should have to endure this, she told herself, sitting in the dark. Was it that way for you, Dorothy? she asked, palming her ears, shutting out any sound of a potential answer.

VIII

While Dorothy was working, he listened to the tape of the answering machine in the apartment. It was sufficient justification for his earlier discomfort. As he had suspected, she had been too indiscriminate in her zeal and had dredged up unlikely candidates. Of the three messages, he noted that one had been scared off by her recording.

The recordings indicated that he had to amplify his strategy, invest more time and money. He bought her additional dresses, and together they began a furious round of cocktail parties, diplomatic receptions, pre-dinner cocktail hours, whatever event seemed likely to attract Washington's powerful elite. Obediently, she proffered her card to senators, representatives, diplomats, and high administration types. Not that he recognized all of them. Sometimes he had to ask fellow guests, always eager to oblige, as if knowing who was important somehow increased their own status.

Is the man newsworthy? As always, that was his principal criterion, although there were others. He naturally looked for married men, although single men were equally vulnerable. But those who reached the pinnacle of power were careful to preserve the married state. Even when they divorced, they quickly remarried. Marriage, they'd all learned, was good for their careers. He marveled at how simple it was for a beautiful woman to make contact with a powerful man. Youth and physical beauty transcended all barriers and the promise of availability was a powerful ice-breaker. Under all the discreet politeness and articulation, under the finery and finesse, there was a pervasive predatory instinct. People searched and scrutinized each other like eagles alert for prey. Whether the prize was power or profit, the event itself formed the boundaries of the jungle and everyone hunted for their own reasons.

The new strategy brought its rewards, vindicating his tenacity. The calls she was now getting pleased him.

Dorothy basked in his admiration, relating her own effectiveness and self-image directly to his reactions.

"I did good?" she asked, after she told him who called. He had carefully briefed her on how to respond. He had also drummed into her some basic caveats: Never be seen with them in public. Tell as little about herself as possible. Put them completely at their ease. Never talk to one about any of the others. Remember as much as possible about what they said and keep them coming back to the apartment. He was truly confident she could do that.

When she grew curious, he offered vague explanations that satisfied her, at least for the moment.

"It's who you know that counts," he told her. "And what better way to get to know important people than this?"

"Are they really important?"

"Very."

"And will me knowing them help you very much?"

"You, too, Dorothy."

"How?"

"Having friends in important places is the name of the game. It's called Vitamin P."

"Vitamin P?"

"Pussy Power," he added playfully.

She giggled. Sometimes what she was doing troubled her and he had difficulty dispelling her blues.

"And you're not jealous?"

"No. Because I know that what we're doing is strictly business."

"Business?"

"That's what it all adds up to, Dot."

"Then I guess that's okay. As long as nobody hurts anybody. They're really very nice."

"Hurt anybody? Where did you get that idea?"

"Sometimes I feel, you know, funny. Like it's wrong." She would pucker her lips and her brow would wrinkle.

"Wrong?" He looked at her sternly. "Just do it, Dot. If anything's wrong I'll make it right. I promise you. I know you don't fully understand, but trust me. Do you trust me, Dot?"

"You know I do."

"Then don't worry about it. Everything will work out for us. Just trust me."

"Sure, Jason. I'll do anything you want. Anything."

"Just this, baby. Just this."

Soon she was juggling three men around, a schedule that required careful coordination since he had decided that it would make sense for her to continue at her job. To be unemployed implied that she was a prostitute, a role that would seriously diminish the ultimate story.

He was overjoyed at the two others who had fallen into the net: Senator Charles Hurley, majority whip of the Senate and a close friend of the President, and Army Chief of Staff Edward Templeton, a four star general. Arthur Fellows continued his weekly visits.

Fearful that the debriefings would become a chore for her that would induce boredom or forgetfulness, he encouraged an air of lightness, of fun. Often, she dissolved in giggles as she described some sexual variation.

"He makes me paint my tits with lipstick and he likes me to paint his thing with little squiggles."

"Squiggles?"

"Like wormy little circles."

She was referring to General Templeton, who had other special preferences as well. Like watching them doing it in the mirror. And talking baby talk.

"It's fun," she said, imitating the general. "Sometimes he spanks me like a bad little girl."

"But what does he talk about?" It was always a persistent refrain.

"His wife can't get it off without a vibrator."

"He told you that?"

After awhile, the sexual oddities, which she would dwell on in detail, became repetitive.

"The general's wife sounds horrible. She gets drunk a lot and he keeps her locked up in her room all day long. I feel sorry for him. He's a very nice man."

"Does he say anything about his work?"

"He calls some man the chairman. Says he's an asshole."

"You're kidding." Despite his professional glee at receiving such information, his excitement was always tempered with a personal revulsion. Every man, after all, was entitled to his dirty little secrets.

"He's also very worried about the Army boys. Says they're not worth shit as soldiers. Too many spics and coons."

"He said it just like that?"

"What's wrong with that?" she asked innocently.

Always, once she'd falter, either from boredom or lack of anything more to say, he would ask, "That's it?"

Expecting it, she always seemed to withhold something for that last moment, as if to especially please him.

"He gave me this little pin." She opened her robe to show him a little silver four star pin fastened to the crotch of her panties. Accepting gifts was another caveat. If they gave her anything of value, she had to turn it over to him. It was, after all, tangible evidence. But the pin didn't amount to much and he was feeling so good about the material that she was providing that he let her keep it.

He might have been even more generous after the Senator Hurley debriefing, only the senator provided no little gifts. He had come to her very drunk after a dinner at the Saudi Arabian Embassy, but it hadn't fazed Dorothy. She was used to that.

"He was very mad about something. He called the President a Zionist bastard." A frown gathered on her forehead. "I think that's what he said." She obviously had no idea what it meant and shrugged it off.

"Did he say something else?" He wanted to keep her train of thought running.

"He said the ambassador from Saudi Arabia gave him a bad time. That he'd made a deal and was being double-crossed. I can't remember. He kept going on and on about it."

"What happened?"

"I undressed him. He couldn't get it up. So I made him some coffee and gave him a massage. He loved that. He said I was the most beautiful girl he'd ever been with." Such compliments never failed to please her and she remembered them and their source long after they were spoken.

"So nothing happened?"

"Oh it did. I danced for him, like at Johnny's."

"That did it?"

"No. It wasn't until he danced for me. He was cute. He loved doing that dance. It gave him a hard on."

The image of the overweight senator doing a dance with an erection made him burst out laughing.

"He got so excited, he came in the middle."

"You're kidding."

"He was cute. Like a little boy. He had a great time."

"Did he say anything else? Anything about his job?"

"Oh, he hates that. He told me so."

"It's unbelievable," Jason said with astonishment. "The things they tell you."

"Why?"

The insight excited him. A lover was better mental therapy than any priest or psychiatrist. She apparently had qualities beyond even his earlier imaginings.

"You're fantastic."

"Me?"

"You set them free," he told her, patting her on the head appreciatively.

"We have fun. I like them, Jason."

"Just don't like them too much."

She watched him, pouting.

"Not the way I feel about you, Jason. Not like that."

After a month of debriefings, he had enough information for a big story. But he wanted a bigger one. Even when it became apparent that Webster had planned to keep him out in the Fairfax Siberia indefinitely, he resisted. He wasn't ready. Not yet.

"I'm working on something really big," he told Webster one day as they passed in the city room.

"Great."

The response was overlarded with enthusiasm, the kind given as a placebo, without sincerity. He had the impression that the editor had actually forgotten his name. Angered, he was on the verge of expanding the hint, but by then the editor had moved away. Not yet, he decided. His send-up was still not strong enough; he would keep to his original plan.

But it was not without its minefields. He had to be more cautious about where he exhibited Dorothy. Not only did he want to keep the principals in his little drama separated, he did not want to risk them observing her in active pursuit of others.

Their outings on the party circuit grew sparse and he would not make a foray if he couldn't manage to get the guest list in advance, a tactic that considerably diminished their activities. When too many questions were asked, he quickly retreated.

"No more parties?" she sighed. Sometimes she would try on her party dresses and prance around the Capitol Hill apartment. Between trysts, he tried to keep her amused. They went to lots of movies, mostly horror films at her choosing. He also bought her movie fan magazines.

Because of his caution, the infrequent parties he took her to didn't provide good pickings and, usually, they left early. He detected a growing restlessness in her.

Fortuitously, Arthur Fellows provided a welcome breakthrough.

"He wants me to meet a friend of his," Dorothy told him at one of the debriefings.

"Who?"

"Some man named Tate. A congressman."

"Tate O'Haire?"

"He just said Tate."

Tate O'Haire was chairman of the powerful House Ways and Means Committee.

"Great."

"You want me to meet him?"

It was, of course, an unexpected windfall that had come just in time. Dorothy was becoming less sharp about their debriefings. Her concentration meandered and his rebukes only made it worse.

"Why must we keep doing this, Jason? It's hard to get new things."

"You're doing just fine, baby."

"Sometimes it seems silly. I mean, telling all that private stuff." She shook her head. "And them not knowing that here I am telling you all about it. Sometimes it just doesn't seem right."

"You're only talking to me," Jason said, sensing that he was on dangerous ground.

"And that thing?" She pointed to the recorder. "Why do we need that?"

"It's important," he said.

"But why?"

Hadn't she surmised it by now? Surely she had some inkling, but if she did, she was keeping it to herself. If she was confused about his intentions, it didn't inhibit her willingness to meet new men.

Jason had flattered her by telling her that the man, Tate, had seen her once at a party and was dying to meet her. What Arthur was doing was simply passing her along, a blatant bribe. Apparently, the

White House minions were under pressure to get some legislation passed to which Tate O'Haire held the key.

"We really had a good time together," Dorothy told him as the tape recorder whizzed. Her concentration had returned. She had needed the injection of new blood.

"He likes me to tie him up."

"Tie him up?"

"He brings this special kind of rope. It's a silly game. I tie him to the closet rod and close the door."

For a moment, he was so shaken he turned off the recorder.

"What's wrong?"

"He's one of the most powerful men in the country," Jason said with amazement. "No money is spent, no tax laws are changed without his approval." It was the furthest he'd ever gone to explain any of it. She looked at him blankly and shrugged.

"It's just a game."

Jason shook his head and turned the recorder back on. He made her describe in detail the man's reactions, which she did as if she were describing the plot of a movie, replete with "and thens." This time he had to deliberately turn away from her, afraid his reactions would seem judgmental.

"He cries like a baby. I tell him I won't let him out of the closet until he promises to be a good boy."

"My God!"

He had always thought of such behavior as aberrations. In her descriptions, after the initial shock, they sounded like no more than a mild form of recreation, like playing bridge or going to a ballgame.

Even his elation at having been given such a juicy morsel could not temper his amazement. The idea of it also left him unguarded.

"What a book it will make."

"Book?"

Quickly, he backtracked, sensing a ripple of indignation, not quite expected.

"I mean if someone wrote about that."

"Why would anyone want to do such a thing?"

"Because people are interested," he explained patiently.

"They are?"

"Makes important people seem human. Just like us," he continued, although he detected some lingering confusion. Actually, he was more puzzled than she. There was some odd equation between sex and power. Maybe being in the public arena was so repressive to a person's id that when the pressure was off, they got weird. Was it Dorothy that brought out these oddities? It was as if she had the ability to recreate an entirely new code of sexual behavior, a completely different set of morals.

Or maybe conventional morality, the accepted rules of sexual conduct, wasn't the truth at all, but merely existed as a protective facade, made to hide a humanity that didn't fit the concept of the Christian-Judaic ethic, squaring off human instincts to fit the perfect rounds of manufactured convention. It surprised him to probe so deeply, but it explained what he had only dimly understood before. Aberrations sold because recounting them secretly reassured people. It amazed him to see how his original idea had grown, expanded, become important in a larger context. He was becoming an instrument of greater awareness, of a philosophical truth. The great middle class and their packaged notions about themselves and their leaders was a pack of lies and he was going to be the first to blow the lid off them. It was their false indignation that made them so vulnerable and made what he was doing so valuable. He would actually be doing a great service to society, contributing to the highest goals of life, knowledge, awareness, insight.

With four men to keep track of, her scheduling required careful balancing, playing havoc with her attendance record at Saks. On Wednesdays, her normal day off, she began seeing two of her lovers: Arthur Fellows in midday and General Templeton in the evening.

During their debriefings she often got them mixed up, much to Jason's irritation.

"I'm merely trying to ascertain where Arthur stands in the power struggle at the White House." His frankness only confused her. She had no idea which little detail was especially relevent to him.

"I keep forgetting things."

"Try to remember."

Sometimes in Dorothy's recounting, the paths of the two men figuratively would cross in a single day.

"It's a small, exclusive club and it meets on the pinnacle of a pyramid," he sighed.

"Arthur says Eddie may not get to be chairman," Dorothy told him, comprehending little. Jason forced himself to remain casual.

"Did he say why?"

"Something about the President favoring Mulligan's man." Mulligan meant Ed Mulligan, Arthur's rival for the President's ear, the other Presidential counsel.

"I feel bad for Eddie," she said. "He wants to be chairman more than anything in the world. And he thinks he will be. Arthur is all for it."

"You discussed that?"

"I just listened. Like you told me."

"Good girl."

"Is it very important?"

"Very."

The paths of Dorothy's other two lovers also crossed in conversation.

"Charlie had lunch with Tate today."

"Did they?"

"They have lunch all the time."

"What do they talk about?"

"All I know is that Tate is going to run for the Senate and Charlie is going to try to get lots of money for him to run."

"But they're different parties."

"Gosh." He wondered if she understood.

Jason had discovered another factor that seemed to take the sting of evil out of what he was doing. The men seemed to have a genuine affection for Dorothy and she enjoyed being with them. Not only did she, too, enjoy the sex, but the men's company entertained and amused her.

Sometimes after a debriefing, he would ask her questions that had a special relevance for him alone.

"Do they ever ask about you? Where you come from? How you live? You know, questions like that."

"You said I should tell them as little as possible." She paused. "I tell them about Pennsylvania. Growing up in a coal town. Things like that. I also tell them how I feel about things."

"Like what?"

She thought for a moment and smiled. "About how much I like the snow. And the springtime. And clean things. But mostly they talk about themselves."

"Egos," Jason said.

"They're like little boys."

She was more like a little girl herself, he thought. And they obviously didn't want the reality of Dorothy to interfere with their fantasies of her, as if they could create her whole, just the way they wanted her to be. It was, of course, one of his secret fears that one of them, or some of them, or all of them, would fall in love with her. Emotional betrayal brought out the killing beast, made reactions less predictable. Also, he feared that she, too, might fall in love with one of them. That would complicate everything.

Sometimes, in the middle of the night, his paranoia would take control and he would shake her awake.

"Do they talk about love?"

She always slept deeply, what seemed like a silent dreamless contented sleep, and prodding her awake was always an effort.

"The men. Any of them talk about love? Loving you?"

"Me?" Slowly, she emerged out of the fog of sleep. "Of course, they love me. Why do they come to visit me?"

He shrugged and moved to embrace her.

"Like you love me, Jason," she whispered, cuddling into his embrace.

"Like me?"

Though not reassured, it was a subject he preferred not to explore further. He made love to her instead.

The Czech ambassador literally picked her up at Saks. Although he spoke English fairly fluently, his understanding of the tongue was faulty. He assumed Dorothy also sold perfume. When she protested, he persisted stubbornly.

"You are a pretty lady. You will know what I should buy."

It was an odd hour and the store was too busy.

"I am the Czech ambassador," he said, obviously used to pulling rank when the occasion called for it.

Reluctantly, she helped him, after telling one of the salesgirls in perfume that she would let her write the sale so she could get the commission.

"What kind do you use?" he asked finally, after he had sniffed all the available scents.

Before he was through, he had his card in her hand. She read it and knew instantly how to pronounce his name.

"I'm Polish," she said, explaining that she used the name Curtis because it was easy to pronounce.

"A fellow Slav," he said, putting out his hand. He was a chubby man in his middle forties, blond and good-humored with a high-pitched, easy laugh.

"May I call you?" he asked. "If you don't mind going out with a communist."

"I never met a communist," she told him.

As with all her encounters with men, she told Jason everything. It was becoming second nature to her now and she studied his face to read his reactions.

"Another windfall," he said happily. After considering it for a while, his enthusiasm abated. As an ambassador from a communist country, he was obviously under complete surveillance. And he was married. It would be dangerous for the man to take risks and give the Americans a weapon that could be used against him by his own government. But he did not reject the idea outright. He had, of course, contemplated that a diplomat would one day fall into the net, but he had never calculated that it would be a communist diplomat, truly a bonus. The Profumo case in England came to mind. Profumo was the English defense minister, who shared a prostitute with a Russian naval attaché. It made worldwide celebrities out of all the participants. She hadn't read or heard about it, of course. Nor would the implications have hit home if she had.

The risk of his plan was premature discovery. He dreaded the possibility of losing control of the material, even though he had Dorothy sign a paper giving him worldwide marketing rights to her story.

A communist diplomat! The idea was intriguing. Surely the man was clever enough, knowing that he was under surveillance, to throw them off the scent when he was pursuing an infidelity. When he appeared again at Saks, this time under the pretext of buying make-up for his wife, she had been fully briefed, reporting the conversation back to Jason.

"He asked me to meet him at a hotel," she said, giggling. "He really is very cute."

"And direct."

"I said what you told me to."

He had instructed her to tell the ambassador that she was frightened of going out with a communist, that all ambassadors were under surveillance, that their lines were tapped and their whereabouts carefully monitored.

"He just laughed and told me not to worry. Although, he did look around and lowered his voice when he spoke. 'I have my ways,' he told me."

"What ways?"

"He didn't say, but he told me not to worry, to trust him and no one would ever know."

He wondered how many people had been deceived by such an imperative? Especially Dorothy. Weighing the alternatives, he decided to tempt fate. Bagging a certified communist was worth the risk.

"Invite him to the apartment," he told her. It was too good an opportunity to enhance the story and increase its value. And value in raw monetary terms was an extremely important consideration. The cost of the operation had stretched his finances to the breaking point. He was behind on his bank note and Jane had begun legal proceedings to collect back support payments for Trey. His last few phone conversations with his ex-wife had ended badly, and he had begun to worry about Trey's future.

"I'm working on something big, Jane," he'd said. "A book. I should get a solid advance and catch up."

"I've heard that before." She had hung up abruptly. She was right, of course.

"You'll see," he muttered into the dead phone.

For the first time since he had begun the adventure, he felt the pressure of time.

On the evening of the Czech's assignation, Jason sat in his car outside of the townhouse to make sure the man wasn't being followed. From his vantage, he had an excellent view of the quiet street. He could see the windows of the apartment and he'd instructed her to keep the lights off and watch the headlights of his car. If she saw them go on or heard the motor start, she was not, under any circumstances, to buzz open the front door.

In order to keep this vigil, he had to miss an important meeting of the Fairfax County Council, although he had made arrangements to have it covered by one of the reporters from a weekly paper, a chancy business at best. To do this was a violation of all his professional instincts.

He looked at his watch. The ambassador was nearly fifteen minutes late, which he attributed to the inefficiency of the communist system. It also gave him second thoughts about the chance he was taking. It could ruin everything. Perhaps it was a sign to abort the whole idea. He grew increasingly impatient as he watched people pass, hurrying homeward. He observed each person carefully, watching for signs of surveillance as well. An old man walked haltingly down the street, slightly bent and unsteady. The man carried a paper bag in his arms as he meandered in his direction. Ignorning him, Jason turned his attention to the rearview mirror to check the other end of the street. When he looked back he noticed that the street was suddenly deserted.

At the same time he saw that the lights had come on in the apartment, giving him a brief glimpse of Dorothy as she drew the draperies.

"Son of a bitch," he muttered. It was the old man . . .

He'd obviously evaded the American security system. Too bad it would be a futile victory, he thought with delight as he gunned the motor and moved out of the parking space.

But, by God, they had bagged themselves an ambassador.

IX

Love had split Fiona into two persons. One of them was coldly rational, a sensitive observer, relentlessly self-critical, a brutally honest judge of the other. That other was preposterous, adolescent, sickeningly romantic, capable of violent mood swings from glorious euphoria to extreme anxiety and depression.

Even now as she lay embraced in Clint's arms, one could not resist ridiculing the other. The absurd other had let this man materialize beside her at 6 A.M., fresh from his legitimate marriage bed. They had always avoided any references to sex in connection with his wife, as if by evading the subject they might deny its existence.

She wondered how many other Washington mistresses allowed such an early morning assignation to occur. It did not, after all, interfere with one's work day. He could pop off to his office and, after a long day, a stalwart hard-working husband and father could return to the legal nest, still master of his kingdom. For some reason, too, mornings did not induce the heavy angst of an evening tryst, as if the day still held the promise of a resolution in favor of true love.

True love! The sensible part of her berated the other part for letting herself get caught in the coils of such hopeless folderol. If there was a shred of individuality and backbone in the other just moments before he would arrive, it would quickly disintegrate under his warm kiss. Soon he would be naked beside her, showering her with kisses, loving her body as well as her soul. (This other put a very high premium on spirituality.) At this moment of his arrival, she was the object of a formidable attack on all her vulnerabilities. The sensible one could only observe and try to understand. Not that it mattered—the other, the wild one, soared on waves of selfish pleasure.

Because he was the dissimulator, she had to accommodate herself to his meandering schedule, knowing it could only be worked around the rhythm of his married life. This made his wife, the formidable and mysterious Ann, the true manipulator of their time together. That humiliation alone was enough to revolt her sensible self, fill her with shame and humiliation and curse her fate as the natural twin of the other.

"You're wonderful," Clint told her. "A gift."

"And you my darling."

"I love you."

"I love you."

Under normal circumstances, they could thrash around together until nearly eight. Then a somewhat pale and enervated Clint would shower and dress and be off to face his morning's duties. She wondered if anyone in his office ever noticed his temporary exhaustion. For her part, she would rise after he had gone, energized and rosy-cheeked, ready to take on a thousand eggplants and whatever strenuous assignments the day had to offer. Unfortunately, the pain of forced separation was getting worse now that their meetings had become a ritualized pattern, like getting one's meals at a set hour.

That morning she had to confine their lovemaking to a mere hour, although she didn't explain her physical greed until it was time to hop out of bed. Yet even in that time frame she managed to induce his usual orgasmic quota, three, an accomplishment that never failed to make him marvel at his masculine prowess. Even that had become a part of the ritual, an expectation that seemed beyond their control, as if their desire for each other needed tangible validation.

The eggplant had called an eight o'clock meeting of the entire homicide squad. The teenage killer had struck again. More significant was the fact that the new killing had taken place while the Marine suspect had been in custody.

Nor was there time to dwell on the more important question between them. Had he told Ann? And if he had, what then? It was the impermanence of it as well that had begun to unravel her. Despite her liberation, she discovered that, like all good Irish girls, she really wanted to be married. That revelation grew more and more powerful with its denial. It jarred her. Having such conventional desires would have warmed the cockles of her parents' hearts, had she told them. As it was they'd simply given up on her ever marrying.

She bent over him to implant a goodbye kiss. As she did so, she suddenly thought of Dorothy. What was the real commonality between them? Naturally, the passionate one would hear none of that. It was the other that was pursuing Dorothy's imaginary killer, if only to prove a point.

At the meeting, she forced herself to concentrate on the eggplant's every nuance, making sure that when his eyes drifted her way, she showed rapt attention. Actually, she was still thinking of Dorothy. If the eggplant knew what they were up to, he would explode.

"I want every available man on this case," the eggplant ordered, as if they were all to blame for this affront to the dignity of his office. When he was in this state, the force became all male again. It was not, of course, the appropriate time to remind him of her gender.

"Think I should fill him in on the Curtis case?" Cates whispered during a lull in the speech as the eggplant pored over an assignment sheet. She assumed he was joking.

"Only if you're planning your own castration."

The eggplant began another tirade. Once he'd spent himself, the meeting broke up and they were assigned to follow up on a series of call-in leads. The chief had authorized the newspapers to print the usual "Any information on the teenage killings, etc." and offering a police number which came directly into their office.

The result was a maze of confused leads, an endless descent into fantasy and anxiety. They talked to parents of teenagers, who swore they knew the killer, tips that proved worthless, especially those instigated by revenge. They spent the day in the heavily populated

black ghetto areas of Northeast Washington, walking up stairways
and through corridors of incredible filth.

But the wide publicity given to the murders and the race of the
victims had stirred the ghetto community, feeding its paranoia. Many
of those to whom they talked were certain, as some had been during
Atlanta's similar crisis, that the beginning of the crusade to violent-
ly eliminate all blacks had begun. Guilt-ridden whites continued to
give money to the fund for the victims' illegitimate children.

Cates's unenthusiastic response to the assignment and bored
demeanor throughout their interviews was not surprising to her. The
ghetto was as foreign to him as it was to her.

"What are they going to tell a honky and an oreo?" Cates asked,
knowing that it was futile, a ploy for the eggplant to show that
homicide was working double time. They both knew it was an exercise in bureaucratic hypocrisy. Still, they checked things out with
obstinate efficiency.

During their afternoon break, Fiona took time out to cajole
Flannagan on the phone. He was the man in charge of the Mobile
Crime Lab, to whom she had come often for favors, invoking the old
ethnic tie.

"Come on, Mick, give it a dust-off for a daughter of the old sod,"
she begged him. Both of them knew the case wasn't strong enough
for an official Mobile Crime Lab sweep.

"And what do I get if I do?" It was his typical response, more ban-
ter than proposition.

"Satisfaction. And you'll go to Irish heaven."

"And stink through eternity of corned beef and cabbage."

"Would that be heaven or hell you're talking about?"

"Hell. Heaven is an authentic Irish pub with Guinness hisself
servin' the brew . . ." He paused. "Oh shit, Fiona, why do I have to
be pressed in the middle of an earthquake? You saw him this morning. Apoplectic."

"How can you tell?"

"He turns ebony-black."

The fact was that the commonality between them was racial as well as ethnic. The dwindling numbers of whites drew them closer together. The blacks didn't object. It gave the whites an opportunity to learn the pains of being a minority.

"I'll get on it as soon as I can," Flannagan said finally.

"Thanks, Mick."

"He finds out, he'll have my ass."

"Who the hell would want your ass?" she said, hanging up, knowing she had pushed as hard as she could.

As expected, the leads turned up nothing of significance.

"Home?" Cates asked as they got into the car.

"Hell no."

"There again?"

"It's not on the taxpayer's tab."

He shrugged and headed for the dead girl's apartment.

"And suppose we do find evidence of murder. What then? It would have to be proof positive. You saw him. He has a one track mind."

She nodded. He was right, of course. What was one more dead honky?

Entering the apartment, she sensed something immediately awry.

"What is it?"

"I don't know," she admitted.

He went to the kitchen and opened the refrigerator.

"They're still there."

She began to move around the apartment. Somebody had been in this place since she had last been there. It was her police training, she would have argued, if someone had suggested that it might be intuition. A matrix in her mind had been disturbed.

She began poking into the closets again, opening the medicine chest, cautious now about smearing prints, berating her earlier carelessness. It had always been difficult, even under the best conditions, to look for something that had not yet become tangible in her mind. She felt Cates watching her, confused, as she stood in the center of the bedroom, surveying it, taking mental inventory of each object, then comparing it with the subconscious memory of her previous visits.

"Anything?" Cates asked.

It occurred to her slowly at first, a blip on her memory screen that grew each time her eyes washed over the white chest in which Dorothy kept her underwear. She inspected it from every view. The blip grew in her mind until it focused on the upper drawer of the chest. Although it was closed, it wasn't flush against the edge. Not that she could remember if she had actually pushed the drawer to its furthest point, but it was enough awry to trigger her curiosity and she opened it. Without having to go through the neat pile of white panties, she knew immediately. The large sizes were gone. Opening the lower drawer, she checked the stockings. Gone. The shoes, too, were gone.

Cates had been observing her, understanding immediately.

"El kinko."

"What?" But it was coming to her as well.

"Our man. He's a dress-up freak."

She felt the flush begin at the back of her neck and spread upward and around to her face.

"Very common," Cates said authoritatively.

"I'm either very straight or very dumb," she conceded.

"That makes me an expert in kink."

"I'd never have guessed. It could explain the caller."

Suddenly there was no time to dispel his confusion. The door to the apartment began to rattle and she heard the sound of metal. Someone was obviously picking the lock. With hand signals, she directed Cates to the other side of the door. Both drew their pieces. The sound of the metal pick continued. They could see the knob begin to turn and the door swing outward.

They heard voices. There was no attempt to be clandestine. At least two of them, Fiona thought, holding up two fingers, tensing as heavy footsteps crossed into the apartment.

"Jeez," Flannagan screamed, a vein palpitating in his jaw. One of the cops behind him had reacted quickly by stepping back into the hallway and flattening himself against a wall.

"Sorry," Fiona said, putting her piece back in its holster, relieved. In retrospect, she knew, it would probably be deemed a mistake to have drawn, a needless risk. If Flannagan had reacted badly, they might have had a huge problem on their hands.

"I'm doing you a favor, Fi. I don't need to have the shit scared out of me."

"We got nervous," she said apologetically, as two technicians entered the room with their equipment.

"What I need most is a good set of prints," she said, drawing Flannagan aside and explaining about the drawer. "Dust the inside as well. Closets, too. And the cans in the refrigerator, the Beluga caviar."

Flannagan shook his head and smiled. Despite their kinship, Fiona suspected he didn't quite take her seriously.

"Anything else, your bigness?"

"One other place. The toilet seat. Especially that spot that a man uses to lift it."

"Gross," Flannagan said, chuckling.

Latent fingerprints, at best, were always a problem. And without a real crime, she wasn't sure how she was going to handle the situation. She'd wait and see.

Fiona and Cates went for hamburgers at a little bar not far from Dorothy's apartment. The waitress set down two beers and they sipped in silence for awhile. Observing Cates, she realized he was getting an odd lesson in unorthodox procedures. She was actually corrupting him, a thought that made her uneasy. Obviously, he had enough problems. He was a black man with white features and a white view of the world. Reflecting on it, she felt a flush of sister-ly warmth.

"You said it could explain your caller," Cates said.

"Can't you guess?" she teased. He tensed, reacting exactly oppo-site to what she intended. He must have mistook it for a put-down. She realized suddenly that she really hardly knew the man.

"He wanted to see if the apartment was empty," she said, hoping that she did not seem smug. ". . . to get his unmentionables."

"But you said he didn't respond. How could you know it was even a man? And you said hello. It wasn't Dorothy's voice."

His interrogation increased her uneasiness. She was presenting theory as fact, superimposing imaginary circumstances.

"Don't you see?"

He shook his head, still unconvinced. "I don't see."

"But the clothes are gone."

She was begging him to understand, seeking vindication. But his eyes darted from side to side, revealing his mind's wanderings.

"Your theory," he began, cautious not to offend her. "Its hypothe-sis is based on him knowing she was dead. How would he have known that? It wasn't in the papers."

His deduction surprised her. How indeed? He was right.

"He knew," she stammered.

"How?"

It was like coming into a dark room with all exits locked. He did-n't let her suffer long.

"Martin," Cates said softly. "We told Martin."

No, she decided, the man on the phone was not Martin. That man was frightened, with something to lose, something big.

"Martin is the logical one," Cates mused, reinforcing his affirma-tion. "That is . . . if your theory holds."

"Sounds reasonable," she said without conviction.

"That's still not murder," he said gently, revealing the soft edges of doubt. Was he mocking her?

"But it is a motive," she pressed.

The waitress brought their hamburgers.

"People kill for less," he said.

No, she decided. A deeper fear was the issue here. Clint's kind of fear. How could she possibly convey that to Cates without confessing how she had discovered it?

"We still don't have a victim."

"But we do." She felt on the edge of hysteria.

"A murder victim?"

"Soon," she said. "You'll see."

He shrugged and bit into his hamburger.

Back at the apartment, Flannagan had just begun wrapping up. Seeing Fiona, he shook his head.

"Miss Tidy lived here. All spit and polish. Bet most of what we found is yours or his," he said, pointing to Cates. "And the girl's. But not many."

"You think someone might have wiped them away?"

"That's police stuff. I'm only a flunky."

He pinched her cheek. "We dusted where you said. I got nothin' under the seat," Flannagan added, smiling.

"We got one good two-hand set," he said, his professional instincts showing now. "Some good takes on the inside of a drawer, the one with the undies."

"And the caviar cans?"

"Smears."

"Where was the two-hand set?"

"Damnedest place. The closet rail. Good and clear."

"See," she said, turning to Cates. "We're just missing pieces."

"I'm with you, Fiona. Partners, remember?" She wondered if he was humoring her now.

He handed her the batch of prints, separated into a plastic envelope and marked. She quickly dropped them into her purse.

"It would have taken longer if we really did it right, Fiona,"

Flannagan said, as she walked him to the door. He had lowered
his voice.

"Look," he said. "It's all the time I can spare. He finds out I've taken
time away from the other, he'd shit." She pecked him on the cheek.

"Thanks, Mick."

She was already calculating the problems that lay ahead. She
couldn't deal with Slaughter, the latent prints man. He guarded his
domain with more than the usual paranoia and would probably ask
too many questions. Somehow, she knew she'd have to enlist the
help of the FBI. Another personal favor. So much of police work
depended on personal connections. What she had in mind, however,
was a little too personal—Tom Gribben.

He was an agent now assigned to FBI Headquarters. Working with
him on a case had led to a couple of dates, a consequence of her inex-
perience. She had, she recalled, deliberately aborted his interest, much
to his confusion. It was his attitude she remembered most, because he
didn't take kindly to her rejection, especially after they'd once slept
together. For him, apparently such an act became a bond of fealty. It
had set off in her a total revulsion against dating anyone in law enforcement. They needed too much praise, especially about their lovemaking.
No, she had decided after Gribben. No more cops as lovers.

"Let's split," she said suddenly, effecting a yawn to cover her agitation. It was nearly midnight.

"Do you really think we're on to something?" Cates asked. It was
obvious that he, too, wanted to get his hopes up about what might
show up in the prints.

"Yes," she answered firmly. "It may not be police business, but we
are on to something."

Back in her apartment she took a cold shower, perhaps a subconscious punishment to that other illogical female victim trapped
inside of her. You can't be me, she rebuked that other self.

Now listen, her logical, police self reasoned as she sat on her couch in an oversized terry cloth robe that she shared with Clint. She wore it as a security blanket, recalling his presence. She was, of course, directing her conversation to the phantom Dorothy, not the broken horror lying in the creek that day, but the sweet, soft, vulnerable female sister who apparently could not extricate herself from that mysterious illness, the male malady.

Was the pain of it so unbearable, she wondered, that the only solution was to fling one's self to death like tossing away a used candy wrapper? Or was it necessary for her to be deliberately eliminated in order to protect some male fantasy of ambition, some public lie? Was the sexual game of dress-up so disgusting to confront that the man had to eliminate the witness to the supposed aberration? And was it really an aberration?

She thought of herself and Clint, watching their sexual performance with that other observer's eye. It was a rather silly exercise really, grunting contorted bodies, a mad frenetic animal's dance. Was the human compulsion to pursue orgasmic ecstasy so powerful that the veneer of civilized behavior fell away like that other wafer-thin membrane? Recalling her times with Clint, she was certain it was. No part of them had gone unexplored, as if it were some immutable law that their flesh be joined together, melted as wax into a single conformation. And love? That, she knew, was the mind's way of initiating the process, completing the total oneness.

She craved him now, a hunger powerful enough to trigger the entire spectrum of loss: longing, loneliness and despair. Nothing, she knew, was worse than being alone like this. Death could offer a tantalizing escape. Had it offered that to Dorothy?

Then suddenly she was crawling out of a deep pit, conscious only of incomprehensible pleasure as she stirred in a bath of warm jelly, letting whatever was happening happen. In the soft dream, she felt the ecstasy begin, a release so pure, so powerful and delicious that it lifted her beyond happiness.

"My God," she cried when her mind reluctantly accepted consciousness again. She was locked in his embrace, speared, in a literal sense, to the couch, his body still throbbing in the paroxysms of his own pleasure.

"I couldn't resist," he said, when he had quieted. "Lying there so lovely and inviting. It was a sight to tempt the dead."

"That was the most wonderful dream I ever had," she said. "You just can't imagine . . ."

"I have eyes," he whispered. "And other antennae."

"Thank goodness for that." She lovingly caressed him and he seemed to harden instantly.

"Must be the forced absences," he said. The idea always filled her with panic. Was that at the core of it? Would their relationship disintegrate with permanence?

"How quickly you erase the pain," she said later.

"Pain?"

She hadn't meant to say it. It was essentially the wrong time to trigger his guilt. Instantly she wondered if she had been deliberate. He closed his eyes and lay silently next to her. She watched as a tiny tear trickled down the side of his face.

"I don't think I can hack it, Fi," he whispered.

She turned away, watching the bright lines of the sunlight filter through the drawn blinds. Not now, she wanted to say, but her will had frozen. Why had he chosen just that moment?

"Hurting you. Hurting the kids. Hurting her. We've been at it nearly twenty years. I need you. And I need them."

Her? Do you need her? She wouldn't ever ask that question.

"I suppose I have no courage," he continued. "But the fact is, Fi, I can't do it. I can't break it up. I can't tell her. It's horrendous, selfish. I never thought we'd get in so deep and I also can't bear the idea of your being just a mistress. I love you too much for that."

Through her anguish, she felt the sense of revolt begin. No, she thought, I won't let him off the hook so easily.

"Are you kissing me off?" She said it tautly, swallowing a back-wash of tears. She wanted to hurt him, lash out, hang tough.

"You have a right to a life."

"Without you?"

"You don't understand," he said. "I can't put you in this position. This town is full of other women. It's debilitating."

"You meant a closet fuck." Her growing anger was making her stronger. "I've seen what that can do," she said, thinking again of Dorothy.

"It's just not worth it, Fi." He had also regained his composure. Were they being civilized now?

"Why not? We can play these games indefinitely. Until you get caught." She said it with a deliberate note of sarcasm. "Then it gets tacky. Now that you're a public figure. One way or another, it will hurt your career. Not to mention that you owe your job to your wife's boss." Did you go through something like this, Dorothy, she cried to herself.

"Don't make it any more difficult, Fi."

"Difficult? For whom? It's always been difficult for me."

"I didn't twist your arm," he said. He was also capable of quick anger.

"Precipitate an argument. Go ahead. It's an easy way out." Throwing down that gauntlet, she knew, was unfair. But didn't she have to test his resolve?

Despite the harsh exchange he remained beside her naked, their bodies still touching. Her other self saw the humor in the scene, especially the costuming, or lack thereof. Aware that it might be their last time together, she suddenly started to trace patterns on his body with one finger, drawing curlicues down his chin, along the bony ridges of his neck, over the hump of his Adam's apple, down the forest of fur, circling the tiny hard nipples, downward still along the single strand of haired ridge. Her head had moved onto the hard shelf of his chest where she could hear his heart pumping, a steady, strong beat. She felt his hand caressing her forehead, sweeping the hair back, patting it lightly.

Mysteriously, like some gorgeous beast rising from the dead, that special part of him twitched with renewal.

"I'm making it hard for you," she thought, with giddiness, a message conveyed from one self to the other.

"I wish . . ." His words trailed off, whatever thought it implied masked by a sigh of futility.

"A goodbye gesture," she whispered bitterly, watching the smooth twitching organ now in her hand. She moved lower, caressing it with her lips, making tiny forays with her tongue. In her work, she saw it as an object of ridicule; their Johnson, they called it. They were always grabbing at it, clutching it, scratching it as if they needed to know it was still there. It was a terrible thing to be enslaved by something beyond your control, dependent on an involuntary nervous trigger.

Salivating now, moving her lips along the smooth shaft, fingers touching the soft crenelated sacks and below, the tight hard gut of arousal, she wondered how many times it would take to defeat him, to destroy the arrogant potency. Suddenly, he was reaching out with his hands for mutuality, which she avoided by a surreptitious twist of her body downward, where he couldn't reach.

Against her ear, she heard the giant pump of it, the surge of pulsating blood. For a few brief moments more, she would control him. Perhaps in his mind now, he was thinking that she was offering a tribute to his vaunted masculinity. Let him have his delusion as a parting gift. He tried to move, but she held him there, her mouth and hand pinning him.

"I want you," he cried out the words as if it were a plea for mercy. "I need you."

No more, she told herself. That part of her was out of bounds for him from this moment forward.

"Please," he begged.

Never!

The army of herself attacked, determined that his last foray would land impotently in the air. See me now, she cried out to the nuns of her schooldays to whom the object in her hands and mouth was the ultimate symbol of the forbidden. Is this the beast you railed against, she wondered, her eyes open now, alert to what she believed was her final victory. With methodical deftness and clinical observation, she watched the thing twitch and spurt, offering its last gasp.

Soon he was still, the giant pumping generators at rest as the proud knight slowly nodded. Am I free now, she wondered?

She left him there, lying prostrate, his eyes hidden in the crook of his arm. He did not reach out to touch her as she slid away and went into the bathroom. In the shower, she rubbed her body raw, hoping to rid herself of the last vestiges of the affliction, urging the final ascendency of her rational self.

By the time she'd dried herself, stimulating her skin with an aggressive toweling, she was freshened, renewed, stronger than she'd felt in months. The entire episode with Clint, nearly six months of madness, seemed already a thing of the past. As if to test the alertness of her new self, she concentrated on the various objects on the bathroom shelf, rearranging them neatly, her bath salts, her toilet waters, her perfumes. He had given her Arpege, a favorite of his, which she promptly poured down the sink. The gesture increased her new sense of well-being. Before the day was over, she vowed, she would rid herself of everything that reminded her of him.

It annoyed her to see that he was still in her bed. Apparently he had fallen asleep. She decided to ignore him and dressed carefully, paying uncommon attention to her makeup. She put on a blouse and pleated skirt, demure clothes but still feminine, not the usual pants suits she wore to buttress her sexual neutrality. Surveying herself in the mirror, she decided that, whatever the anguish, it had not ravaged her. She was complete again, confident, the cobwebs blown from her mind.

Her first act that day would be to rid herself of the compulsion to continue to investigate Dorothy Curtis's suicide. That was total madness. The eggplant had been right. As for Cates, she would offer no explanations. He had been reluctant to pursue it in the first place.

Usually she made coffee and offered him a cup before leaving, an idea she quickly rejected. She wanted no more post mortems. Clint was right. She was not cut out to be a mistress. Too many traditional mores against it had been programmed into her to keep it from working. It was time to devote herself to her work again, to regain control over her life. Once she'd been determined to follow an unwavering track in order to become the first woman police chief in the history of the MPD. Indeed, the first lady chief in the United States. Admittedly, she'd been side-tracked, although all she'd lost was time in the process. She was still the best goddamned detective in homicide, wasn't she?

Tiptoeing around the apartment, she selected a pocketbook that matched her outfit and transferred her belongings. Then she buckled on her piece, shifting it round so that it rested on the back of her hip.

Not looking at his sleeping figure in her bed, she started toward the door, the new and restored Fiona ready to tackle the world. Before she could grasp the knob the telephone rang, breaking the silence. Her first reaction was to avoid it, turn the doorknob, flee. Instead, instinctively, at the second ring she rushed to pick it up. Peripherally she saw him stir, the arm move as he hoisted himself on his elbow, watching her.

"Fiona?" It was Dr. Benton's voice.

"Yes, Dr. Benton."

"I tried to get you last night."

There was a pause at his end. An ominous urgency flickered inside of her, as if the new Fiona was wavering.

"I got the toxics back," he said. "On that woman."

"Dorothy."

"Nothing," he said. "She was clean."

She felt a sense of disorientation, remaining silent, turning her back to avoid Clint's stare. What had she expected?

"Did you think she was poisoned?" he asked.

Her heart lurched. Was Dorothy betraying her now? A nerve palpitated in her temple.

"Yes," she admitted. By something, she added to herself.

"It's only a suicide, Fiona." There was a long pause. "Why did you think otherwise?" Like the others, he was dismissing it, writing it off.

"Are you all right, Fiona?" he asked gently.

"I m not sure, Dr. Benton," she sighed.

"Leave it alone, Fiona. Accept it."

Accept what, she wondered, disoriented again, the earlier resolve disappearing.

"She didn't have to die," she said.

"It's not police business, Fiona." He paused for a moment. "Oh yes," he said, "the vaginal smear."

She had forgotten.

"Evidence of recent intercourse," he said. "And that's no crime either, Fiona."

"Depends," she said, her resolve cracking. So she was with a man before she died.

"It's not a crime, Fiona," he repeated before he hung up.

The image of the ravaged young body returned to her thoughts. I won't desert you, Dorothy. On the table near the phone were the prints that Flannagan had given her, tossed aside now.

"Damn," she muttered, retrieving the plastic envelope and slipping it into her purse.

She heard Clint's voice.

"Fiona?" It was tentative, slightly hoarse.

"Close the door on your way out," she said, without looking back. "There's no need to make the bed." It was a gratuitous remark, merely for effect, filling the void.

He had never made the bed anyway.

X

When Jason saw the account of the council meeting in the paper the next morning, comparing it to what he had heard on the radio, he knew he had it wrong.

"You screwed me," he shouted into the phone at the man who had subbed for him, a stringer for one of the weeklies. The Fairfax County Council had voted to rescind a sewer moratorium for one of the sewer districts. Later, apparently after the man had left the meeting, they had tacked on an addendum, putting a 60-day limit on the moratorium. A minor point, perhaps, but not for *the* Washington newspaper and for a reporter under in-house surveillance.

"So they'll print a retraction," the stringer said. Jason had given him twenty-five bucks. "It's not that important."

"You don't understand."

"Want your money back?"

He had hung up in a rage. He was too close to have something go wrong now. The result was predictable. The editor of the Virginia section called him into the suburban office, a tiny clutch of desks in a storefront with word processing computer connections to the main building.

"You fuck up, it's my ass," the editor told him. He was a thin young man with an Adam's apple that bobbed up and down as if he'd swallowed a ping-pong ball. Taking it from such a lowly flunky taxed his self-control even more. Barely listening, he tried to think other thoughts, of Dorothy and how far they had come in engineering his plan. Don't blow, he warned himself, not now.

"It's not that important," he said, repeating the stringer's line.

"It is to me," the editor replied, inspecting him contemptuously. "I'm too young to be a has-been."

No you're not, Jason thought, a broad smile forming inwardly behind a taut mask. You're going to be a never-was. Little did the poor bastard know that standing contritely before him was a man who was sitting on the juiciest story of the century, a man about to make history.

What he dreaded most was losing his accessibility to Webster, who, despite other misgivings, would know a good story when he saw one. Hang in there, baby, he told himself.

"I'm sorry," he said to his young superior. "It won't happen again."

It mollified the man, but indicated to Jason that time could be running out. They had to move faster.

Time!

It had come down now to the management of time. Dorothy's time was being programmed like a computer. She was having affairs with five men at once, a feat of planning that sometimes approached farcical proportions. To keep them separated they had to resort to all kinds of creative subterfuge. At first, when there was a conflict, he had instructed her to say she was having her period. But they soon found out that keeping track of her cycle in five different stages was almost impossible.

Finally, they managed to force the assignations to some regularity. The men were all married. Most of them operated in a goldfish bowl with assistants who scheduled their time. Also, the men were perpetually going out of town on short trips, although keeping track of those schedules sometimes proved formidable.

After a month of rotating the five, the scheduling process boiled down to weekday evenings, one lunch hour and one weekend evening, usually Sundays. The general seemed to prefer Sunday evenings, when he was allegedly playing tennis at the club. The Czech had reserved Tuesday and Friday evenings, the senator Wednesday, the congressman Thursday and good old Arthur Fellows kept his lunch hour free every Monday

"We should make a time and motion study," he told her one day after a repetitious debriefing. She didn't understand and he didn't bother to explain it. The sexual parts had become, like a bad porno-graphic movie, somewhat of a bore. But he continued to probe for any information slippage that might be potentially embarrassing. In her wonderfully naive way, Dorothy had filled up enough tapes with their indiscretions to fill volumes. Still, he was not ready to end it. There seemed always to be more to find out.

They were also making an interesting collection of odd gifts. Tate O'Haire wrote her erotic love poetry, scribbled in his own hand, mostly describing their genitalia and his feelings about them:

> *My sword of love stands firm*
> *Awaiting thy secrets to confirm*
> *Let me prove its power*
> *In that special bower*
> *And convert its hard steeling*
> *To the ultimate joy of feeling.*

Jason read the poem out loud, doubling up with laughter. Dorothy became oddly disturbed by his reaction.

"He's sincere," she protested.

"Sincere?"

When she continued to pout, he let the matter drop.

The Czech ambassador gave her exotic foods. Senator Hurley brought her leather souvenirs from his home state. And Arthur gave her matchbooks from Air Force One and the luncheon menu from the White House mess.

"What's that?" she had asked, looking at the special of the day. "I hate fish."

He made her bring all the gifts back to his Capitol Hill apartment, where he stashed them with the tapes in his safe deposit boxes.

"What do you do with these?" she asked him one day after she had seen him snap out a used cassette and slip it into his pocket.

"I keep it in a safe place. Just in case."

"In case?" Her brow furrowed into a frown.

"Wouldn't want it to get into the wrong hands."

She thought for a moment, her frown deepening.

"That would be awful." It seemed a half-satire, and he could tell by her hesitation that more was coming. "Are they helping you, Jason?"

"Who?"

"My boyfriends. I hope they're helping you . . . like you said they would if I . . . you know."

"Oh yes," he said, remembering. "They are." It was, he knew, a vague assurance. Somehow he caught a warning in her words and it troubled him. He hadn't expected the reminder. "Just trust me," he said, knowing it was a weak response, but hoping she would understand his emphasis.

"You know I do, Jason."

Just the same, he was still troubled.

The taped information continued to grow in volume and value and he found himself perpetually disgorging the information in his mind, putting it into palatable journalese.

Another strange thing was developing between them. She seemed to be soaking up information subconsciously, like a transmission line, inert but alive. It was as if some built-in sensor was picking up signals and translating them back to him. She had become a medium and the bits of potentially damaging information strewn around in her mind were being quickly converted into a battery of lethal weapons.

The general, aside from his outspoken views on his colleagues, the secretary of defense, and even the President, whom he also called an asshole, was particularly vociferous on the inability of the army to function. Bad weapons. Bad manpower. Bad planning. Bad leadership.

Senator Hurley's verbal indiscretions revolved around the sexual peccadillos of his colleagues. He confessed to her that he was having affairs with other women. He also revealed that he was thinking of running for President.

"He asked your advice?" Jason asked her, stunned. "What did you tell him?"

"I said it would be good if he could still come to visit me."

"You said that?" It staggered him. These are our leaders! The revelations were positively lip-smacking. Was it possible? Could she be inventing this?

"He also said the minority whip was a fag. I didn't understand. I thought that whip stuff was something else."

When Jason laughed, she enjoyed it all the more.

"I really like these guys," she told him.

"Just don't like them too much," he warned her. That look he'd seen on her face once before returned, disturbing him in a way he couldn't fully comprehend.

What was incredible was that he, too, continued to make love to her, and she responded with equal passion. It was as though all of his past knowledge of female behavior had been trashed and remade.

The Czech ambassador brought her exotic foods and bragged about his ability to circumvent the security apparatus of the United States, the Soviet Union and his own country.

"They are all stupid," she reported the Czech to have said, "especially the Russians."

He had her repeat it for the benefit of the recorder. It seemed to spill from her mind with uncommon clarity.

"He said he likes the renewal of the cold war. He keeps telling his country that the U.S. is planning trouble, so they keep him here. He says he made nearly a half-million smuggling out certain Czech works of art from the U.S."

"He told you that?"

She shrugged, indicating a dubious comprehension, but it did not stop the flow.

"And they got paid in diamonds. His wife smuggled them out in her cunt."

"My God."

"He said they couldn't get them out. He had to search all over town for long thin tongs."

It was incredible. Again, he made her repeat it into the tape recorder. Would they believe this? he wondered.

From Arthur Fellows, Dorothy relayed a picture of backbiting and intrigue that had spilled over into violence.

"He said the secretary of state hauled off and hit the secretary of defense, breaking two teeth. He said he was the only witness and had to separate them. But/ not before the defense guy kicked the state guy in the balls."

She had to repeat that as well.

"Should be worth another fifty thou . . ."

"What?"

"Go on."

"Also, he said the President's wife demanded the resignation of the secretary of energy because she overheard him call her iron pussy." He remembered the language of the Watergate tapes and the great gap they illustrated between the private and public person. Tearing away the facade of probity had become big business and he, by God, was going to be chairman of the board.

"So that's why he resigned," Jason recalled. "I thought he said something about personal commitments."

"He also said the President is taking drugs to control high blood pressure. He said he's the only one who knows that, besides his doctor. The prescriptions are made out to Arthur."

What she had told him moved from the bizarre, to the fantastic, to the incredible. Was it her ingenuousness that was so disarming? It was not possible for her to be inquisitive. Yet he was beginning to acquire a nagging presumption that she knew more than he had imagined. The things they confided seemed appalling. Was their need for expiation so strong that they felt compelled to empty their substance, psychic and sexual, onto this absorbing human blotter? Indeed, perhaps she was becoming more than that . . .

"What is it in you that makes them feel so safe?" he asked her.

She smiled proudly. "They're good old boys. They trust me."

Not once had she indicated a sense of being used or abused by any of them.

"It's all going to make you rich someday, Dot," he said.

"Rich? How?" Her concern was tangible. Had he seen panic in her eyes?

"You'll see."

As always, he quickly squelched any further explanation.

The tapes, after two months, had filled up three safe deposit boxes. Still, he wasn't ready. If he were to discredit the entire checks and balances system, he would need a member of the Supreme Court. It was the final mountain to be climbed.

Accessibility posed the biggest problem when it came to members of the court. They were outside the hurly-burly of politics and did not need to mix socially, except as a form of entertainment.

Using the *Washington Post* library of clippings, he pored over everything he could find out about the personality of the men on the Court. A female member had narrowed his choices down to eight. Four were eliminated because of age. Not a breath of scandal emanated from the remaining four. They were all upright family men of sterling character, long tested in the crucible of peer investigations and public conduct.

Another obstacle was their natural reclusiveness. They shied away from publicity and rarely granted interviews. What he could glean from the clippings was mostly dated or peripheral knowledge. One was a weekend sailor. Another a part-time cabinet maker. Only one seemed to offer the remotest hint of accessibility, Associate Justice Orson Strauss. His hobby was walking. He walked every day from his home, an apartment in Shoreham West, two blocks from Dotty's place, to the Supreme Court building, a distance of five miles.

Because it was a daily thing, it had a predictability that intrigued him and the man himself was, according to some accounts of observers, open and gregarious, a reasonable possibility.

He and Dorothy stalked him for three days, sitting in Jason's car parked near his apartment house. He came out at precisely five forty-five every morning, wearing a gray jogging outfit, walking at a steady pace. His path was invariable. He would move east on Calvert Street, turn south on Connecticut Avenue, continue to Seventeenth Street past the old State Department Building, then along the great parade route toward the Capitol and his office in the Supreme Court Building.

"Can you do that?" he asked her after they had confirmed the regularity of Justice Strauss's schedule.

"Hell, yes," she said proudly. "I've always walked a lot."

Looking at her, her eyes wide with a special pride, he could not resist hugging and kissing her. For the first time since they had begun, she seemed more eager, more dogged than himself.

"A Supreme Court justice. Now that's something," she said.

"You're getting quite a lesson in how America works," he said, somewhat facetiously.

"Yes, I am," she responded with intensity.

"Soon," he whispered, leaving the comment unfinished. It was a matter he was not yet ready to deal with.

"Soon what?"

"You'll see."

She looked at him archly. It was an expression that he had never observed before. Soon, he told himself. The sooner the better.

He had decided that whatever happened with Orson Strauss, this would be the end of it. He set a time goal in his mind—a week. If she couldn't get Strauss by then, he would go with the five. The lucky bastards, he thought. He was about to make them immortal.

"Bet you can't snag him in a week."

"Bet I can."

"Just follow him and try to talk to him."

That was the only instruction he gave her. Nature and her intrinsic talent would do the rest. He was sure of that.

In three days, they were walking together.

"He's very shy."

"That's understandable."

He had instructed Dorothy to tell Strauss that she worked on Capitol Hill, parting from him near the steps of the Capitol, then walking the few additional blocks to their Capitol Hill apartment, where she showered and had coffee with Jason before going off to Saks.

"Remember, one week," he reminded her, pointing his finger as if playfully rebuking a child.

He was not sleeping well. When she sensed his restlessness, she would comfort him in her special way, and he found that her love-making would often calm him. Now it just increased his agitation. Often, in the night, he would study her face as she slept. Before, it had been serene. Sleep was absolute. Now she, too, seemed restless, as if something foreign, disturbing, was thrashing around in her mind. Even her own questions were becoming more and more frequent.

"Just accept," he assured her. "It's all for our future."

"As long as it's what you want, Jason." There was a tentative ring to her response that hadn't been there before.

"It is, baby. It is."

He became increasingly short in his answers and wondered how long he could deflect her growing and still inarticulate curiosity. Although he tried to deny it to himself, she seemed to be changing in some way. He could not define it. Some intangible growth, per-haps, but he sensed an odd awareness in her, as if her exposure to these men and the subsequent debriefing was opening her mind. He had not anticipated that. Had the experience awakened a latent intelligence? How would she respond to notoriety?

It was a path that he'd never tracked before. When it worried him he would take refuge in his original premise, that what he was doing was necessary. The public needed to confront its hypocrisy. Journalism need-ed the shock out of scandal mongering; the government needed it. Sometimes he felt like a director in a kind of theater of the absurd. In the end, he knew, it would make sense. He didn't care about the men whose

present careers would be destroyed. What troubled him most was
Dorothy and her reaction to the revelation. Surely, she would understand.

At first, the justice had been understandably reticent, but after
the fourth day, he was chatting amiably, enjoying the company.

"He asks lots of questions," Dorothy told him.

"About you?" Of course he would, Jason reasoned.

"I always try to tell him the truth. About where I grew up. The
mines. Things like that. Never about us," she added hastily.

"He's probing. He wants to be sure. Testing the waters."

"He tells jokes, too. I laugh. They're very funny."

"And you flatter him. Tell him how wonderful he is. How smart.
How handsome."

"He likes that."

"Has he made his move? Hinted at it?"

"Oh no. He wouldn't do that."

Jason felt foolish. That was her expertise, her talent. Suddenly, he
wanted it all to be over.

"Just a week," he said.

"I know, Jason." She said, pausing. "He's such a nice man."

"Do you think he will . . . ?"

"Oh yes, Jason. He will. You'll see."

Vanity, Jason sighed. They were all vulnerable.

It took exactly a week.

"You're a miracle worker," Jason told her.

"Not a miracle," she said matter-of-factly. "I just know men." The
remark came as a surprise. Although true, he hadn't expected her to
be able to articulate it. Perhaps she was growing too sophisticated.
The idea frightened him.

Soon the associate justice was eschewing his walk for a twice-
weekly session at the apartment.

"He's very scared," Dorothy told him, during their first debriefing.

"I can understand that."

"But I made him feel good," she said happily.

"I knew you would do that."

"There's nothing for him to be scared about, is there, Jason?"

"Of course not."

"He's such a gentle man. A good man. I think I like him the best of all the others."

"Don't get carried away."

"You're still my number one, Jason," she said.

"Just remember that."

He continued to debrief her and the tapes became increasingly repetitive. All that was needed now was to embellish on the relationship with Orson Strauss.

"Does he ever talk about cases?" he asked.

"Cases?"

"He's a Supreme Court judge."

"Yes. I know."

It was the nuance, not the substance, that troubled him. Was she holding back?

When she told him about the justice's dressing up in women's underwear, he had difficulty keeping a straight face.

"I bought him stockings, panties, a bra, a garter belt, and high heels. He looks cute."

"Cute?"

"One day I put lipstick and rouge on him and lots of mascara. He loved himself and couldn't tear himself away from the mirror." She smiled broadly. "Sometimes he wants me to call him Sally."

"Sally?"

Surely this is satire, he told himself. Who would believe it? She seemed to enjoy making the man happy. Making all of them happy. Most of all, it was making *her* happy.

As the time to end it grew near, he became increasingly edgy. With Dorothy's tapes as documentation and her physical presence as evidence, their denials would quickly break down in any confrontation. Some might choose to play hardball, continue denials, hide from the press, feign ill health. Others might opt for a full confession, throwing their reputations on the secret mercy generated by every man's sense of guilt. "It was wrong. I did wrong. I made a mistake in behavior and judgment." Whatever path they chose, it was all grist for the mill.

He had also developed his own fall-back moral position, a righteous posture. In that special role, he saw himself as an exploder of myths, particularly the great myth of probity and sexual purity in those who bubbled up as leaders in the democratic process. Sexuality, whatever its expression, in or out of wedlock, was no criteria to demean character. Indeed, it was a harmless expression of human character, a function of mind and matter, no less common than breathing or voiding one's wastes. The fact that it gave pleasure and joy did not make it any less human. Besides, the technology of birth control had put sex into the category of recreation. Romantic illusion, an anachronism, was finally being put to rest.

He viewed his effort as the last great sex scandal of the century. He was convinced of that, imagining himself and Dorothy telling their story on the nation's talk shows, offering themselves as a sacrifice, a kind of delicious martyrdom to hypocrisy and cant. Perhaps, after this book, which would be manufactured as a paean to ludicrous prurience, he would offer these special views and at last put the great sexual revolution in the sixties in its true perspective.

Listening to Dorothy's matter-of-fact debriefings, he sometimes felt he had not gone far enough. Where was sodomy, lesbianism, bestiality, necrophilia, the whole panoply of aberrations? That, he decided, was toying beyond the pale. And it would also be far outside the realm of the experience and interest of the mass audience he was shooting for.

Once Dorothy's relationship with the justice was insured, all that remained was for him to explain to Dorothy what he intended to do with the material and how she was to play her future role.

That was the moment he dreaded most.

XI

Fiona had substituted one magnetic field for another. Now she hurtled in Dorothy's as powerless as she had been in Clint's. Each step, she knew, had its own inexorable logic. And professional dangers.

Tom Gribben watched her, his melancholy stare attesting to his continued interest in her as a woman. She knew the signs, of course, but until that moment, confronting him, his hurt had not mattered.

He had led her through the maze of corridors in the FBI building to the cafeteria, where they sipped coffee in a quiet corner.

"I have one good set and a partial," she told him, showing him the plastic envelopes. His eyes evaded them as he continued to search her face. She knew what he was looking for.

"You're asking me to stick my neck out, Fi?" he asked, with exaggerated astonishment.

"It's a professional favor."

"What happened to your regular channels?"

"Do I have to explain why?"

"I'm not going to do it," he said, although she detected a kind of subtle temporizing. He had his own set of macho values, a shrewdness that belied his bland exterior. He had been one of Hoover's later young men and still clung to the amenities. A gallant knight, she had once dubbed him sarcastically.

"I was entitled to a better explanation," Gribben persisted. He was determined not to let their old affair die.

"It wasn't in the cards," she said gently. "At the time."

The tacked on phrase was specious. She had no right to lead him on to a dead end. But it was too late. He had already caught her drift, and she made no move to correct the impression.

"We had some good times, Fi. You have to admit that."

141

She could barely remember what they had done together, except that one abysmal experience. "Yes, we did."

"And could again."

"All I want is an ident," Fiona said. A wry smile formed on Gribben's lips.

"No," he said, shaking his head, eyes furtive, searching the cafeteria. "Besides, you guys at MPD are a bunch of idiots."

"Look at our statistics," Fiona said, prompted to defend the department. She had to admit that they did often look like bungling idiots, but when they made a case it usually stuck. "Yours are still not so hot."

She remembered now how she had taunted him, how she had paraded FBI failures before him, citing their inability to get convictions. He had taken it as it was meant, a personal put-down, and she turned the knife to get at his smug FBI loyalty. Despite all the recent FBI earthquakes, most agents were loyal to a fault. For this reason, defensiveness made him vulnerable.

"You can put them in. It's like a gum ball machine. Out will pop an ident and nobody's the wiser."

Once he had explained how it could be done and she had tested him with near-perfect results. The full set, she knew, would create no problems. The partial could be risky.

"I'm not just ready to go official. Not yet. My boss has his hands full with the black teenage killings. Besides, I'm not even sure there's a case here."

"We're not friends anymore, Fi. Not lovers either."

He had put too much stock in that at one time. Without it, they still might have been friends.

"Hell, Tom, I'm not asking for the moon."

She had, of course, miscalculated his reaction. Remembering, she supposed that ducking his calls had been cruel. Unfortunately, she hadn't let him down lightly and the bruised ego had not faded over time.

"I don't owe you anything," he snapped, then suddenly grew nostalgic. "We had good times, Fi." He paused, showing the old hunger. "We could again." His implication was clearly stated.

Alarms went off inside her head. They were always doing that—Dorothy's magnetic field persisted, leaving her floating in space, trapped in invisible parameters. Putting herself in jeopardy was not the issue. There was Cates, Flannagan, now Gribben. *I did not die by my own hand.* Dorothy's voice now seemed loud and clear in Fiona's mind. *It could also be the beginning of a nervous breakdown,* another inner voice added.

"Come on, Tom, do it. For old time's sake."

"So you admit it. We did have old times," he said, misinterpreting again.

"The moon was in the wrong phase is all."

Son of a bitch, she thought, smoldering ashes of resentment catching fire. It wasn't only Tom. It was all of them, the manipulative bastards.

"Okay then. We'll try again," he said, obviously satisfied. *In a pig's ass,* she thought, casting herself loose from the last trace of professional ethics. Her anger accelerated, but she didn't let him see it.

"Deal," she said, forcing the edges of her lips to curl into a smile.

"I'll put them through. Then we'll have a drink and discuss the future. Fair enough?" He was absorbing all the disingenuous signs like a sponge. She put her hand over his big fist, knowing he would think of it as a caress.

By the time she arrived at the office, she had worked up a full head of steam. She saw herself as the beleaguered female, a lone rangeress, patrolling the swamp of the male ego. She'd fight them at their own game, with their own weapons and win. *I'm coming, Dorothy baby,* she thought to herself.

"What's with you?" Cates asked. It was time, as well, to set him straight.

"We have to talk." As her partner, he had a right to know. Sitting in the car, she filled him in on what Benton had said and what she had done with Gribben. There were other things she intended to do, but held back, waiting for his reaction.

"What can I say?" he shrugged. "No victim. No hint of murder."

"And I don't know where it will end. You're more vulnerable than I am. He'll say you've been pussy-whipped and haul your ass out of homicide with a reprimand sheet as long as your arm."

"It's something to consider."

"I can get you out anytime you say."

"I know." He hesitated. "But I feel that maybe I'll be missing something. I hate to stop anything in the middle."

"I'm giving it to you straight, kemo sabe," she said, watching him mull it over. "It'll mean double duty for the next week or so. And we're going to fall behind in the regular work. Also, we can scare up a hornet's next. Harassment. Entrapment. The whole list."

"Why can't we just go to the eggplant and have him sanction it?"

"When we have enough, we'll shove it down his throat."

He stroked his chin and contemplated his position.

"Before you get my decision, Fi, I have only one question." It was not a simple decision for him, putting his career on the line. She, after all, had the protection of her status as a double minority. Bracing herself, she knew what was coming.

"Why?" he asked.

He was not entitled to that knowledge. Their professional alliance did not change the essential situation. Nature had put him in the enemy camp.

"Because it's there," she said facetiously. He laughed, but did not press the question. Maybe there was a level of subtle communication between them after all, she thought, quickly dismissing the idea. Such things watered down resolve.

"Okay," he said, resigned to not getting a complete answer. "We're partners, and I'll go along with you, no matter what." So he was hooked on that myth. She hoped he wouldn't regret it.

They spent the day tracking leads on the teenage killings, as usual, without anything significant to report. But her mind was on Dorothy and the identification of the prints.

Back in the office, she settled behind her desk and began typing out the reports of their investigation. On another level, she felt quite proud of herself. Thoughts of Clint had receded into the background. Her concentration had returned, allowing her to devote the remainder of her time to Dorothy. I'm coming, she told herself again, ripping the report from her typewriter.

The mood in the office was still tense. She could hear the eggplant ranting and raving at someone behind his closed door.

"The mayor's down on him now," one of her former partners muttered. He was sitting beside her, struggling with his own report. She looked up, catching a view of his ruddy complexion. It was obvious he was hitting the booze pretty hard these days, trying to tough it out until retirement.

"They need a goat," he burped, moving closer, his breath foul with last night's drinking. "He's perfect for it. Fits him like a glove."

"Poor bastard."

"We bring him one more potentially open case, he'll shit."

Cates looked up and frowned.

"Drink?" Cates asked after they had filed their reports in their case sackets. She consented, welcoming the idea which rescued her from the prospect of going back to an empty apartment.

They went to the F. O. P., the Fraternal Order of Police, club. He ordered double Scotches and brought them to a corner table, a big bowl of popcorn between them.

"Sooner or later, I suppose I'll understand it," he said after a long sip of his drink.

She was sitting with her back to the wall, watching the line of cops. Most of them wore sport shirts and uniform pants. Everyone, according to regulations, was armed. It always reminded her of a bar in a movie western and more than once some cop had gone for his piece in an argument. That kind of altercation was quickly hushed up.

"Understand what?"

He scooped up a handful of popcorn, chewing one kernel at a time.

"Why I'm going along with this."

"Don't get too analytical."

"I'm really depending on you. Trusting your instincts."

Trust! They had these holy rules about only trusting one's partner, an idea that might have been true before they began to mix things up. She had never quite trusted any of her male partners and they had, she was sure, never quite trusted her.

"You know what they say," he laughed, ribbing her. "Never trust a woman."

"I'm a woman."

She said it too fast and he looked at her strangely.

"You're a cop. Like me." She wondered if he was trying to convince himself.

"You're a man," she snapped. She wanted to tell him that, despite all of society's new contrivances, there remained that unbridgeable gulf between them. Never the twain shall meet. No, she decided, he could never understand about Dorothy.

He shook his head and smiled.

"We're just people then," he said.

"We're different. That's the truth of it. I'm the alien here. I've muscled into a man's business." She couldn't stop now. "Look at the statistics. Who commits most of the real crimes? A woman sees things differently. A woman thinks in a different way. A woman reacts differently. A woman . . ." she hesitated. "A woman loves differently." Again, she thought of the dead woman. "Man is the killer."

Her vehemence surprised her. She looked at him and saw that he was, understandably, confused by her outburst.

"Shit," Cates said. "I'll still take my chances."

"That's just macho talking, Cates."

"Maybe," he said seriously. She could feel his eyes probing her face. "Why don't you ever call me by my first name?"

"I didn't know you had one."

"Timothy."

"Okay, Tim."

"Not Tim. Timothy."

"Okay, Timothy."

Despite herself and her long harangue, she felt him getting closer, burrowing in. She knew she was crossing a Rubicon.

"Tell you what," she said suddenly. "Let's order some Chinese and go up to my place."

His hesitation told her that the sudden suggestion of intimacy startled him. Hell, it startled her, too—maybe what she needed most now was friendship.

Or maybe she was just reluctant to go back to her apartment alone.

He went off to the China Palace on Ninth Street while she subwayed home.

"Damn," she said, exasperated, as she opened the door to her apartment. Clint was sitting in the dark, slumped in a chair, his feet sprawled in front of him. Apparently he had been sleeping and the sudden light made him shield his eyes in a kind of sloppy salute.

"I was waiting . . ." Clint said, clearing his throat. He looked forlorn and empty. Feel no pity, she urged herself.

"This is childish," she said.

"I know. I wanted to explain."

"You don't have to, Clint." She was determined to be firm, and went into the kitchen, bringing out plates.

"I'm caught between a rock and a hard place," he said.

"So are we all."

"There's something I wanted to say. Something you deserve to know." He crossed his legs in front of him. Must he? she thought silently. She was running out of activities to invent. Finally, she sat down opposite him. Confession time. How she hated that, remembering her childhood and all those Hail Marys.

"I told her," he said, taking in a gulp of deep breath to renew his strength.

"Jesus," she snapped. "Do I have to go through that?"

"I told her about us."

She stood up.

"I don't want to hear this."

"You know what she said?"

His tone was ominous, and she knew in advance it was something she definitely did not want to hear.

"She said I hadn't fooled her for a minute. That she knew all along."

"Knew it was me?"

"That, too. She followed me once, in the morning. Can you imagine that? She knew all along."

"Dear Ann," Fiona said. "A good little actress."

"I thought I was going to really hurt her. I went through this elaborate preliminary and she knew all along. I couldn't believe it. She lived with that."

"Such martyrdom," she said, unable to hold back her sarcasm.

"I begged her," he began, then faltered.

"Must I listen," Fiona said.

"She said she was content with the present arrangement. I mean that's a pretty wrenching experience for a man of my generation, still obsessed with doing the honorable thing."

"Clint," she said. "Leave it alone."

"She said that someday she'd let me have a divorce. After the last kid leaves the house."

"It's none of my business."

"I wanted you to know, Fiona," he said, valiantly trying to hold himself together. "I love you. I want . . ."

"Stop it please . . .

He was obviously hurt, on the verge of some inner hysteria. Was this his way of lashing back? "Are you trying to hurt me?" she asked gently.

"Hurt you?" he sighed. "I'm not in control, Fiona. I even owe my job to her. Maybe . . ." he paused, "I'm testing if you really love me."

"And you expect me to fall at your feet, beg you to come back?" She moved her head from side to side. "Uh uh." What she really wanted to tell him was that indecisive little boys disgusted her. "It's your trap. Not mine. I'm out." She hoped she sounded deliberately cruel. He had no right. Not now.

At that moment, the door buzzer rang.

"It's Cates, my partner. We're having Chinese food. Care to join us?"

He seemed startled and she realized suddenly that he seriously believed his confession would bring them together again. The buzzer became insistent. When she opened the door, Cates walked in holding two brown paper bags.

"Still hot," he said. Clint stood up awkwardly and put out his hand. "This is Clinton Chase. I asked him to join us. Timothy Cates."

"Really, I can't. I've got to get going," he said, fiddling with his keychain. She directed Cates to the kitchen.

"I'm sorry," Clint said, handing her the key.

"So am I." A sob caught in her throat. Cates came back into the room.

"Believe me. I bought enough for four. I always over-order this stuff."

"Thanks," Clint said. "But I really . . ." His voice caught as he hurried through the door. Behind her, Cates clattered plates, feigning normality. As the sob burst, she leaned against the wall in the little entrance alcove. She struggled to pull herself together, thankful that there was someone in the room, another human being. Hurrying into the bathroom, she splashed water on her face, observing herself in the mirror. Life has hardened you, little Fiona, she told her image as she pulled herself together, taking a secret pride in her strength.

"Look at that," Cates said pleasantly, pointing to the neatly set dining room table, taking pains to avoid any reference to what he had just seen.

"You like soap operas?" she said, sitting down.

"It's none of my business."

"Damned straight," she said, reaching for one of the concoctions, wondering if she could generate an appetite.

Before she could take a bite, the apartment buzzer rang again.

"Maybe I should go," Cates said.

"No. Stay."

Perhaps Clint had left something, she thought.

"I'll hide in the bathroom," Cates said, disappearing quickly. This is a farce, she thought, as she went to the door, expecting to find Clint. Instead it was Tom Gribben. He came in without a word, tight-lipped, his face flushed. A nerve palpitated in his neck; the anger was obvious.

"I can't believe you'd do it deliberately."

"Do what?"

He paced the room like a tiger. From his pocket he withdrew the plastic fingerprint envelopes and tossed them on the couch.

"This," he said. "I stuck my neck out, very nearly got my head chopped off." Taking a bottle of Scotch from the little glass pushcart that she used as a bar, he poured a heavy shot into a glass and drank it swiftly. "I wouldn't even trust the damned phones. I was lucky. I think. I had a buddy working the computers. He nearly shit when they coughed up those names." He looked at her and shook his head. "When you take advantage, you take advantage."

"I don't know what the hell you're talking about, Tom."

"Them." He pointed to the prints. "Don't tell me where you got them. I don't want to know. I want to forget about the whole thing."

"Whose were they?" she asked, expectant now, the illusive professionalism returning.

"You owe me, baby," Tom said, eyes narrowing.

"Who, for Christ sake?" She was growing impatient.

"The good set belongs to Tate O'Haire, majority whip of the House. The fucking House of Representatives."

She sucked in a deep breath. It whistled through her teeth.

"And the other is a goddamned associate justice of the Supreme Court. Orson Strauss." He shook his head and poured himself another drink. She sat down on the couch stunned. A moment later he was next to her.

"I don't want to hear about it," he said. "All I know is you nearly got me into a bind. I'm not even sure whether or not I've had it. Who knows if I can trust my buddy?" He looked at her. "Or trust anybody?"

"I didn't know."

"It's heavy, Fi. Whatever it is."

He put his drink down on the floor and turned toward her. "I really stuck my neck out for you, baby." He started to stroke her arm. She felt little goosebumps spread toward her shoulder.

"Are you sure about the names?"

"Listen. Me you gotta trust."

"I didn't question that."

He moved his hands up to her shoulder and caressed her ear, moving closer, embracing her.

"I stuck my neck out for you, Fi." He said it again, this time gripping her shoulders. He bent her backwards and lumbered over her. She could smell the whiskey on his breath.

"Don't, Tom," she said gently. "Please."

"I'm entitled."

She squirmed in his embrace. He pushed himself forward, pinning her with his body.

"I said no," she shouted.

Cates was instantly at her side, glaring down at Gribben, who flushed scarlet with embarrassment. He stood up quickly.

"Spades now." He shook his head. She saw Cates's fists tighten.

"No," she said, getting up to restrain him.

"You fucked me, lady," Gribben said, livid with rage. He rushed out of the apartment, slamming the door behind him.

XII

A windswept April rain pounded Jason's car. He leaned his head against the edge of the seat and smoked a cigarette. Through the smoke and the droplet-dotted side window, he squinted toward the lights of the apartment. She was with Tate O'Haire. Big Teddy Bear Tate, she called him. He hated the implication of warmth and security.

All of them now bore her special labels. Templeton was her little toy soldier. Once she had brought a little wooden soldier doll from the store, painted in a shiny blue uniform and a flat pink face with rosy cheeks and round black eyes.

"Little Eddie," she had giggled, showing it to him. It offended him now, staring blankly from the highest bookshelf in their Capitol Hill apartment.

She called Arthur the "duck," buying a cheap little Donald Duck charm, an image that belied what Jason knew of him, which was that of a hard, selfish, conniving man. Her perception of all of them seemed distorted by a peculiar prism in which she saw these frenetic, ambitious men merely as mischievous little boys. Could that be what they really were?

She called her Czech "Checkers," a pseudonym he must have enjoyed, donning alternately red and black bikini shorts in honor of the color chosen. Somehow they made what passed between them into a game of checkers, of sorts.

"Tonight we do a triple jump," he would tell her, dutifully reported later in a chorus of giggles. Apparently he was able to execute the move as well.

Senator Hurley was "the whip," hardly an appellation of irony although when she explained it, she became so bent over with laughter she couldn't continue.

153

"Whip it out. Whip it in," she mimicked. When she repeated it, he didn't laugh. No. He had discovered that he was definitely enjoying it less, somehow losing control.

As for "Sally," he could only summon disgust. Sally! How was it possible to weather that impending storm? The man would have to disappear from the planet.

Enough, he had decided finally. It was time to stop the game, convert the material into commercial forms. The *Post,* of course, would be the clarion. Webster would watch him, bug-eyed and slack-jawed, as he played the tapes and showed him the various geegaws of proof, the little gifts; the exhibit of Dorothy herself.

His plan was fully formed now, the marketing effort carefully outlined in his mind. He envisioned a three-part series on successive Sundays in the *Post,* five thousand words each with appropriate art. That would begin the worldwide drumbeat. Then would come the books, serializations, movies, foreign rights, and collateral material. By then, he was calculating in real dollars, setting prices. A million net is what he wanted for Dorothy. He'd be content with half that amount for himself, part of it to be tucked away in a trust fund for Trey. The rest would be a nest egg for himself, a cushion against any future ass-kissing.

Perhaps, after the smoke cleared, he and Dorothy would go away. Maybe Ibiza or Sardinia or Corsica. Somehow he had fixated on islands, as if the surrounding water could purify the rest of their lives and keep them safe. He could not envision his future without Dorothy.

What remained was to confront her with the truth of his intentions, an idea that continued to fill him with dread, especially since an odd element of suspicion had crept into the debriefings. Who was questioning whom?

"Why do you want to know that?"

"It's important."

"But didn't I say it before?"

"I want to hear it again."

In the end, she would obey. Then she would come at it again, from a new direction.

"You don't tell me what they do for you, Jason. I mean, how they help you."

"Us, baby. Help us."

"How?"

"It's very complicated."

"Sometimes I want to ask them."

The remark struck him like a blow.

"Don't you dare," he snapped. "Have you ever mentioned me?"

"Never."

"And are you telling me everything?"

"Everything I can remember."

"You're not conveniently forgetting?"

His own suspicion frightened him. Whenever it hit him he would stop the session, embracing her, changing the subject. What frightened him most was the nagging feeling that he was losing control. Could she—had she—grasped all of the implications? All she had to do was follow his directions. He would, of course, assure her of his devoted protection. That would certainly be enough. Or would it? Was there reason to doubt that? Had she changed that much? Developed guile? Lost innocence?

He hated this nocturnal waiting. He had had quite enough of that, quite enough of seeing her, smiling and happy, bouncing toward the car, as if he were picking her up after an ordinary day's work.

Tonight, he told her, he was coming in to talk. At that point, he even hated to enter the apartment. It wasn't really his place, just a prop to be discarded after it had served its purpose. Still, he knew she had become attached to it. Had she also become attached to the others? It gnawed at him now. He discovered that through it all he had never quite transcended an underlying jealousy that, until now, had been denied.

He looked up in time to see the bulky figure of Tate O'Haire slipping out of the front doorway into the rain. Since the downpour was sudden he was caught hatless and without a raincoat. A Teddy Bear? More like a jackal, Jason thought. They were all jackals. The lot of them.

When he was out of sight, Jason ran across the street and let himself in with his key. She had already tidied up and was in the shower, giving him time to take what he hoped might be a final reflective inventory. The apartment would have to be preserved intact, living evidence, perhaps to be used as a set for a TV documentary. Dorothy would show the viewers around. No, he thought, it was not going to be easy.

When she came out of the bathroom, she was damp, sweet-smelling.

"He was so cute. Wanted to stay the night."

That was another prohibition. Nights were leisure time, his time. She moved to his lap and he smelled her flesh, breathed it, as if it had vaporized. All traces of the others had been scrubbed away. Hadn't she always come to him miraculously renewed, the grime peeled away?

"I'm afraid we're going to have to say goodbye."

Having turned it over in his mind for days, he had decided on just those words, a swift body slap. Saying goodbye was her primal fear. He felt her stiffen with panic.

"Not to me. To them," he corrected, knowing that he had deliberately created the space to save her in the nick of time. Instead of reassuring her, it confused her.

"To whom?" The frown lines deepened in her forehead and her eyelids flickered nervously.

"To them." His hand swept the room. "The six wise men." As his contempt for them had grown, he had begun to refer to them as such. "It's all over."

"Over?"

"It's the end. We've finished what we set out to do."

"Finished?"

"We have enough now."

"Enough?"

My God, she was making it difficult.

"I'm going to make you a million dollars, Dorothy. Would you like that?"

"A million dollars?" She giggled nervously. "Who wouldn't?"

"Tell me what you would do with a million dollars." She contemplated her answer, but he didn't wait. "You know what you could buy? Anything you want."

"Anything?"

"A Rolls-Royce. A beautiful house. You could tour the whole world. How would you like to come away with me? To a beautiful island. Just you and me."

"Gosh," she said. But the frown persisted.

"That's why we've done all these things, Dorothy. That's why you've talked to me after each time. That's why you made those friends. Now comes the time when it has to end."

"Is it something I've done, Jason?"

"In a way," he said, caressing her damp hair, rubbing strands together between his fingers. "Now what we're going to do is write about all your experiences. We're going to tell the whole world."

He had been watching her face, observing the clean soft skin, the shine in her eyes, where the whites were perfect and glistening, outlined by her thick black lashes.

"You mean tell other people?" she whispered. Her face suddenly turned ashen.

"The world," he said gently. "And people are going to pay for it. And pay well. And you're going to wind up with a million dollars."

"Tell everybody about what I did with them?"

"It's not meant to harm anyone," he said quickly, the hollowness easily apparent, even to her.

"All those things I said?" She paused and smiled. "You're kidding me, right Jason? You're not going to tell everybody what I told you."

"Do you trust me, Dorothy?" It came out abruptly, more like a challenge. Her eyes probed him, still confused.

"You're my man," she said, barely audible.

"And don't I always do right by you?"

She seemed in pain. Why should it hurt so much, he wondered? These men didn't deserve her pity.

"You just can't tell people," she said softly.

"It's like show business. Like exhibiting yourself at that bar in Hiram. Nothing more. I'm just going to tell your story. People will eat it up, Dorothy."

"My story?"

"You'll be a national celebrity. Everybody will want to talk to you. You'll be famous."

Why couldn't he just order her, he wondered? Instead he was groveling, pressing for her approval.

"I can't tell people about the way they do it, about Sally . . ." She got up and moved away from him.

"It won't really hurt anybody. Besides, there's something important about it. Don't you see?" He could not believe what he was doing, mouthing moral platitudes as if he were feeding peanuts to some slow-witted elephant. The animal images troubled him. Were they genuine insight, or an illustration of something lacking within himself, a basic sense of humanity. The six wise men were jackals. Webster a fox. Dorothy an elephant. And himself? What was he? A misshapen hyena baying into a moonless sky? He felt disgusted, but he couldn't stop.

"Don't you see? We'll be making fools of them, showing how their vaunted moral code is a fraud. All their churchgoing self-righteous pontificating about the structure of society, our democracy. It's all bullshit, and we're going to blow the lid off it! So our great leaders fuck in strange and different ways, one step removed from the animals." There it was again. Was this the way self-loathing began, comparing humans to animals, stripped of civilization and evolution? "We'll be telling them that important people are just as human as the rest of us. It'll embarrass them, but it'll also make them reassess themselves."

It was like throwing darts against a stone target. Nothing penetrated.

"I can't, Jason."

Through the obscure softness came the cry of her rebellion. A thousand hosannas, he thought sarcastically. Cause to rejoice. So she had elevated herself from a slab of sexual meat to a deeply compassionate woman. The revelation came like an epiphany. I love this woman, he cried in his heart. And I hate myself for what I must do.

"People will laugh at them," she said.

"So what?"

"I don't laugh at them, Jason. If I did, I know it would hurt them."

"Dorothy. Do you think that they give one damn about you?"

"Of course they do. They all love me. They're my friends."

"Friends? You're kidding me."

"I respect them and their privacy. They believe that what they tell me is secret."

He was appalled by her arguments. Couldn't she see?

"They used you. That's all."

"They did not," she snapped back angrily.

He couldn't believe it. Still, it wasn't a complete surprise. It was his secret dread come to life, made real.

"You said they would do you favors. That's all. I did it because I thought they were helping you."

"They are. That's the truth."

Her agitation grew. The color did not return to her cheeks.

"You lied to me, Jason."

The accusation was jarring. Hell, he had rescued her from a slag heap. He had the power to make her wealthy.

"You never told me it would be like this, telling everyone about it." She was shaking her head in obedience to some inner caveat, but there was no mistaking the decisiveness.

"I don't even know why we're discussing it," he said firmly. "You have no choice. We're going to do it."

"How can I tell them, Jason?"

"Tell them?" Was she serious? His laughter was high-pitched, mocking. "You're not going to tell them anything. This is it. We're closing shop." He had that planned well. She would simply quit her job and go underground until he was ready for her to surface. Tomorrow, he decided at just that moment, he would see Webster.

"Do you mean I'll never see them again?"

"Christ, Dorothy. You've been playing sex games with six men. Don't you think it's about time you stopped?" He struggled to hold back his fury.

"But I thought . . ."

"That's the problem," he said. "Suddenly you're thinking. What did you think the purpose of all this was? All of this?" His hand swept the air. "It all cost money." He shook his head, as if to edit the new tangent he was following. Money was the least of it.

"The fact is that it will bring you freedom. Nobody will be able to kick dumb pollack Dorothy around anymore. Do you know what that means? Nobody will ever be able to use you again. Like Jim. Like those men. Like . . ." He swallowed hard. "Like me." The argument sickened him. Come what may, she would always be dependent, manipulated and misused. It was the only choice she knew how to make.

"I'm afraid, Dorothy," he said, controlling himself, "that if you don't go along with me on this, I mean be real cooperative, we're finished."

Her body began to tremble, a paroxysm that he'd never seen before, she was transformed before his eyes. Her ashen complexion turned dead white, the skin tightening over her face. It frightened him and he came forward to embrace her. Her body was cold.

"I'll never leave you, Dot," he said. "Forgive me for saying that."

My child, my love, he wanted to say.

"But it's time you stopped being a toy for others," he said, holding her still, his breath a tiny breeze trying to stir a dying flame. "These men know how to survive. They're shrewd. They'll know how to roll with the punches." Hadn't he convinced himself of that?

"But why are people so interested?" she said sadly.

"Why did they want to see you dance naked?"

"Nobody got hurt. It made them feel good to watch me."

Was he losing his ability to influence her? Before she didn't need elaborate explanations. But now . . . Why couldn't she have tossed them off like turning tricks?

"Dorothy, it's impossible to be emotionally involved with six men," he said, still holding her, feeling the sweetness of her flesh. She was a miracle, like a divining rod that could seek and find man's pleasure.

"I truly love you," he said. Sacred words. Had he locked them away for just this occasion? Never once had she told him that. Now he yearned to hear it more than anything he had ever wanted. Say it, he begged in his heart. But she said nothing, seemed lost in thought. He tried to kiss her, but she turned her face away.

"Must we?" she asked.

He stroked her spun hair, then caressed her face, feeling the moisture of fresh tears. It was the first time he had ever seen her cry.

"It'll only hurt for a little bit," he whispered. "And I'll be with you no matter what," he added, not sure it mattered any longer.

Her lack of malice would be an asset, he thought. The public would love her, identify with her . . . America's innocent darling. They would look at her as a beautiful fool manipulated by a cynic. Svengali's doll. That, of course, was the real story. The other was simply where the profit was. Writing it was going to be painful as hell.

"Can I stay here for a little while longer?"

She got up and moved to another chair.

He debated for a moment. There was no harm in that.

"I do love this place. All white and clean." She looked around and caressed the arm of the couch.

"Fantasy land," he murmured. It was a shock to have discovered that she was capable of another life. More specifically, a life without him.

"I want to stay here."

He studied her face, a mask now, no longer as comprehensible as before.

"I don't," he said, "I hate it here."

"By myself," she whispered. Again he fought to hold back his anger. You can't take her screaming and protesting into the arena, he reasoned. The entire credibility of the enterprise was at stake. Without her complete cooperation, the thing would disintegrate. He hadn't even considered that possibility.

"This is ridiculous, Dot." He moved toward her again, lifting her gently. She was as cold and rigid as stone. "Dammit," he muttered, releasing her. Without him, without his protection, his love, she was like a reed in the wind. He sensed that her balance was delicate, her calibrations foreign and mysterious. There was too much at stake to impose his will by force.

"They're not worth it."

She had turned her eyes away as if to hide them from him.

"They're my friends," she whispered, between deep swallows.

It was the final straw.

"I'm trying to give you a life," he said, his words spewing out in a great flume of frustration. How dare she do this to him. "You're nothing but a goddamned bitch," he said, his vehemence beyond control. "A goddamned ungrateful bitch!"

He came back to where she sat and lifted her out of the chair.

"Don't you understand? Nobody cares. All these sons of bitches care about is manipulating other people to satisfy their own egos. To them you're nothing but a piece of meat. A whore. A toy to be played with. Is that what you want to be all your life? I've figured out a way to make you a person. To give you enough so you don't have to be anybody's slave. Can't you get that into your thick skull?" He paused, choking on the words, gasping in a sudden coughing fit.

Her eyes still averted, she remained impassive.

"You wait," he continued, when he had stopped coughing. "Wait till that beautiful body starts to corrode and fall apart. It does that, you know. You'll be dry, shrunken, worthless. Those tits." He pinched her breasts. "Like wrinkled melons. Soon it won't be just people who fuck you over. Nature will take its course. It'll chew you up and spit you out like it does everybody. And what will you have left? What will you be? Nothing. For crying out loud, I'm trying to save your life. I'm trying to set you free." He paused again, lowering his voice. "Me as well. No more ass kissing. No more hypocrisy. Can't you see it? We'll be getting even. Fighting back. Don't worry about those assholes. Not one is worth the candle."

As he spoke, she had slowly turned away again. He felt impotent in his frustration. He wanted to lash out at her, pummel her into submission.

"All right," he said. "You stay here by yourself. There's nothing but lies here anyway. Fraud. Bullshit. You'll crawl back. Crawl like a fucking lizard, begging me to take you back. You push me too far, I'll wash my hands of you. Send you back to Hiram. How would you like that?" Behind his eyes a great wave of blood seemed to break, boiling with foam.

"You stay then," he shouted. "You stay. I can easily make this thing work without you."

Striding out of the apartment, he slammed the door behind him. In the car he slumped behind the wheel, enervated. Sitting in the cool, silent night, it was as though another wave broke inside of him, and his body was suddenly wracked by sobs, his entire being flooded with sorrow.

Dorothy, he thought silently as he peered at her lit window, I didn't know it would be like this either.

XIII

Fiona and Cates sat in the waiting room of Tate O'Haire's massive office in the Rayburn Building. Ironically, it was not far from Bruce Rosen's office. In the two years since she'd last seen him, she'd thought of him only occasionally. Another dead love. She had a strange talent for getting involved with the wrong man. Another sweaty-palmed politician gearing up for the next election, she sighed, observing O'Haire's intense young staff, puffed up with arrogance and self-importance.

Yet, it was because of Bruce that she was in O'Haire's office instead of that of Justice Strauss. Every experience teaches, she assured herself. Because of her relationship with Bruce, she knew more about congressmen, their fears and vulnerabilities.

"The name of the game is re-election," he had told her, and in so doing reflected the principal concern of his life.

"Some of them would sell their mother," she muttered to Cates, realizing that the bitterness of her affair with Bruce still lingered. She was assembling quite a rogue's gallery of her own.

It was their regular day off, making the risk of interrogation even more dangerous. It implied officially sanctioned police business, which, in the technical sense, was a lie.

"Are you sure?" Cates had asked when she told him she was going to see O'Haire.

"I'm not sure I'm sure."

What she was sure about was that there could be no turning back. As for Cates, he had made his decision. In the light of her experience with indecisiveness, that was something worth admiring in anyone.

"Martin. Strauss. O'Haire." An odd trio. They spoke them aloud, wrote them down, mulled them over, speculated.

What were O'Haire's fingerprints doing on the closet rail in Dorothy's apartment? The prints of Justice Strauss were easier to explain. "El Kinko" was the way they referred to him.

"She was a busy lady," Cates had said. "But was she a murder victim?"

"If she was," Fiona said, pausing to consider her own determined reaction, "I intend to prove it."

They had appeared at O'Haire's office without an appointment, a typical police investigatory ploy—catch them off guard if you can.

"Let me be the heavy," she'd said to Cates.

"Be my guest."

From Bruce, she learned they were a crafty lot, intimidating and arrogant under a thick patina of charm. She reasoned that their relationship wasn't a total loss, after all. When the receptionist tried to put them off, Fiona flashed her badge.

"Police business."

She glared at the young girl, who looked bug-eyed at the shield. "Confidential."

"I'll check," she said, leaving the room. "Have a seat . . ." Returning quickly, she said, "The congressman will be with you in a moment."

The wait would give him time to carve out a position, create a public posture. It also gave Fiona time to hone her own approach. Above all, she had to hold herself back from making any overt accusations. In a way, he had the advantage. She was dueling in the dark.

O'Haire was a large, florid-faced man in his early fifties, bulky and well-groomed with a fresh boutonnière in the lapel of his pin-striped suit. Shanty, she decided immediately, using her ingrained ethnic instinct. Takes one to know one. His eyes were steel gray and although his lips smiled, his eyes inspected.

"An O'Haire can never refuse a FitzGerald," he said, leaning back in his chair. His stubby fingers played with a ballpoint pen. "What's your pleasure?" Noting her dominance, he had dismissed Cates, who sat impassively beside her.

"I'm investigating a death," she began, her throat suddenly dry. She cleared it with a cough.

"The great leveler," he said. There was the barest hint of an affected brogue. She studied him carefully. She had deliberately said death, not suicide. She took out her notebook.

"Just routine," she said, looking at Cates, whose chocolate complexion had lost its gloss. "A woman. A young woman. She went under the name of Dorothy Curtis."

"Dorothy Curtis." O'Haire lifted his eyes as if the name might be engraved on the ceiling. "No," he said, showing not the slightest difference in attitude.

"Early twenties. Worked in the makeup department of Saks. Lived on Cathedral Avenue."

Still no reaction. Fiona's stomach tightened. The whole exercise was meant to connect them. It wasn't going the way she had expected. He was too impassive, too slick, a good actor. She stole a glance at Cates, who turned away, looking at the pictures on the wall.

"You didn't know her?" she asked.

"She might have worked for me."

He straightened in his chair and pressed a buzzer before she could stop him. "We'll see." A middle-aged woman came in. "What was her name again?" he asked, turning to Fiona.

"Curtis. Dorothy Curtis."

The middle-aged woman looked thoughtful, obviously searching her memory. An old warhorse, Fiona thought, used to such ploys. Usually these women knew more about their bosses than they did about themselves.

"Not familiar." Her face brightened. "We had a Bob Curtis once."

"Wrong sex," Fiona said pointedly, looking at O'Haire.

"Thank you, Mrs. Armbruster," O'Haire said, dismissing her, making it clear that if Mrs. Armbruster didn't know then no one would. When she left, he settled back in his chair and began to play with the pen again, challenging her. He was a cool number, Fiona thought, thinking of Bruce. They were all cool numbers. But this one was a lying bastard.

"Is there anything more?" O'Haire asked pleasantly. He was playing with her now, feigning profound disinterest. What he was doing was waiting for her to unreel information, although he betrayed none of the curiosity that must have been eating at him.

"Well, I guess that's it then," Fiona said, slapping her notebook shut. Two can play that game. She had often used it in her interrogations. Setting bait. Dangling it on the hook before the startled fish.

"Anytime I can help the MPD," he said, standing up, thrusting out his hand. She felt his stubby cold fingers. This one, she decided, was used to power, used to winning. Cates rose as well, but O'Haire didn't offer his hand. She turned her back and started for the door, calling his bluff.

"I hope you have better luck elsewhere," he said, forcing her to turn. He was still smiling, but his fingers had whitened as he gripped the rim of the desk.

"It could have been a mistake," she said, watching his eyes now. Had she caught the glint of fear? "Probably was." She turned again and reached for the doorknob.

"A death, you said." His words tumbled out. There it was, she thought. She had the bastard.

"That's about the only thing we're sure of," she said, turning again. Beside her, Cates shifted nervously.

"I don't understand." Despite what seemed like a valiant effort, his smile collapsed.

Easy, she told herself, excited now by his unwitting confirmation.

"We found her in the ravine under the Ellington Bridge."

"A suicide?" The bit was in his mouth now.

She deliberately hung her hesitation in the room like a tinsel mobile to tinkle in the breeze.

"Maybe." It was a bloated maybe, pregnant with possibilities.

"I see," he said. "Are you talking to others? Other congressmen? Mrs. Armbruster can check around. See who she worked for."

He was snapping voraciously at the bait, obviously wondering if he had been singled out. It was the one bit of information she was determined to withhold. Not yet, she cautioned herself.

"That won't be necessary," she said pointedly, opening the door now. She did not look back.

Sipping coffee at Sherry's, she was feeling proud of herself. A mighty man was dangling in her rope. All she had to do was tighten the noose and . . . and what?

"Smooth as silk, that one," she said. "But I got to his gut. He definitely won't have a good night."

"No. I guess not," Cates said morosely. He was obviously troubled.

"You saw it. He's scared out of his wits."

"Yeah," he said, avoiding her eyes.

"Now all we have to do is wait."

"Wait?"

"I know those bastards. He's hiding something and he thinks we know what it is. He can't live with that. No politician can."

"So what will he do?"

She hadn't moved that far ahead.

"He's guilty of something," she said, ignoring the question. "He was in Dorothy's apartment. We know that. We also know that somebody wiped away evidence. Or tried to."

"The justice?" He said it by rote, forcing his interest. Was he simply another weak man, she wondered, getting cold feet?

"We're pretty sure of that one. He thought he had cleaned up all his garbage. Imagine. A damned Supreme Court justice. We'll get to him as well." She felt her heart pound. "They think they can get away with anything."

"Like murdering Dorothy?"

"Maybe. We've got one hell of a motive. Fear of exposure. That's the big enchilada. I've seen it. When it comes to that, nothing stands in their way."

"You think Dorothy threatened to expose them? That it?"

What other weapon did she have? she thought. How dare he question that? She thought of Dorothy, waiting. Always waiting. A thing to be used at their whim, always ready at their beck and call. She knew what that meant.

"We'll flush them out," she said, her excitement at the prospect growing.

"I'm sorry, Fiona, but I just can't see them as killers."

"They are. I know they are." She felt the wave of hysteria begin and hid her trembling hands under the table. "One way or another."

Cates shook his head, lifting his eyes to observe her.

"But where is the crime?" he asked softly.

She let her mind cool. It must sound reasoned, calm, squeezed of emotion.

"It's there. I know it is."

"How do you know?"

She felt the condescension. He was talking to her as if she were a child. He was a man. How could he know?

"They use people," she said. "They think nobody can touch them. They think they own everything."

"It's getting heavy, Fiona. I'm sorry. We still have to prove a crime."

"We will."

"How?"

"I know what I'm doing. If you want out, say so."

"It's getting out of hand, Fiona. You're pushing too hard. It's not . . ." He hesitated, his reluctance palpable. He can't possibly understand, she thought. ". . . professional."

"Well then . . ." She got up indignantly, glaring at him. Continuing to sit, he looked at her and shook his head.

"You're foreclosing on other possibilities. She could have been a part-time hooker."

"Hookers aren't jumpers. They don't suffer. They just do business." He can't know what I know, she thought as she turned to walk away. He came after her.

"It's that guy," he said, following her into the street. "That Clint. I'm not stupid, Fiona. I could see it."

"Fuck you."

"He's made you crazy, right? It's not just the jumper. Dammit, Fiona. Can't you see that I'm worried about you?"

She continued to walk away, leaving him behind. Worry about yourself, buster, she muttered. I know I'm right. I'd stake my life on it. My life—the image scared her. Clint, I need you now, she cried, walking swiftly. At a telephone booth, she stopped and dialed Dr. Benton's number. His smooth voice soothed her, offering the promise of solace.

"I need to see you, Dr. Benton. I'm coming right over."

"Of course," he said quietly.

Taking a cab, she was at his home in Northeast Washington quicker than expected. He was still in his robe. As she sat down in his neat, book-lined living room, with its pictures and memorabilia of his dead wife, she realized that it had been a long time since she had gone there. Up until now Clint had filled all her needs, making her whole.

"A woman alone is an unnatural state," she said, after he had brought coffee and cookies. Oreos. They had had a good laugh over that on other occasions. His were always the light ones with chocolate inside.

"Anybody alone is an unnatural state," he replied, glancing at a picture of his wife.

She reached out and he took her hand.

"Maybe I've got the cop's malady. Overidentifying with a victim."

"The girl? The suicide?"

"It's not suicide," she said quickly.

"Not suicide?"

The hysteria began again and she took a deep gulp of air to calm herself.

She looked at him and shook her head. "Put on your white collar, Dr. Benton." He remained quiet and squeezed her hand.

"I'm out of control. I saw her as me. Dumb me, maybe trapped like her. I can't believe I let it happen, falling for a married man . . . Anyway, I forced the issue. I mean this case. Like it was me, with no place to turn." He started to speak. "Don't say anything. I'm fighting it. It's worse than giving up cigarettes, I can tell you that. It is the most horrendous emotion, this love thing. It debilitates the brain, crowds out reason. Makes your body turn to goo. And inside I'm screaming with unrequited whatever. Jesus. Don't I sound freaky?" Breathing deeply again, she leaned her head on the back of the chair.

"A little hysterical maybe."

"Too bad I have to uncork it on you."

"Who knows, maybe someday it'll be me bottled up."

"You? Never. You got it out of your system." She waved toward his wife's picture.

"One woman. One love. No pain in it though. Only joy. Except once . . ." Lowering his eyes, he swallowed, and she lifted his hand and kissed it.

"When He wants you, He gets you. The least He could have done was coordinate it," Dr. Benton said.

"I'm making you morbid."

"Maudlin. Not morbid," he responded cheerfully.

"One bad thing leads to another," she said. "Clint led to Dorothy."

"Dorothy?"

"The jumper. My reaction to her. It galled me to see her lying there. A beautiful girl all busted and broken. Men did that." She paused. "See, there I go again."

"Men?"

"Three." She thought of the cans of caviar. "Maybe even four. At least two are among the mighty."

She told him about the fingerprints, Gribben, the identification, her visit to O'Haire. He listened patiently as the room darkened. When he turned on the lights finally, she felt emptied of anguish, calmer. Her hysteria had gone.

"Maybe I should leave it alone," she said, getting up and stretching.

"I'm going to the office a little later today. Care to go out for dinner?"

"Best offer today," she answered cheerfully.

A telephone rang and he went off to the kitchen to answer it. When he came back, he looked troubled.

"I'll bring in some fried chicken," he said.

"I thought . . ."

"That was your favorite man. Captain Greene. Your eggplant. He was fuming. Says you should stay put until he gets here."

"How did he know I was here?"

"He's not as dumb as you think."

XIV

Back in his Capitol Hill apartment, Jason poured himself half a tumbler of Scotch and tried to sort out his tangled emotions. He wished he had a meeting to cover—anything to take his mind off the earlier scene. It was impossible for Dorothy to sustain that kind of rebellion, he reasoned. Nothing more than an adolescent tantrum. She was being deliberately self-destructive.

He finished his drink and glanced at the door. She would crawl back. What he had to do was assemble himself, plan a response. When an hour passed and the level of Scotch in the bottle had considerably diminished, he began to pace the room, stopping periodically to look at the telephone. She would call. She would be frightened, contrite. She would beg him to forgive her.

What were those men that she should worry so much about them? Garbage, the lot of them. Where did she get the idea that they thought of her as a person? In a moment the telephone would ring or she'd be coming through that door, needing him. Only him. He was her protector, her savior. And after it was over, after the deals, the talk shows, the promotions, after the dollars had changed hands, he'd take her away. Travel. See the world. Just the two of them.

When the telephone rang, he took a deep breath, relieved at last of the burden of uncertainty. Let it ring, he told himself. Two. Three. Four. He counted them out. On the sixth ring, he picked it up, smiling into the receiver. Vindication was sweet.

"You son of a bitch."

A male voice in a hoarse whisper, like an obscene phone caller, sibilated in his ear.

"Who is this?"

"Your old FDA buddy," the voice said.

"Arthur."

"Not now," Arthur said, his voice scratchy and harsh. "Meet me."

Jason looked at his watch. It was nearly midnight. He thought of Dorothy.

"I can't."

"Yes, you can."

He felt disoriented. The booze, the tension, the aggravation had unnerved him. There was no mistaking Arthur's desperation.

"Where?"

In the long pause, his mind cleared. Government officials were paranoid about telephones.

"The back parking lot at the Key Bridge Marriott."

Jason knew the place, a high rise motel at the Roslyn end of the Key Bridge.

"A half hour," Arthur said before hanging up.

He immediately dialed Dorothy's number and got a busy signal. He tried again. It was still busy. He tried a number of times before he went out. Maybe she had taken the phone off the hook. No sense flogging himself with fantasies.

As he drove, he listened to heavy rock music, nostalgia for him now, a symbol of another time and place. He had believed in the sweetness of his aspirations, the goodness of his motives. The truth was his holy grail. How delicious it had been to ferret out the liars at the FDA, to prick their bloated bureaucratic egos and watch the slime seep out. He was a journalist, goddammit, a noble heroic soldier in pursuit of truth. Even now. He'd make them see how far they had drifted away from the meaningful, the relevant. He smiled. It had been the operative word of his time. Everything had to be relevant. Suddenly a Beatles number floated into his consciousness. "I Wanna Hold Your Hand." Remembering it, his eyes watered and tears spilled down his cheeks. He could barely see the entrance to the parking lot when he reached it.

He drove the car slowly through the crowded lot to the rear of the hotel. He circled it a few times until he spotted headlights flashing on and off near the rim of the lot. Parking his car, he got out and headed toward the other car. As he approached, the door opened and he slid in beside a distraught-looking Arthur Fellows.

The man stared straight ahead into the darkness. He wore a tie-less dress shirt and his jacket lay rumpled between them on the front seat. A fetid smell seemed to emanate from him, something more pungent than simple body odor.

"You're a scroungy cocksucker," Arthur said, his voice tremulous. A shaking hand wiped away a patch of sweat over his upper lip. Confused by the outburst, Jason said nothing.

"She called me."

"Who?"

"Who? Queen Elizabeth, you asshole."

Suddenly Arthur turned to him, his face distorted with fear and anger. He made a gargling sound, like a death rattle, then opened the car door and stepped out. Jason followed him to the tree line beyond the lot. Arthur lit a cigarette and coughed.

"Thought you gave that up," Jason said. He couldn't bear to ask the obvious.

"Should have stayed with cigarettes. Given up other things."

He coughed again and spat a ball of phlegm on the ground. "She called me," he said, turning toward Jason. "She told me that you set us up."

"Come on, Arthur. She doesn't talk like that."

"She said you were going to tell everybody about me and her. That that was your idea all along."

"She said that?"

No, Jason protested in his heart. Not Dorothy.

"You know what she wanted me to do?" He shook his head and made croaking sounds, half-laughing, half-crying. "Take her in. You know. Into my house. Can you believe it? Take that cunt into my house. She said she'd do anything. Be a maid. Anything. I couldn't believe it."

"So what did you say?"

"What do you mean what did I say? Then she told me what was happening, what you were planning to do. At first I said no. Couldn't be." Jason felt Arthur's eyes boring into him.

"Then I began to think about it. Shit. The bastard is really going to do it. You lousy prick. You've been manufacturing stories all along. You're going to put me away. At first I said to myself, she's crazy. This cunt is crazy. I'm the counselor to the fucking President of the United States. You're just a goddamned pimp reporter. You can't destroy me." He pounded a finger into Jason's chest. "And you're not going to do anything either, buster. Because I'm not going to let you.

"Is that what you told her?"

Arthur flipped the half-smoked cigarette on the ground and smashed it with his heel.

"I told her that if she ever opened her mouth, I'd get her."

"Get her? What does that mean?"

As a journalist, he was used to threats. They goaded him. His reaction, always, was to stonewall, get tougher.

"You know what it means," Arthur hissed. "And . . ." Again, he pounded his finger into Jason's chest. "That goes for you, too."

"I'm creaking in my boots."

He stepped backwards to avoid the persistent finger.

"You said it was safe stuff. Now I find out it was you setting me up." His voice softened. "I can't believe you would do this, Jason. Not you. We were friends. Asshole buddies. And now you're planning to destroy my life. My kids. My family." He gagged suddenly, doubled over and vomited. When he straightened up again, he wiped his mouth with a handkerchief.

"Haven't you got any pity?"

"Pity?" Jason thought of Dorothy. She really believed those men cared. She really believed it. He was more angry with himself for not seeing this coming. Now she'd know he was right.

"You're not going to get away with this, Martin. Nobody's going to buy it. It's blackmail. Webster won't be party to that. Besides, I'll deny it." He moved closer and Jason could smell his sour breath. "We won't let you get away with it."

"Who's we?" Jason said, contemptuously. "You and O'Haire? Remember who fixed him up. If she called you, she called him."

"My God. So that's why he's trying to get me." He leaned against a tree for support.

"He was another one of the regulars," Jason said, watching Arthur's face contort in pain.

"One of the what?"

"Regulars." He paused. "She had six."

"Six!" The knowledge seemed to slowly seep into his comprehension. "You've really lost your mind. Do you really think you're going to destroy six guys with this? Who are the rest?"

Jason told him. He watched him clinically, as the shock registered on his face. He wondered if he should make this scene part of the book. Hell, it added a whole new dimension. Fear. Pathos.

"You think they're going to let you do this? No editor will buy it. There's a criminal intent here—you engineered it. Entrapment. That's what it is. These men have families. Shit. They're powerful. A lot more than you think you are." His body sagged, but he couldn't stop. "What's the big crime that any of us committed? We went out and got laid. What's the big deal?" He began to laugh. It was forced, hysterical. "We'll deny it. To a man. It's our word against that stupid little bitch's. And yours. There won't be any sympathy for you. You're a fucking monster. That's what you are." He shoved himself away from the tree and brought himself up, ramrod straight. "I don't know what I'm doing here even discussing it with you. You haven't got a chance in hell to pull this off. Hell, this is America. I'm personally not going to let you get away with this. I've got more clout than you. You're just a flunkie. You want to see muscle? I'll show you muscle. Hell, if she called all those guys and

told them about you . . . then goddammit . . . you better head for
the hills."

He was winded, spent. Jason watched with indifference as he
struggled for control. Soon he would learn that the mighty only
think they can get away with anything. Arthur started back to his
car, stopped, shook his head and came back to confront him again.

"I'm the big asshole here, right? It's for money. Of course, it's for
money. You're looking for money from us. Right? What kind of a figure do you put on it? Six guys. Ten thou apiece. Or more. I'm not going
to pay shit. That's actionable. You forget, Jason old salt, I'm a lawyer."

"That's why I'm not worrying about you, Arthur. You'll make
out. You always do."

The rain, which had abated, started again. Arthur continued to
glare at him, unsure of how to proceed. Jason shook his head, thinking again of Dorothy. She had really believed they were her friends.
Now she surely would come crawling back, her innocence betrayed
once again. Now she would understand that she had one friend, one
dear loving friend. Nothing would stand in the way of what she had
to do now. Nothing.

The rain began to sweep over the lot in slanting sheets, soaking them.

"You're both going to pay for this," Arthur said. "Pay dearly. Her
word against mine."

"I got it all on tapes, Arthur," Jason said. "The room had a live bug."

Again, he staggered back, leaning against a tree.

"Bullshit. It won't stand up."

"Stand up where? She told me everything. All those little backbiting things you said about your colleagues. Yeah, Arthur. That, too. It's
more than just a dirty little sex scandal. It's got everything, including
foreign intrigue. We got it all. And she's going to back it up."

"The hell she is. She hates your guts. She didn't want any part
of it."

"That's when she thought you were all her buddies."

He stood in the rain, looking at Jason for a long moment. You won't find pity here, Jason thought. Too bad for him. He wasn't a man to inspire pity. Not that it would do him any good anyway. It was too late for that. Jason turned and walked toward his car. By now Dorothy would be back at their Capitol Hill apartment. Perhaps she was worried about him. He'd let her stew.

He heard the angry roar of a car, the screech of tires. Turning he saw it hurtle toward him, barreling down on him at an accelerating speed. He started to run, tripping on the slippery asphalt. Still the car came, a relentless lethal weapon now. He threw himself on the ground between two cars. Arthur's car missed him by inches, crashing against the fender of one of the cars, then pulling back and speeding out of the lot.

Squinting into the rain, Jason got up slowly. A new dimension had been added to the scenario. Desperate men did desperate things. Until now, the possibility had been a vague one, but he realized that Dorothy, too, was now in danger. Physical danger. He was sure of it. He got into his car and headed swiftly for Capitol Hill.

XV

The eggplant arrived at Dr. Benton's house in an ominous mood. Brushing past them, he grunted a perfunctory greeting and helped himself to a shot of brandy. His black complexion seemed grayish, a sure sign of his inner turmoil. Taking off his jacket, he showed dark sweatlines under his armpits. He did not look at Fiona at first, not until he had finished one drink from a brandy snifter and poured himself another.

"I can leave if you like," Dr. Benton said. Despite his calm wisdom, he could be obsequious in the face of authority.

"No. You stay," the eggplant roared, turning bloodshot eyes on Fiona. He took another deep swallow and refocused on her.

"Might as well. He's your rabbi."

It was a police term. Everyone in the office knew that Fiona and Dr. Benton had forged a special friendship, one of the department's many odd couples. They all knew, too, that Dr. Benton was no boat-rocker and could be trusted with anyone's secret. Except the secrets of the dead. What she suspected, too, was that the eggplant needed a reliable witness.

"All they send me is assholes. Used to be a time when they'd send me real cops. Now it's deadheads and . . ." She could see him struggling to hold back the hated word. "Feeemales. This time the mayor's in it." Fiona looked at Dr. Benton, who shrugged, not comprehending. A new law had given the mayor absolute power over the police, one more thorn in the eggplant's battered hide.

"It was bad enough that we can't get a handle on this crazy who's wasting little girls." His bloodshot eyes narrowed as he looked at Fiona. "Black teenage girls. That's bad enough."

"No leads at all, Luther?" Dr. Benton asked. It was a particular concern of his. He had done the autopsies on the victims, a terrible chore for him. "I can't take the youngsters," he had often said. "Why do they kill the children?"

"That would be bad enough," the eggplant said, lighting a cigarette. He was already working on creating a little mound in an ashtray.

"It'll kill you, Luther," Dr. Benton said.

"One way or another," he said, "if this one . . ." He pointed to Fiona ". . . doesn't do it first." He waved a nicotine-stained finger at her nose. "This time I think you've bought it, mama." He turned to Dr. Benton. "I'm going to do her in for insubordination, malfeasance, harassment. The book. And I'm through eatin' myself up alive over it. White woman or not. She's gone too far."

They let him talk. He was all wound up in his bitterness and Fiona braced herself. She had sensed it was coming anyway.

"He was mad as hell, the mayor. I had to stand there in the big nigger's office listenin' to him rant and rave about appropriations, about his career, about honky power. You name it. I got both barrels. And I stood there holdin' my Johnson like a dummy wonderin' what the hell he was gettin' at. Then he started to talk about some jumper. Oh shit." His face glistened with oily sweat. "What jumper? What the fuck has he got to do with a jumper? Here I'm tryin' to find some crazy killer and he's layin' this jumper on me." He looked at Fiona. "You know what jumper? Your goddamned jumper. The same one. The one you said smelled funny. Well it sure as hell does smell funny. Only it's me that smells. I didn't know what the bastard was talkin' about." He stopped, took a deep drag on his cigarette and poured himself another brandy. "Your jumper, mama. I'm sure you told the good rabbi here all about your jumper."

Dr. Benton nodded. Fiona wanted to interrupt, but thought it wiser to remain quiet until he burned up more venom. By confronting O'Haire, hadn't she begged for this?

"I checked your reports, too. That was after. Just to make sure." He turned toward Dr. Benton. "You did a toxic and smears. Right? This is one persuasive little bitch. And what did you find?"

"Evidence of intercourse . . ." Dr. Benton began.

"Since when is fucking a crime? Evidence of intercourse," he mimicked. "I had to stand there while the fat-assed mayor dressed me down for her stickin' her nose where it shouldn't be. You can't manufacture a criminal from the air. Some dumb honky broad snuffs out her own lights, which is her privilege, and the great detective here . . ." He upended his drink in one gulp. "Intuition, right? That's where it is. Intuition. Pretty little white ladies don't throw themselves over a bridge after they get laid. The hell they don't. And it's none of your damned business. Like I told her. Leave it alone. Leave it alone."

"Maybe I overreacted," Fiona said quietly. Dr. Benton watched her, comforting her with his eyes. You're in trouble, Fiona, she told herself. And the eggplant knew it.

"I had enough on my plate without this," the eggplant said. "There's just so much one human bein' can take." He was wallowing in self-pity now, a typical ploy of his.

"I didn't mean to . . ."

"Didn't mean shit," he shouted, banging his fist on the table, scattering the cigarette butts.

"Easy, Luther," Dr. Benton said in in his soft voice.

How was it possible to explain anything to this raving maniac? She could never tell him about Clint. He would ridicule it, trivialize it. In this state, Fiona knew, nothing could placate him.

"Murder. So it was murder, was it? There's not a shred of evidence. Not a shred. Did you see anything, smell anything?"

Dr. Benton looked at him helplessly.

"And you." He glared at Fiona. "Any evidence of a crime? Not one iota." He got up and lumbered across the room, then poured himself another drink.

"I've suspended Cates pending an inquiry," he said. "And you, too, FitzGerald."

"Isn't that harsh, Luther?" Dr. Benton asked.

The eggplant came back to the couch and banged his glass down on the table. Fiona's stomach tightened, the lump of fear expanding. Suspension. Inquiry. So he was finally testing the power of the double minority.

"I had no choice," he said, quieting.

"And if you did?" Fiona asked, her voice breaking.

"Maybe I would. Maybe I wouldn't." He glared at her.

"Typical."

"Easy, Fi," Dr. Benton warned.

"You think I got it easy," the eggplant said. "To some of you, I'm a joke. The eggplant. You think I don't know that? Sometimes I can't tell who's worse." He looked up at the ceiling. "You. Or the damned killers. I don't know who gives me more shit."

"Well, you sure as hell pass it along," Fiona said, drawing courage from her welling anger. "You're like the guy who comes home from work and kicks the dog. Only some of us are the dogs."

"Fiona," Dr. Benton interrupted sharply.

"Let the bitch talk," the eggplant mumbled, pouring another drink. "My department doesn't respect me. Least of all her. The token white princess. Well, this time she's gone and bought it. The laugh is, that it wasn't me who did it."

"Not you?" she asked, momentarily confused.

"Mayor's orders. Not that I wouldn't have done it myself, but he's the boss. I told you. I had no choice. He had me there with my pants down."

"I hadn't realized . . . So I really did get to that bastard O'Haire."

"Who?" the eggplant asked.

"O'Haire. The majority whip of the house. You mean his name didn't come up? That's the one I leaned on."

They exchanged looks of confusion. The eggplant shook his head like a dog rising from a long sleep and stood up. He began pacing the room.

"Why exactly was I suspended then?" Fiona asked, watching him. "I have a right to know. And Timothy Cates. That's a real bad rap for him. It wasn't even his fault. I . . ." she hesitated, glancing briefly at Dr. Benton, "I pussy-whipped him."

"I told you. He took it out of my hands."

He turned to Dr. Benton.

"Maybe I am an asshole," he said. "But one thing I do is defend my own people. If they screw up, it's me that gets the poker."

"Well, you didn't defend us," Fiona muttered.

He stopped pacing and glared at her. "Even I got limits, FitzGerald. What do you know about it anyway?"

"What did the mayor tell you," she said gently. "I have a right to know that."

The eggplant sat down again and lit another cigarette.

"The White House. One of the President's top guys . . ."

"That high up?" Dr. Benton said.

"A man named Arthur Fellows. He said you were messing in areas that are very sensitive. That the President was upset. That unless there was solid evidence of foul play in this suicide you'd better stop messing around. He made me check, so I read your reports. There is no evidence. He said you were apparently working on your own, harassing people and you had to be stopped."

"He didn't mention O'Haire?" She could have understood O'Haire. Even Martin. They, at least, had a legitimate gripe.

"No."

She tried to assimilate the information.

"The White House. Is it possible?"

"Hey, woman. You know the games they play. They all jerk each other off. Clout. Remember that word. They trade things around with each other. Appointments. Favors. Who the hell knows? Maybe the mayor thinks he's going to lose next time out and wants to be ambassador to Zululand. It wouldn't be the first time the White House scotched an investigation. National security or some shit like

that. Besides, it's not like we're squelchin' anything. FitzGerald . . ."
He raised his voice. "There's no crime here. No fucking crime."

"Well, there sure as hell is a lot of other shit going down," she
said sharply.

"What the hell is that supposed to mean?"

She looked at Dr. Benton, who shrugged and turned away.

"Shall I tell him?" she asked.

"I can't make that decision, Fiona," Dr. Benton said.

She knew his courage was faltering, that he would have rather not
heard anything. It wasn't cowardice, she knew. Just surrender. He
loved his work and knew the survival techniques of the bureaucracy.
Knowing too much wasn't one of them.

"I'm sorry, Dr. Benton, to have dragged you into it."

"I'm the goddamned boss and I don't know nothin," the eggplant
said with disgust, sitting down in a corner chair, crossing his heavy
thighs. As she talked, she watched him. Every word she uttered
seemed like the blow of a blunt instrument. His jaw grew slack and
his bloodshot eyes seemed tired. The glass trembled in his hand.
There was, she knew, a sense of evil power in her explanation as she
told him about Justice Strauss, the oversized underwear, O'Haire,
the cans of caviar, the four-star pin, Gribben, Jason Martin.

"An investigative reporter," she emphasized.

Hearing it come out in her own words, she was startled by the
tangle of events. Was this all because of Clint?

"Lord have mercy," the eggplant said when she finally finished.
He took out a handkerchief and mopped his face. "Is that all?" he
asked, obviously stunned.

"No. I don't think that's all," she said. She poured the last remains
from Dr. Benton's bottle into a glass and drank it in one gulp. The eggplant slumped back in his chair, as if his bones had suddenly dissolved.

"I tried to tell you. It did smell. You've got to admit that."

When he didn't answer, she continued, feeling the heat of the
brandy roll inside her.

"She could have also had a friend in the White House."

"Who needed this?" the eggplant mumbled.

"I'm sorry. I really am sorry." She felt her contrition deeply, knowing it was too late for that.

"At least she wasn't black," the eggplant said, emitting a forced chuckle. Fiona looked from his face to Dr. Benton's, connecting with their anguish. It's like we were playing bridge on the Titanic, she thought. Minding our own business.

"That dumb nigger mayor," the eggplant exploded. Again, Dr. Benton and Fiona exchanged glances. The signs were obvious. He was winding up once more. No one could ever accuse him of being a quiet brooder.

"That White House fucker knows his niggers."

Suddenly he seemed to abort his temper and grew quiet, his eyes drifting as he played with his empty glass. "You gonna cooperate, FitzGerald, or do we all have to go through the exercise?"

He was obviously pleading. It was too big to cope with. "Unless you're a good liar, and I don't think you are, we can't go through an internal inquiry. Not with all that shit going down. Everybody loses. Except maybe you, FitzGerald. The avenging white angel."

"I didn't ask to be suspended," she snapped. No, she wouldn't want to go through it, either. Sooner or later they'd get at the root of it. Maybe even to Clint.

"What do you mean, cooperate?" she asked.

"I'm not sure," the eggplant said, drifting again. "Just let it pass. Blow over. I'll try to talk him out of suspension."

"Without telling him?"

"I'm gonna try. Why should I give that son of a bitch a club? Rule numero uno. Never trust a politician." He paused, waiting for her answer. "Well?"

"Do I have to answer now?"

She looked helplessly at Dr. Benton.

"They're too big to play with, FitzGerald. We're little guys. The big guys don't like little guys messin' with their shit. Somewhere along the line we all get it. Dig? So they were playing around. We're not the . . ." He laughed, a sad little bleat, ". . . the moral minority."

Maybe, she thought, her loyalty ought to be to the living. Sorry, Dorothy, she told herself. Dead is dead. It was, she knew, because of a bit of power that had fallen into her lap, undeserved. But she could show them her loyalty, her commonality with them, crossing all racial and sexual borders. She'd be one of them and they'd owe her for that, she mused, upset by the nastiness of the thought. When all was said and done, they were her people. Just cops. Like her. Like her old man. She had finally made it, she told herself, wanting to cry, but holding back. She would never show them that.

"Sure, I'll play," she said, feeling the room spin.

"And Cates?"

"Timothy? I'm sure he'll play, too."

"Thank the Lord," the eggplant said, getting up.

And what about Dorothy, she thought. Had she played along, too? The question persisted, leaving a knot in her stomach that she couldn't ignore.

XVI

"Dot."

Before he turned on the lights, he called out. It was a useless effort. He knew she wasn't there. Wild hope had driven him through the heavy rain back to his Capitol Hill apartment. What he had failed to calculate in his scheme, excised by sheer blindness, was the power of desperation. If he hadn't moved quickly, Arthur Fellows would have run him down without pity or remorse. In cold blood. He shivered, less from the chill than his fear. Had she escaped as well?

He picked up the phone and called the Cathedral Avenue apartment. He let it ring five, ten times, praying to hear the sound of her voice at the other end. Without changing, he jogged through the rain back to his car. Please God, no, he begged, as he sped toward her.

Absolution was what he craved. He would get down on his knees and beg her forgiveness. In the car, he held tightly to the wheel, feeling the chill permeate his body. He began to shiver as he maneuvered the car along the Southwest Freeway, forcing his alertness to be sure he took the right cut-off and not the one that led to Virginia. It could lose him as much as half an hour.

Please be safe, Dot, he begged God. God! It was, he discovered, suddenly not just a figure of speech. He was beseeching a tangible source, a protector of his childhood. Don't punish her, he pleaded. It was my evil, mine alone. It wasn't her fault.

It was frustration, he beseeched. It had corrupted him, destroyed his sense of morality, melting good and evil into an indistinguishable mass. Hadn't he once done good as a journalist? All he wanted was to prove a point, illustrate hypocrisy. Wasn't that good? To satirize their phony standards? To bring back relevance?

As his thoughts whirled, he headed the car up Seventeenth Street
to a deserted Connecticut Avenue. The light drizzle continued. The
street lights, set for heavy traffic, inhibited his speed, and he pounded the seat beside him every time he was forced to stop. He was
afraid to go through the reds. Being stopped by the police now
would only slow him further.

By the time he reached Calvert Street he was pleading to Dot,
offering justifications to her as well. No. He had no right to deny her
feelings, to force her into this against her will. "Never," he vowed in
desperation. He would protect her forever, take care of her, make
amends. He would destroy the tapes. They would go away together.
He would get another job in some other place and spend his days and
nights loving her, demonstrating his sweet love in a thousand ways.
The idea energized him and for the first time in months he felt real
elation. Finally, hate had gone. Just give me the chance, he begged.

There were no parking spaces near the house, forcing him to double park. The lights were still blazing in the apartment. Thank you,
God, he thought, rushing out of the car and fumbling for his key,
bursting with the news of his, their, liberation. His fingers trembled
so badly, he couldn't fit the key into the slot and he pressed the
apartment buzzer.

"Dot," he called. "Please. It's over now. Please. Open the door."

When she didn't answer his buzz, he steadied himself and managed to get the key in the slot, hoping the door would not be
chained or bolted. Surprisingly, it opened freely and he rushed in.

"Dot. Dorothy? Please. Where are you?"

When it was apparent she wasn't there, his mind filled with
dread, searching for an answer. Was it possible that one of the men
had actually offered her a haven? Perhaps she did mean more to one
of them than even he had suspected. If that were true, she was in
good hands. He deserved it, deserved to lose her.

The thought of her escape calmed him, but not for long. Looking
in the closets, he had seen nothing amiss, nothing out of place. Nor

had there been signs of her taking anything out of their Capitol Hill apartment. She would not have left without taking something. Inspecting the apartment, he noted its extreme neatness, even neater than it had been earlier. In the kitchen and bathroom, everything gleamed. The contents of her drawers were perfectly placed. Her little nest was spotless.

But in the kitchen trash can, neatly lined with a white garbage bag, was a piece of crumbled plastic, the kind used to protect dry-cleaned garments. It was the only thing in the can. Had it been there earlier? He looked in her clothes closet and as he fumbled with the neatly hung clothes, searched his memory for a dress that might be missing. The white cocktail dress, pure white, lacy. It had been her favorite. He was genuinely puzzled now, roaming through the apartment, searching for other clues. Where was she? Under less tense circumstances, his journalist mind would have thrived on speculation. Now it seemed blocked. Nothing she had done in the last few hours seemed in character. She was not the Dorothy he knew.

For a little while, he was able to hold back any further morbid thoughts. She had simply gone away. It had been too much to handle. One of them must have helped her.

So this was the way it was going to end. Another dead end. Jane had been right from the beginning. Everything he touched was doomed. He thought of his son. Was he, too, doomed? Another generation of tainted Martin genes. Like his old man. Another life aborted by impossible dreams.

His mouth felt parched, and he went into the kitchen for a drink of water. Standing before the sink, glass in hand, waiting for the tap water to cool, his eyes drifted toward the window. Not far was the string of lights across the Ellington Bridge. They seemed so close. If he reached out, he felt he could almost touch them.

The bridge—suicide bridge! No, he told himself. Morbid thoughts begot morbid thoughts. But the idea persisted, and soon it crowded out everything else. Never, he assured himself. Never.

But the morbid itch had, finally, to be satisfied. It was absurd, but when he remembered how Arthur Fellows had nearly killed him, he shuddered with anxiety. Letting himself out of the apartment, he went into the deserted street and walked quickly to the corner, making a left on Calvert Street. A few cars passed by, but not a soul on foot was in sight. The span began at the edge of a large apartment house and the low concrete railings were broken periodically by a circular platform that the builders had evidently designed as observation posts for nature lovers. What the builders hadn't anticipated was that they would be used for more bizarre purposes, mainly by those contemplating suicide.

Stopping at the first one, he peered over the edge. Heights always made him queasy and he could feel the tingle of fear in his groin. Although it was still dark, the lights provided some illumination of the terrain below, and the occasional headlights from the parkway offered a brief, sweeping view of the trees and vegetation that lined the edges of the ravine.

He rebuked himself for his morbidity as he moved further over the bridge to another platform. Peering over, he could see the shiny thread of the creek, reflecting the passing headlights.

At first it had seemed like a crumpled newspaper drifting at the edge of the creek, and he had dismissed it until a blast of light had given it more definition. Again he denied the possibility to himself. The events he had lived through that night had already diluted the edges of reality and part of him had begun to insist it was merely a dream, and he had no control over the twists and turns of the subconscious plot line.

Denying it still, he moved from the platform, crossed to the end of the bridge and headed downward into the ravine, holding on to the scrubs to keep his balance. Slipping and scudding downward on the soaked ground, he cursed the anxiety that was driving him, knowing it could not be true. Soon he would hear the familiar sound of his alarm clock, the reassurance of reality.

The downward thrust of gravity was relentless, propelling him toward the creek. But he could not deny to himself the ultimate feeling of aloneness, the desperate sense of an impending rendezvous with horror. By the time he was halfway down the ravine, he recognized the truth of it, and finally in front of him, a broken doll in a white party dress, was Dorothy. He kneeled before her, struck dumb with terror as the empty eyes peered back at him. Forgive me, God, he cried into the night, looking upward, tasting the rain and his tears.

He did not know how long he knelt there. Time had no logic. Only the inertia of his will moved him. There was something he had to do, but it had not yet reached reason. The first texture of dawn began in the thickly clouded sky and he clambered upward. He had wanted to bend down and kiss her lips, but when the whitening light revealed her face, he was certain that the real Dorothy had long departed, that this misshapen, broken form was not her at all. Struggling upward, he reached the summit of the ravine's edge and ran to the apartment again, hoping that his beating heart would explode his ribcage. Once inside, he closed the door and leaned against it as if his weight could keep out the pursuing spirit of vengeance.

Yet, even in this blind anguish, his mind asserted itself. He searched the apartment again. No note. Nothing to indicate what she was about to do. She had even left the lights on, as if she were certain to be back. A fleeting thought speared out like flotsam to a man caught in a whirlpool. She was coming back. Soon. She would be back soon. That broken lifeless figure was merely wood and sawdust, a castoff doll. He felt better, but only for a moment. Why? Was it to punish him? Them? Now the idea emerged again. Them. One of them. Arthur Fellows would have run him down in cold blood.

Breathing in great gulps of air, he tried to calm himself. He must fight grief, a new enemy, and he scoured his mind for some thread of redemption for himself. And for Dorothy. His own life was worthless now. Had it ever been worth anything? All he had to show for

time spent was Trey, and even Trey was denied him. Dorothy at least
had her innocence, a rare gift, a talent. His grief was slowly trans-
forming itself into anger. Anger was good. White hot. Anger gave
sustenance. Anger gave him back his reason. He called Arthur
Fellows at home.

"Yes."

The voice was irritable. In his job, Jason supposed a call in the
early hours would be routine. Important White House business.

"You must come," Jason said.

"Who is this?"

"We got problems, Arthur."

"You again."

There was a long silence, but Jason could hear Arthur's breathing
at the other end, waiting. He didn't hang up.

"She's dead."

"Dead?"

"Very."

"Where are you?"

"At the apartment. You know."

"There?"

"You had better come. Now!"

"You think I'm crazy? No way."

"You'd better trust me now."

"Trust you? Of all people."

"You have no choice. You better come. And fast. Or I'll blow you
out of the water right now."

He hung up and tried to form a pattern of action. Somewhere in
the distance of his thoughts it was taking shape, sustaining him. Had
one of them done away with her? It was a speculation that would
never be far from his thoughts. Or had she killed herself? Was her
innocence so pure? Again, he had to tamp down grief, recall anger.

With a towel, he cleaned himself off, then wiped every surface that
he could find. Nothing went untouched. Sills. Windows. Furniture.

Every piece of tell-tale surface. The floor as well. He detached the answering machine, gathered every scrap of paper that might bear witness and placed everything, including the towel, in a plastic bag.

By the time Arthur arrived he'd finished. The ring reminded him that he would have to wipe the doors clean and the railings and the buttons. In his early days as a journalist he'd been a police reporter—he knew too well that the inanimate also had eyes and ears.

Arthur was in a state of blind panic. Deep pockets had etched themselves below his bloodshot eyes. He seemed to be breathing too deeply, as if he were unable to bring his body to its usual rhythms. His hands shook.

"This isn't some kind of trick?" His natural bent had always been skepticism.

"No trick. She's dead. Off the bridge."

"Bridge?" He didn't wait for any explanation. "Oh my God."

"I'm not sure whether she jumped or was pushed."

"What are you implying? You know where I was."

"I also know what you tried to do to me."

"I wanted to scare you. I'm not a killer." He sat down. "I'm a fucking victim. I was taken in and you know it." He covered his eyes, trying to maintain control. "You want to destroy me. My family. It isn't fair, Jason. I don't deserve it and neither do they."

"It was never a question of that," Jason said. "It's too late for regrets, I'm afraid. I've just done that bit. It's penance now."

"What does that mean?" Arthur said, looking toward him.

"I've got an idea." He paused before proceeding. "I want it secret. I'm going to destroy the tapes. It was sheer madness."

Arthur seemed relieved and the color began to come back to his cheeks.

"There's no note. I looked everywhere. Still, maybe it was suicide." He was suddenly speechless with fear. Maybe she was poisoned. Or there was a wound. He hadn't looked. "Maybe," he said finally. "Unless one of you people went crazy."

"Good God, Jason. We're victims. We're just people. Not killers."

"You said that before. But you nearly killed me."

"I was desperate."

"So are they."

"Then when I calmed down, I said to myself, what the hell. I had a good run. It's the humiliation of it . . ."

"I told you. I'm destroying the tapes."

"Thank God."

"Don't get too grateful." He felt his stomach tighten and his heart pump heavily. Arthur looked at him warily, his eyes had narrowed and his lips fell slack. "Just hold on," he said to placate him. "It's not as bad as you think. Very simple, in fact. Nobody is going to get off scot free. I want money."

"Money? So it is money."

"It is now."

"I figured it wasn't the end of it."

"Don't look so contemptuous. It's not for me. It's mostly for my kid, for his education. How's that for decency?"

"How much?"

"Twenty thousand apiece. No big deal." He felt his growing strength. The idea was emerging painlessly. Even Dorothy would be happy about that. When he would speak of Trey, she would grow misty-eyed and upset.

"You can have mine in the morning," Arthur said, quickly standing up, looking arrogant again. "All in cash, I presume. I suppose in exchange you'll hand over the tapes to each of us. Unless you've dubbed them."

"It'll be a clean deal. I promise that."

"Your promises. What are they worth? Deliberately destroying other people. For what? It makes no sense. What did we ever do to you?"

"Or Dorothy . . ." Jason muttered. But he didn't want to go into that now.

"She went nuts."

Jason ignored the remark.

"There's just one more thing, Arthur."

"Still more?"

"You're going to be the collector."

The blood drained out of Arthur's face and he had to sit down. "Me?"

"You're a great communicator, Arthur. Hell, you're the best."

"I can't be a party to that."

"I'm afraid you'll have to be. I'm just being practical."

Not practical, he knew. Malignant. Even the most fleeting sense of compassion lay dead with Dorothy. He was being deliberately diabolical. It was no longer a child's game. Yet, he seemed to himself, oddly reasonable.

"Hell, Arthur. You've got credibility. Access. You're one of the people who runs America. Right hand of the President. They'll believe you. I also don't give a shit what you tell them. Name names. I've got nothing to hide."

"You're being satanic."

"Manipulative. I prefer manipulative—like you. I only hope you get no objections. That, of course, would put it out of my hands completely."

"I feel ill."

"Fight it, Arthur. You'll need your strength."

He looked at Jason and shook his head. "You're not leaving me too many choices. And no guarantees. You're really turning the knife, Jason. Does it give you pleasure?"

"No, I'm afraid it doesn't. But it would have been worse the other way. I'm just thinking of myself for a change. I've got a kid, too."

"And he'll be real proud when he finds out where the money came from for his education."

There was a long pause.

"Suppose the police get too nosy?" Arthur said, considering all the angles.

"I figure if there was no sign of foul play, they'll write it off as a pure suicide. This MPD is no great shakes. But if they come up with any strange evidence, then we're in the soup. Me, too."

"Then what? You use the tapes?"

"Every man for himself."

"You are the most disgusting human being I have ever come across. Worse than any killer."

"I know. And I hate myself for it. But I'm not going to let self-loathing interfere with what I have to do for my kid, for my own peace of mind."

Arthur got up and walked to the door, pausing, his finger on the knob.

"Be careful," Jason said. "I have to wipe those prints away."

He removed his hand from the knob as if it was electrified.

"Don't worry," Jason said. "I've wiped off everything and I've removed everything that could be incriminating. At least I hope so. Most of the time I made her bring her stuff home."

"Home?"

"She was my girl. She lived with me."

"You're a pig," Arthur said.

"That, too."

"No conscience? No remorse? How can you possibly live with yourself?"

"I'm going to have one hell of a tough time," Jason said, glaring at him. "Think of poor Dorothy," he said. "She actually thought you were wonderful. All of you. Her buddies. What did you tell her on the phone? Live with that."

Arthur shook his head. "I'll have to try. And I'll try on the other. You'll hear from me tomorrow. I hope you're right about the police. But I can't conceive of any of the men doing that to her. I really can't conceive of it."

"I can," Jason said. He felt himself smile. It was more sardonic than warm. "Hell, Arthur. Consider yourself lucky. What if those tapes were in the hands of a really vicious man."

The door slammed shut. Jason looked at it for a long time, then began to wipe off the knobs. Yes, he thought, they were lucky. They were always lucky.

XVII

The early April rain had coaxed open the cherry blossoms around the reflecting pool exactly as scheduled. The delicate pink buds on trees donated by the Japanese before World War II formed a magnificent display, one of Washington's prime tourist attractions.

From where Fiona and Cates stood at the north end of the pool, they could see a panorama of American history—the Jefferson Memorial, Arlington Cemetery, Memorial Bridge, and the Pentagon. Behind them was the U.S. Mint.

"It's the helplessness that really hurts," he said.

"Hell, that's just the other side of power. No fun being powerful if the victim has choices." She watched the lines of tourists walking along the path that snaked around the waterside. They leaned against a railing and Cates flipped tiny pebbles into the water.

"Just don't talk about fair," she said. "I don't think I can take fair."

"All right, I won't say fair. But you got to admit, Fiona, we started something, stirred things up a bit. The damned White House. That's heavy duty. Sounds like a football play—Congress to White House to mayor."

"To eggplant to Cates to FitzGerald. A round robin."

"That's not football," Cates muttered, flipping a pebble far across the pool. "What the hell do you suppose we did?"

"Why flagellate? Forget it."

"I can't."

"I warned you," Fiona said. "Erase it."

"And just wait it out?"

"That's the game plan."

"How long?"

"Weeks. Maybe two or three. Then he's going to get us reinstat-
ed and we get our pay."

"But it goes on our records."

"If he's willing to go this far, he'll probably have it removed." She
wondered why she was putting so much faith in a bootlicking lackey like the eggplant. But he always reacted to strength and her information was a formidable hand.

"Now that's fair," he smirked.

"Sure," she smiled. "If it benefits you, it's fair. If it benefits the
other guy, that's injustice."

He threw another pebble in the water.

"You think it was O'Haire got on our case?" he asked.

"Doesn't matter. Up there, they're all in cahoots. Right?" He
searched her face for the sarcasm, found it, and smiled. If she were a
man, he might have kicked her teeth in for getting him into so
much trouble. I warned him, she assured herself. But it didn't chase
the guilt and she found herself still searching for ways to explain it.

"It's bureaucracy. Everybody has to protect the man ahead of him.
Simple as that. That's why we always get the supreme level of medi-
ocrity at the top."

"It still stinks," Cates said.

There was a long silence between them. A puff of cumulus cloud
hid the sun for a moment, then the blazed out again, stinging their
eyes with the sudden brightness.

"What do you think in your gut, Fiona? That's what I want
to know."

He had turned and looked deeply into her eyes, probing, the
pupils dancing.

"You're not supposed to think with your gut," Fiona said, looking
away quickly. "That's why we're in this mess in the first place." She
wanted to explain to him about Clint's being the trigger. He had a
right to know that, but still she held it back. Her temporary weakness had jeopardized his career.

"You owe me that," he said gently.

"Owe?" She felt a whip of anger.

"What do you think really went down? Did the girl get heaved? Was she some kind of a spy? An agent of some sort? How many men did she make? A Supreme Court justice? A top congressman? Someone in the Czech Embassy? Maybe the ambassador? And a four star general?"

"Maybe even someone in the White House."

It seemed utterly impossible to avoid the subject.

"And that Martin guy," he pursued. "We can't forget him. He brought the poor girl to town in the first place."

"Now you're doing it."

"Doing what?"

"Saying poor girl."

"I've been thinking a lot about her."

"Now you," she mumbled.

"Just a kid from the sticks. A dumb bunny. He should have just let her alone."

"Who?"

"The newspaper guy. Something fishy about him."

"Forget fishy," Fiona said. "It's not going to do us much good. We got jobs to worry about."

"Yeah, jobs."

Cates scratched his chin and shrugged. "Just the same . . ."

"Can't you stop it? Just shut up," she snapped. She started to walk down the path and he caught up with her. "I'm sorry," she said, "I got you in. I'll get you out. Just shut up and be a good boy."

"Us boys," Cates said. "All we do is run. When we fight, we always lose anyway."

She tapped her forehead.

"Smart thinking, black man."

"Black man?" he groaned. "My blood's the craziest mixed drink you ever saw. My grandfather was half-white, half-Indian. My grand-

mother was half-black, half-hispanic. My father was a British civil
servant in Trinidad. Half-Indian, I think. My mother migrated here
with me in her gut. And I'm what you call a bastard."

"You think you got troubles. I'm Irish. That's trouble by definition."

They walked in silence for a long time. Cates worried her. His
mind couldn't leave it alone.

"Just hold on, Timothy," she said. "It'll blow over. I made the deal
for both of us. Just have a little patience. We're little people. We
stuck our nose in the wrong place. One way or another, the girl died.
And the mighty are still the mighty. We're not God's avengers."

"So you think they are getting away with something."

"You just can't leave it alone, can you? It doesn't matter." She
paused and looked out at the tranquil setting, the blossoms swaying
in a gentle breeze. "I was the believer. You were always the skeptic.
This is no time for role reversal."

"I sure would like to know how close we came to something really big . . ."

"Dreams of glory. That's what we need in our business. Another
glory hound."

"You're not even curious?"

She took a deep breath and felt her heart flutter briefly. "Not anymore," she lied, patting his back. "Just hold on, kid. It wouldn't be
any fun without the secrets. We're in the den of the ruling class.
They like to play God. We're supplicants. Pay your fucking respects
and shut up."

They began to walk along the path. She had vouched for him with
the eggplant. Her job, after all, was to keep him cool.

"Whadayawannado?" she joshed. "Take in a flick? Grab a hamburger? Go to a gallery? How about the zoo?"

"The zoo." He looked at her and smiled. "I been to the zoo, baby.
I grew up in the zoo. I work in the zoo."

He started to laugh and slapped his thigh.

He'd be fine. She was sure of that. Just fine.

They spent the day in the Museum of American History. It was the beginning of the tourist season and crowds of teenagers in buses had begun to descend on the city.

That was the first way she'd seen it. She had done an essay on "The American Way," and the trip was sort of half-prize since her parents had to pay half-price. She remembered how the first sight of the Capitol dome had thrilled her. They had all stood on the Capitol steps and sang "America the Beautiful," and everyone in their hearts believed that it was true. The perfect Capitol of a perfect world. A man took their picture and they all paid fifty cents apiece for it. Now it stood in a battered frame in her parent's living room "rogues gallery."

"Pick out Fiona," her father would say sometimes, usually to one of their growing brood of granchildren. The kids were never very successful at it. On her visits home, for some reason, she always noticed that picture and the original feeling came back, like a pure fresh breeze.

Maybe it wasn't so perfect. But people weren't perfect and people ran things. Who was she to demand perfection? Her job was to see that people obeyed the written rules. As for those that were unwritten . . . that was none of her business. Let she who was without sin cast the first stone, she thought, smiling at the change of gender.

"What's so funny?" he asked.

"Us," she said. "A couple of idiots. Gribben said MPD was a bunch of idiots."

"He's right."

They decided to spend their suspension seeing the city like tourists.

"Let's see how they run America," she teased.

"Hell, we know how they run America."

"Do we?"

They had dinner at a small Italian restaurant in Georgetown and headed home in different directions. Suspension might not be so bad after all, she thought.

She had just settled into a book, proud to have put all thoughts of the case out of her mind at last. She had washed her hair, shaved her legs and underarms, filed her finger and toe nails and painted them pink. To match the blossoms, she decided. Then she gave herself a facial, tweezed her eyebrows, took a hot bubble bath, and rubbed herself all over with softening lotion, even the bottoms of her feet. It was delicious, she told herself, all this pampering. And she had nearly convinced herself when the telephone rang.

It was Clint. Her stomach heaved, a groan bubbled up from her chest, but she could not put down the phone.

"Still mad?" he asked.

"Mad?" No, she decided. No games. "It's not a question of mad. Whatever we had, which was good and wonderful, is hereby terminated. Why don't you give up, Clint?"

"I can't."

"I'm sorry."

"We're negotiating," he said. "Talking it out. I can't live without you, baby."

She felt the longing begin again, cursing its power.

"You have no right to do this," she whispered. The flesh is weak, she told herself. Help me.

"I need time," he said. "I'm getting it together. I'm just no good without you."

She could not think. The words refused to come.

"Fi? Are you there?" Tears spilled over her cheeks and she held her palm over the mouthpiece. This man was making her miserable.

"Yes."

"I love you, Fi." He paused. "And I know you love me."

She pressed her stomach in, as if the weight could hold in the pain.

"It's not enough, Clint," she said. "I don't feel comfortable about it."

"Comfortable. What has that to do with it?"

"Everything."

Plumbing her depths to find courage, she found it at last and felt the pain recede. "Maybe someday. Not now. There's too much on my mind." She hesitated. "It's me that needs the time, Clint."

"You're not being fair."

Fair again. Please not fair. This is another woman's property, she told herself. No matter what. And the father of another woman's family. It was stealing. A real crime. She laughed at her simile. Her strength flew through her in waves. She had made a deal with the eggplant. If she did that, she could do anything.

"No, Clint. Leave it alone. Not now."

"Please. Let me see you. Tomorrow. I'll be there at six. Like always. Please, Fi. I can't stand it. Have pity."

"I'm going to hang up now, Clint."

"Please, Fi . . . Ple . . ." She pressed the cut-off button and the phone went dead.

You're getting to be a hard case, Fiona, she told herself, trying to settle back with her book. Finally she found her concentration again and read until she eventually fell into a dreamless sleep.

The telephone's ring stabbed her consciousness. Not again. She let it ring and covered her head with a pillow. It didn't help. The persistence was maddening and she picked it up.

"Be dressed in fifteen minutes," the eggplant's voice crackled. "I'll pick you up."

"Fifteen minutes?" She looked at the clock. It was eight-thirty.

"That's an order."

"An order? I'm suspended."

"Fifteen minutes."

He hung up and she dressed quickly, jumping into the shower to remove the grease she had smeared on herself before going to bed. She wrapped her wet hair in a turban, then she put on a slack suit and hurried downstairs. His car was waiting for her, the door open. A cigarette dangled from his lips. He squinted through the smoke at her, nodded and slammed down the accelerator. That told her all she needed to know. Something had gone wrong. When the car jammed in traffic, he turned to her.

"I thought you said you could cool Cates?"

It caught her off guard. Cates?

"We made a deal," he growled.

He was obviously wrestling with his temper. A wrong move by her would set off the eruption. She cautioned herself, speaking slowly.

"I was with him all day yesterday. It was settled."

"You think so?"

"What did he do?"

She watched him as he accelerated and decelerated in quick spurts.

"You're making me nauseated," she said.

"Good."

"So what did he do?"

"You didn't know?"

"No. I don't know. I told you. He was fine."

"Some fine."

He looked at her with contempt, removed his cigarette and punched it out in the ashtray.

"Cates rousted this Martin guy. The newspaperman. Must have been late last night. This morning the guy called the office for you. I took the call. He said he would only talk to you."

"And what did you tell him?"

"I said he talks to you, he also talks to me. We work for the same company."

"Yeah, but I'm suspended."

"He said he had somethin' important to say. He said he was going to stop this shit once and for all. What shit? I didn't know what the hell he was talking about. Then he told me about Cates coming to see him. Apparently the dummy got physical as well. I'll have that one's ass."

He opened the window and spat out.

"I didn't know about it," Fiona said. "Not that it matters now, but I'm really shocked."

"I bleed for you."

He shook his head and sneered, showing a line of yellowed teeth. "I kept my part of the bargain. The mayor agreed. Two weeks. Charges withdrawn. I was also going to remove them. For that, I get this." He looked at her, his eyes narrowing. "You know what your problem is, FitzGerald? You don't know men. You haven't got the goddamnedest instincts about men. Black, white. Any man."

I'll buy that, she told herself, refusing to acknowledge it to him. Of all people, not to him.

He swung the car onto Pennsylvania Avenue. Passing the Capitol, the traffic thinned.

"Where are we going?"

"Neutral ground. Benton's."

For once, she forgave his paranoia. It's a zoo, Cates had said. But he didn't have to walk into the cage.

XVIII

Jason met Arthur Fellows at the Arlington Metro station. It was always deserted. There were no prying eyes to connect the two men, a valuable consideration if denial became necessary. Even the tourists eschewed it since it was too far to walk from the Tomb of the Unknown Soldier and the Kennedy graves, the two most popular sites in the Capitol. They had it all to themselves, especially at that hour. It was 8 P.M.

The visit from that woman detective and her black partner had shaken him up, but only until he realized that they really had nothing. Only that dumb pin. He had been worried about that. Hell, the pin was so obviously a general's insignia, it would have raised anybody's curiosity. He was sure they had nothing more. Dorothy was dead, in any event, and it didn't matter how anymore. At least Trey would benefit from all this horror. A little digging back in Hiram had revealed his connection, but he wasn't really worried about it. The point was that the police had no right to harass him if there was no evidence of a crime. That much he knew. Anyway, he was sure it would soon be over. They had nothing. Nothing but that pin. If they had more, their approach would have been different.

A train rumbled into the elaborate station and Arthur was the only passenger to get off. Watching him come forward, he saw the pale drawn face, the hunched posture. He seemed to have aged considerably in the past forty-eight hours. When he got closer, Jason moved to a bench and sat down.

"You put me through the worst moments of my life, you bastard," Arthur said, falling heavily onto the bench beside him.

"But you did it?"

"Not quite."

Jason coughed to mask his sudden anxiety. Arthur looked at him and turned away, his lips curling in contempt.

"It'll all be over soon," Jason said. He, too, wanted to have it done with.

Arthur breathed deeply and cleared his throat, which was slightly hoarse. Furtively, he looked around the deserted station.

"What a boondoggle," he said. "Typical."

Jason waited. There was no point rushing him now, no point pulling the noose any tighter. For the moment, he chose to ignore the "not quite."

"I saw them all. Every one. I saw the fear in their eyes, the agony. All good men. All they wanted to do was play, have a good time. What the hell is wrong with that?" He smiled suddenly, a leering, toothy smile. "Not one of them had the slightest inkling. Not one. They couldn't believe it."

"But they believed you?"

"Look at me. Do I look believable?"

"Then it was easy. See? I told you."

"Easy. These are men with brilliant careers." Arthur laughed derisively. "The Czech . . ." He paused when his throat caught, ". . . the Czech broke down and cried."

"Did she call them all?"

"Not all. The senator was out of town. She left a message with his wife. Can you believe it? When I told him, he had to take half a bottle of Maalox." He turned suddenly to Jason and scowled. "You know what it means to carry a message from the devil? It's madness. Madness. I feel depraved. Christ. It was all in fun. That's all it was. And they all asked me the same question."

"What was that?"

"Does that man have no pity?"

Jason glanced away and looked at the arched ceiling of the station. No, he thought, he had no pity. Men who have power are not to be pitied. To get where they are, how many lives did they have to ruin, how many people did they have to step on?

"Did any of them show any pity for Dorothy?"

"They were in no mood for pity."

"Neither am I."

"I told them that she was innocent in all this, but they weren't so sure about that. They cursed you both."

"Maybe one of them did more than curse Dorothy. Maybe one of them killed her."

"Maybe," Arthur said. "I can't say that they didn't want to. Maybe kill you both."

"Have we finished with the hearts and flowers?"

Arthur looked at him and shook his head. "You are a bastard. Any one of us can turn you in."

"But none of you will . . . You're all too puffed up with your own self-importance. Too greedy for power. Too ambitious. Hell, so far you've beaten the system, and you'll figure out a way to beat it again."

Jason paused for a moment, reflecting. Now was the time to play real hardball, hold out no matter what. "You said not quite."

"I've got one hold out," he said, his head lowered. "He actually threw me out of his office. The associate justice. He was insulted, indignant. You sure you got him dead to rights, Jason? He was very strong. Very strong. He said if I persisted he would have to report it."

"Always a hardballer in the crowd. There's a fellow so used to power he can't tell the forest from the trees."

"He wasn't afraid. I can tell you that."

Another train rumbled through the station. No one got out.

"I can break the whole fucking lot of you," Jason said, surprised at his own malevolence.

"And yourself to the bargain."

"Who gives a shit?"

"Anyway, the five have already agreed. They'll need a couple of days to get the cash." Arthur's lips curled in a deadly cold smile. "I vouched for your honesty. That's a laugh. Take the five of us and be happy, Jason. The justice is trouble. He'll go down for a principle. I can tell the type."

"We'll see."

"What is that supposed to mean?"

Jason ignored the question, bent on logistics now.

"You'll give me the money and I'll mail you the tapes." He had figured it out carefully. He would mail to each man the tapes that referred to him individually. If knowledge was power, he wasn't going to give any of them that.

"Trusting soul," Arthur said, seized suddenly with a coughing fit. Once he recovered, he grabbed Jason's arm. "I have my money. I want my tapes today. I can't live with this another day. I'll do what you say about the others. But I want anything that relates to me today. I've kept my part of the bargain." He reached into the inside pocket of his jacket, but Jason restrained him.

"Not yet, Arthur. I said all."

"I told you," he pleaded. "He won't bend. I know that kind of guy. A martyr, if he believes he's right. Hell, he's a Supreme Court judge. He'll go to the mat." He looked at Jason and shook his head, obviously annoyed by his obstinance.

"How can you be so sure about the police? Surely, they would have checked her place."

"I tell you they've marked it suicide."

He wondered if he should tell Arthur about the visit from the police, the pin. That was all they had. "I cleaned it up. I wiped all the prints," he said.

"If the police get into it, it's canceled. They all made that clear. These boys are tough." Arthur paused. "Look, what harm is there? The five are willing. I'll make up the difference. Its only money." His fingers tightened on Jason's arm.

"No," Jason said, loosening his grip. "All."

"You're looking for trouble. I know men like that."

"All," Jason repeated. "No one gets off."

He could smell the stench of his own evil. He had already come to terms with his own hatred of himself, there was no problem of conscience. No, he would be adamant. They all had to pay. Even Sally. He could barely suppress his laughter.

Arthur brooded for a long time in silence. His pallid color had deepened to yellow as if his blood had suddenly been freeze-dried.

"Nobody escapes," Arthur said suddenly, the implied threat unmistakable. "Everybody pays sometime."

"You've come awfully cheap, Arthur. Right to the top. One big zoom."

"Is it jealousy, Jason? Is that it? I can understand that. When someone gives me a load of shit, my wife always tells me that. That's a very good way to handle it. The frustration of the loser. Is that it?"

It hadn't occurred to him. He thought for awhile. He wanted his response to be deadly accurate.

"Yes," he said. "But not of your success. Not the substance of it. More the style. How the hell do you do it? The way you press just the right buttons. Make just the right moves. You know just where the weak spots are and you barrel through them like a hot knife through butter. How the hell do you do that? Even now. You may not realize it but you're doing it even now."

"If I told you how, would you call it off?" Arthur smirked.

"No."

There was another long silence. Educational, Jason thought. It was very educational, the way Arthur probed for weakness, faltering, rejuvenating, trying again.

"Dorothy would never have been a part of this. Never," Arthur said. Dorothy again. He would use her now.

"What did you really think about Dorothy, Arthur? Was she just a piece of ass, a bit of fluff? I told her you all thought she was just a piece of meat. Tell me. Was that the way you really thought about her?" He sensed his own weakening now.

"Why should you care about that?" Arthur said, caught off guard. "It's a bit irrelevant."

"Try to think back before you knew she was getting it on with the others. I'm really curious about that."

"You can't stop turning the fucking knife. If I tell you, will you let me off the hook? Give me the tapes?" He patted his pocket.

"No."

Maybe he was not as smart as Jason had imagined. Did he seriously believe that the tapes were floating around his apartment?

"She was the best," Arthur said. "She opened like the petals of a flower, drawing you in. It was wonderful. Wonderful." His voice broke. "I adored her. She was the absolute best. A refuge. An oasis. God, I couldn't wait to see her. I thought about her all the time and wished she would be there waiting for me, always."

"You felt that?"

"Isn't that what you wanted to hear? Or should I try it the other way? Would it make a difference?"

Suddenly, his head dropped to his chest. Jason could hear him sigh deeply. "Actually, I miss the bitch," he said slowly. "I think they all miss her. She was the girl of our dreams."

Jason couldn't bear to hear any more of it and stood up. "You tell the great Justice Strauss that if he doesn't come across we'll get Sally after him." He grabbed Arthur's shoulders and shook him. "You hear me? Tell him Sally will get after him."

Arthur stood up slowly, frowning and confused.

"Sally?"

"Just tell him that."

"I don't understand."

"Better that way. Tell him Sally is all over the tapes."

"And suppose he declines again?"

"He won't."

Jason turned and headed toward the stairs. They led to an overhead walkway across to the Washington bound track. Behind him, he heard Arthur's shuffling steps. When he reached the other side, he slowed and stood at the platform's edge. Soon lights would flash along the rim. Arthur's steps grew louder in the deserted station, gaining speed, as they approached him.

"I need to know one more thing," Arthur said. He was standing very close behind him now. Jason turned, confronting his distorted face. He could smell the man's sour breath. Beneath him, the lights began to flash and in the distance he heard the faint rumble of the oncoming train.

"Did she feel anything for me?" Flecks of moisture came out with his words, showering him. "Compared to the others?" In his eyes, Jason could see the agony. The train's rumble grew louder. He could step away, save himself in the few moments that were left. Instead, he held his ground. Let Arthur make the choice now.

Do it, he challenged in his heart. Push me. Save yourself. Save the others. He stiffened, waiting for the light pressure. It would be over in a moment. He could hear the quickening roar of the swiftly approaching train. Peripherally, he saw the single bright light of the first car, coming forward like a relentless eye, seeing everything.

"We were all one man to her," Jason shouted above the din.

Do it, he urged him silently, but it was too late. Arthur stepped back.

Jason ducked in the door of the deserted train.

When he looked around again, he saw Arthur still waiting on the platform, sullen and forlorn, nursing his pain.

Life for Jason was suspended now. There was little to do but wait. He called his immediate boss in Fairfax.

"I'm sick," he said, picturing his tense, scrofulous face at the other end.

"Shit."

"Thanks for your concern."

It would all be over soon. He would give his notice, take his book of clippings and push on. Journalism, real journalism was dying in America anyway. Perhaps he'd write the book that he had always talked about.

"The book. The book." Jane had always ridden him about that. "How many years do you think you can get out of the promise? I can't stand it anymore. Always pretending that somewhere inside of you is the great book. What book?"

Maybe he would skim off twenty or thirty thousand, hole up somewhere in the Swiss Alps. Mountains always held a literary lure. He'd write the book there. Still, Jane's voice persisted in the back of his mind . . . what book?

Because he couldn't concentrate on anything, he took long walks, as if the physical activity might expunge Dorothy from his mind. It didn't. Did they miss her, too? It had been painful enough removing her things from his apartment, putting them all in large plastic bags and running them out to the city dump. Soon, when the rent ran out in the other place, someone would have to empty her things from there as well. All those white things and the stuffed animals. He knew he could never go back.

It hurt him to know, too, that her body was not yet under ground. Who would claim her? That drunken aunt back in Hiram certainly wouldn't bother, nor would she spend the money on long distance calls to find Dorothy's brothers. Perhaps he could anonymously send them the money to give her a decent burial, instead of the city-paid crema-tion, like they burned the trash. No. That would be too dangerous.

Thankfully, there was no follow-up from the police. He had sensed an eagerness in the woman detective that nagged at him, but his reason dismissed it. If they had something, they would certainly act. There was also not a word in the papers. It was over. He was sure it was over. He would be patient.

Arthur called two days after the meeting in the train station. In the crackle of the pay phone, his voice seemed calm.

"Done," he said.

"Sally as well?"

"Yes."

"I told you."

For the first time in days, he felt his tension ease. They were, after all, reasonable, practical men, bending to conditions that were beyond their control. Like him. He hadn't asked for much. He'd take twenty thousand only, put the rest in trust for Trey and leave the country. Go as far as he could go away from everything. Away from powerful people. From his past. From Dorothy's memory.

"Tonight. Same place," Arthur said. "The cemetery station."

Arthur had every right to be paranoid. One never knows who was listening or watching. Despite the new laws, the Nixon days had not yet faded from memory. Besides, people in power were naturally paranoid.

Jason packed two suitcases, eliminating any extraneous possessions. He'd continue to pay the rent on his apartment. Someday he'd come back, when the pain was gone and he had written whatever book he had to write. He checked his passport and reserved space on SwissAir to Geneva the next evening. Then he went to his bank and made arrangements for a trust account for Trey.

"I'll be putting in a hundred thousand in cash," he told one of the bank's officers.

"No problem," the man said. Cash was cash. No questions asked. Trey's education would be set. He would write to Jane about it.

From the vault, he removed the tape cassettes from the strongboxes and carried them home in a plastic bag. It felt odd, incongruous. In the bag, usually used for trash, he held the public lives of six men. Now that was power, he thought. Real power. Back in his apartment, he separated the cassettes into categories that referred to each man. He had marked each with the day, the date and the name of the man who had been the subject of the debriefing. It amazed him to see how many cassettes had accumulated. Then he carefully packed them into large envelopes, on which he pasted mailing labels. In the post office he got them properly stamped for Special Delivery and carted them home again. He was ready now. The bargain had been struck. Soon he would be free of it. Still, there was one thing more he had to do.

He walked through the *Post* city room, feeling calm, relaxed, knowing that he had in his possession a story that they would have craved. Nodding to those whom he knew, he strode into Webster's office. The editor was on the phone and seemed annoyed by Jason's sudden intrusion.

"What is it?" Webster asked after he'd hung up. He was on deadline. Galleys were spread out on his desk. Some of them had already been marked up.

"I'm splitting," Jason said. "I just wanted you to know, to tell you to your face."

"I'm sorry to hear that." Jason knew he wasn't sorry. He wondered if he even remembered his name.

"I had a big story. The biggest ever for this turkey rag. But I'm not going to give it out. Not to you. Not to anybody."

Webster seemed confused.

"Whatever you say."

It didn't seem to matter either way. The paper was fat now, and the editor was aging. Besides, Jason knew that Webster had long ago lost his cojones. Not that it mattered to him now. Not anymore. Whatever happened, he had proven something to himself. And that would have to be enough.

"You were a good journalist," Webster said, with an accent on the "were." He had certainly said that many times.

"I still am."

"Sorry it didn't work out."

"I'm not."

He looked at Webster carefully. Once he had been God to him. But, like the others, he was only a man, flawed, corrupted by privilege and success. Jason knew what that meant. It was a license to manipulate others.

It had been important to him to say it with just that intonation, in just those words. He had, after all, retired from the game on the one yard line and that took guts. They made the rules which they themselves did not obey. They paid lip service only to the fight against corruption, the public's right to know. It was a game for hypocrites. The good, the true, the innocent always lost. Hadn't he proved that?

He turned and walked out.

The train sped him to where Arthur waited in the deserted station, the irony not lost on him. There, his past would be buried. Dorothy's as well. He had held the power of public death over these men and he had chosen to give them life, because it was Dorothy's wish.

"I can't," she had told him, and in the end he respected that. In a way, innocence *had* won, at least a Pyrrhic victory.

He arrived at the station before Arthur, surprised that he was late. He paced the deserted station, listening for the train, watching the plastic rim for the flashing lights. When two trains passed, he began to grow anxious. From somewhere in the distance, he heard the persistent ring of a telephone. When it didn't stop, he knew it was for him. There was no one else around and he followed the sound to a booth in a little alcove. It was still ringing when he got there.

"It's me," the voice said. He recognized it immediately.

"And me," he answered. The voice was no longer mellow.

"You're a fucking liar. The police. They're still on it. They visited Tate."

"But there's nothing. Nothing. I would have known by now."

"No money. No deal until we make sure."

There was a long pause and this time Jason felt panic. He did not want to stay around this town a minute more than necessary.

"Did they make accusations? Give any hints?"

"No."

"Well, that proves it. They're just fishing, just leaning on people. The same way they did with me."

"With you? They visited you?"

"Just routine. A lady detective and her partner. Nothing to worry about." Still, he didn't tell him about the pin.

"And you didn't tell me? You bastard."

"It wasn't important," Jason mumbled.

"Not important," Arthur fumed. "It was the same two."

"But how did they know about Tate?"

"I don't know."

"If that girl was murdered . . ." Arthur faltered. ". . . and they have some kind of evidence, there will be hell to pay. I'm innocent of that, whatever else I might be guilty of."

"It's that woman detective. She's got some bug up her ass. I don't know why. But if they had something . . ."

"Never mind. I'll find out. I've had enough of your bullshit."

"I get my money or I use the tapes," Jason hissed. "And I'm set to leave the country tomorrow. I've got reservations on SwissAir."

"I'll know by tomorrow," Arthur said.

"What are you going to do?" Jason asked. It was impossible for him to shift gears now. He had already decided, had promised Dorothy in his heart.

"I'll call you tomorrow."

"I'm set to leave at ten tommorrow evening."

"Long before then."

"Look, dammit." Jason felt the perspiration running down his side. Things were getting out of control again, and he'd be damned if he was going to let someone like Arthur Fellows blow it for him now. "If there's no foul play, they have no right pressing people, accusing people, intimidating people."

"Who said you need rights for that?" Arthur said tersely. The phone went dead.

It was wrong, Jason thought, jabbing the toe of his shoe against the wall. "And it isn't fair."

He took the next train back to Washington and walked the few blocks to his apartment. Almost before he opened the door,he knew that someone was inside, waiting, but he couldn't stop himself. Absolution was a hard process. He opened the door.

"I've been waiting for you," Cates said. "We got to talk."

XIX

Jason Martin hadn't arrived yet at Dr. Benton's house. The doctor had placed a stainless steel pot of coffee and some cups on his dining room table.

"No," the eggplant said. "No coffee. Not for him. And draw the blinds."

Fiona knew what that meant. Interrogation was a police art form and it had its conventions. Close off the outside world. Force the subject into a confrontation with himself. No stimulants. No comforts. Dole them out in tiny rewards.

"Where's Cates?" Fiona asked, trying to ignore the eggplant's sullen mood.

"He wasn't home," the eggplant said, raising his bloodshot eyes. "I'm gonna have his ass," he said, knowing that Cates's action could be, for him, the straw that broke the camel's back.

"It seems so out of character." Fiona, too, was angry at Cates. Soon they would know just how much damage he'd done. The climate was very bad for a harassment action.

"Let me see that xerox of the Curtis report," the eggplant snapped at Dr. Benton, who produced the report from an envelope that lay on his cluttered desk. He opened it and grumbled. "Women."

He looked up at Fiona and shook his head. He had every right, Fiona thought, agreeing with him for the first time. We're the damnedest creatures. But it occurred to her that Martin, too, might have had something to hide or he wouldn't have agreed to meet outside of the office. Perhaps, too, the eggplant had already showed him his own vulnerability. For both, she knew, the objective of the talk would be a stand-off. No sense rocking any boats. Not now. Any hint of a coverup could be fatal. For this reason, Martin, wittingly or

227

not, held in his hands the mallet to crush the eggplant's career with a single blow.

Martin's ring was firm, a long press of the button, indicating confidence. She exchanged worried glances with the eggplant as Dr. Benton rose to answer the door. If Martin was startled by the drawn blinds, he said nothing. There was a bruise on one of his cheeks. So Cates had, indeed, been physical.

"I'm Captain Greene," the eggplant said, holding out his hand. Martin took it mechanically and turned to Fiona. "We've met."

He looked slightly thinner from when she had seen him last, more than a week ago. There was the same guarded look, suspicious and defensive. That seemed to be the mark of all journalists. And cops, she thought.

Dr. Benton excused himself from the room as the eggplant sat down at the table, a signal for both her and Martin to follow. She noted that the eggplant was displaying a remarkably sure sense of authority. In the presence of superiors, he always seemed to be groveling.

"I see you haven't found him yet," Martin said as he sat down. The table before them was completely empty and she was thankful for having bolted down three cups of coffee beforehand.

"He wasn't reachable," the eggplant said.

"Well, he reached me all right," Martin said, fingering his bruise.

"I'm sorry," the eggplant said. "As I explained on the phone, he did it on his own."

If there was any hesitation on his arrival, it seemed dispelled now, as if Martin were certain that he had, indeed, the upper hand.

"I've been seriously mishandled," he said. His belligerent undertone was unmistakable. As a trained journalist, he could be an actor as well. As he talked, Fiona continued to observe him. He kept his hands below the table, a sign perhaps that he was frightened, but his voice seemed strong. She wondered if he was sweating under his arms.

"That's why we're here," the eggplant said, nodding. "To hear your grievance."

He waited, making a church out of his fingers, like a priest listening piously. She wanted to burst out laughing.

"First the two of them," Martin said, narrowing his eyes in Fiona's direction. "Then that crazy man last night. Capes?"

"Cates," Fiona snapped. The eggplant rebuked her with a sharp look.

"He shoved me around, as you can see. And I got kneed in other places, like a common criminal."

"It's not police procedure to use violence. Did you give him any cause?" the eggplant asked.

"Don't be ridiculous."

The burst of arrogance seemed to bring the oil to the eggplant's skin, a sure sign of his growing inner turmoil.

"Did he accuse you of anything?" He seemed to be proceeding with remarkable restraint.

"Accuse me? He tried and sentenced me. Said I killed Dorothy Curtis. That's nonsense."

He broke off abruptly and shook his head.

"I think you're all trying to manufacture something out of whole cloth." The voice was more cautious now. "Look. I don't want to make trouble. I really don't. But I do know my rights and I completely understand the vulnerability of the police. First it was this lady." He jerked a thumb in Fiona's direction. "Her implications were quite clear. Then Cates roughing me up, demanding explanations that I couldn't give him. His accusations were wild. Wild. I think that man is unbalanced. Oh, he'll deny everything, I'm sure . . ."

So he didn't know about the suspension, Fiona thought, taking a deep breath. She wondered if a simple apology might suffice and was sure the idea was running through the eggplant's mind.

"If you've got any evidence . . ." Martin began, then he seemed to edit himself. "I can't believe she did that to herself," he said, very slowly, as if he were testing a frozen pond.

"Suppose I told you . . ." the eggplant said, casting an odd glance at Fiona. Don't overkill it, she thought to herself. Just apologize and get it over with. All the jerk wants to know is that he's off the hook.

The eggplant took a deep breath and lit a cigarette, leaving what he had begun hanging in the air between them, a deliberate red herring. She was totally confused.

"How well did you know her?" the eggplant asked, still benign, although she could sense the wind-up within. What the hell was he doing? she wondered, her fingers digging into her palms.

"I brought her here from Hiram. Started a new life for her. We lived together for awhile. Then she moved out. These things happen." He seemed to drift, losing control for a moment. "It didn't end badly. We were friends. Saw each other occasionally." She could see he wanted to stop, but couldn't. "She was a terrific lady." He shook his head and it seemed quite genuine. "I can't imagine her doing this."

"Doing what?" the eggplant asked, suddenly focusing Martin's suspicion.

"Now you. I don't understand any of this."

"Did you know anything about her private life?"

"When I was with her. Yes. But we haven't been together for months." She could see that he was growing more annoyed with his own inability to stop himself. Abruptly, he stood up.

"I won't stand for this. If you've got something on your mind, then say it."

"I was just asking you if you knew about her private life."

"I know what you asked. I also know harassment when I see it."

"Am I harassing him?" the eggplant asked Fiona. "This is a routine police investigation."

"It's not routine."

"Is this routine, FitzGerald?"

"Just routine."

She was surprised at her own reaction. Now she was being a lackey. But his interrogation fascinated her.

"We know an awful lot about her activities," the eggplant said.

"Like what?" Martin asked. Again, the cautious tone.

She was sure Cates must have told him a great deal of what they knew. But it was still no crime.

"Who she was seeing. Things like that," the eggplant said ambiguously, playing with fire. Now *he* was becoming part of it. She couldn't understand why. He's going crazy, she decided. Like Cates. Like her.

"Who she saw was her business," Martin replied, but for the first time his throat had caught.

"You know who she was seeing?" the eggplant asked, with sweet innocence.

His eyes suddenly became frantic as he searched their faces.

"I heard some pretty wild things last night."

"Like what?"

"That's not the point. That's not my business." A thin line of sweat had begun to form on his upper lip.

"Important men like that?" the eggplant said quietly, letting another red herring hang in the air.

"What has any of that got to do with me?"

"That's just the point."

"No, that's not the point," Martin exploded. He sat down and stood up again. "The point is that I've been harassed. And I don't like it. I'm also going to do something about it." He sat down again, sneering contemptuously at them. He was not very likeable, Fiona thought. Did Dorothy once love this man? She quickly dismissed the thought. It was exactly what had gotten them all into this fix in the first place. And there the eggplant sat, helping to dig their graves. Was he deliberately trying to abort their careers?

". . . and I'll tell you why I'm pissed. Really pissed." Again, he edited himself. It was completely transparent.

"Yes," the eggplant said.

"I'm just going to take action. This is ridiculous. It's worse than that." His eyes narrowed as if a new thought had struck him suddenly. "You're trying to cook something up that doesn't exist. There's a lot more here than meets the eye."

"Yes, there is."

"I'm not going to be a party to it. And I won't be a victim. I don't know what you've got, but it has nothing to do with me." He stopped, caught his breath, then drilled a stare into the eggplant. "Are you saying that she was murdered?" But he didn't wait for an answer. "Because if you're saying that . . ." again he hesitated, grimaced and suddenly started to cough. The veins expanded on his forehead and neck. They watched as he attempted to recover.

"It's impossible," he whispered.

"That she was murdered?" The eggplant pressed him now. Fiona was completely confused, digging her fingers deeper into her palms, but still she was fascinated. The eggplant was dissecting the poor man. Poor man? When had he gained her sympathy? I know why you're torturing him, she decided. You got your hooks into a honky.

"She wasn't. She could have been. They . . ." He checked himself. "I . . ." For some reason, not apparent to her, he seemed trapped. He was sweating profusely and his nose had begun to run.

"You . . ." the eggplant said increasing the pressure, coaxing him.

"I saw her."

"You saw her?" Fiona asked. The eggplant threw her a contemptuous look, stilling her with his hand.

"Saw her what?"

He seemed to have begun to shrivel, like burning paper.

"Saw her jump," he squealed, like a man breaking suddenly. Was it possible? Had he pushed her? Had her instincts been right? Her knees began to shake and she had to press them together to stop them. The eggplant reacted like a mad dog, who had picked up the smell of blood.

"What time?"

The man was helpless, his lips moved but nothing came out.

"What time?" the eggplant shot back.

"I'm not sure."

"Where were you? In a car? On the bridge? Why didn't you stop her?"

"I couldn't. She had started to run. I don't remember." He desperately tried to calm himself. "Yes. I ran after her. I couldn't catch up."

"She was wearing track shoes? She was in goddamned high heels." The eggplant had risen and put one of his haunches on the table for balance, bending over the man, pressing. What was he doing? Manufacturing a killer? She was horrified, frightened.

The eggplant called to Dr. Benton, who came in from the kitchen.

"What time? Tell the medical examiner here. He knows pretty near exactly the moment of death. Tell him, goddammit. Tell him." He screamed at the man, who was utterly confused now.

"I don't remember," he said helplessly.

"And you never called anyone. Just let her lay there."

"I was afraid."

"Bullshit."

She wanted to stop him, but her courage had failed. It was as though all the eggplant's pain, his frustration, all the vitriol and bile he had stored in him had suddenly erupted. There was absolutely no evidence of a crime, unless he confessed to pushing her. The idea chilled her. Then he said it.

"You pushed her over, you lousy little turd. You walked her to the bridge and pushed her over. Just like that. In cold blood."

"No," he shouted. "I loved her."

"You don't love anyone, you shitass son of a bitch."

Pushed her. Walked her in the rain in her cocktail dress and pushed her. Impossible, Fiona thought. Even in her panic, her police mind speculated. He could have driven her, but she wouldn't have gotten out on the bridge without a struggle. There had been no sign of a pre-fall struggle.

"A crime of passion pure and simple," the eggplant snapped. "You came in, saw her with one of her bigshot boyfriends. Maybe the con-

gressman. Or the Supreme Court justice. Or the general. Or the
Czech. Or that shit from the White House . . ." He was stabbing
wildly, saliva flecking his lips, the tendons in his neck stretching to
the breaking point.

"All right," the man said. "I did it. I killed her."

He lay his head on the table and began to sob. The eggplant stood
up, lit a cigarette, breathed deeply, and paced the room. Martin's
shoulders shook with agonized sobs. Fiona sat there, stunned, and
Dr. Benton's complexion seemed to turn olive green.

Finally the eggplant walked back to the table and poked a finger
in the man's shaking back.

"You fucking lying little bastard. Covering up for those cock-
suckers. You think anyone will believe your turd shit? Whitelivered
honky liar." He wasn't acting this time. This was genuine anger,
white hot, right from his gut. "Covering up for those bastards."

The man raised his pained eyes.

"Covering up for those bastards?" Jason repeated it between
choked sobs. "She was murdered?" he said, trying to wipe his face
with his sleeve.

"Fuckin' A," the eggplant sneered.

"Who?"

"Why the fuck do you think we're here?" He sucked in the smoke
so deeply that half the cigarette in his mouth turned to quick ash.
"You tell it, baby," he said, the smoke curling into the man's face.
He began to cough again. Then he gagged and seemed to fight down
the urge to heave.

"Not one's worth protecting," the eggplant said quietly. He was
calm now.

They waited for the man to recover. Dr. Benton brought him coffee but the man was trembling too much to lift the cup and Dr.
Benton had to literally spoon some into him. He breathed deeply,
trying to recover himself.

"Which one do you think?" the eggplant said.

He turned his face toward Fiona, squinting in confusion, spent now. Instinct, she thought. The things he always accuses me of. Pure instinct. But there is no evidence of a crime. None at all, unless he was holding something back and she doubted that. When the smoke cleared, she suspected, he would be in bigger trouble than all of them.

"I want it all," the eggplant said. "All of it."

"I . . ." The eggplant inexplicably grabbed the man's shoulder and pressed it. Was it a gesture of manly affection? Were they allies now? The confessor and the confessed. She knew what that meant in a religious way.

"It's all down," Martin mumbled. "I can't speak it. Hear it for yourself. I have tapes."

My God, she thought, comprehending none of it.

They were speeding through the streets again, Martin between them on the front seat saying nothing, trancelike, periodically dissolving into deep sobs.

As they walked up the steps to his apartment, they heard the telephone ring. It stopped when they went in.

"There," Martin said, opening a drawer. Fiona noted the packed bags. The apartment was neater than when she had first seen it, obviously battened down for a long stay away.

"I was going to Switzerland. To write a book." His voice caught in his throat.

He opened the envelopes and put the tapes into six neat piles. She noted the names on the piles of tapes. Hurley. Senator Charles Hurley. The sudden revelation rooted her to the floor.

Martin got his tape recorder and brought out a bottle of Scotch and three glasses. He had begun to recover now, his relief palpable. The unburdening had been therapeutic, a reaction she had seen many times after a confession.

"Hear it in sequence," Martin said, placing the first of the tapes in the recorder. Before he could switch it on, the telephone rang.

"Not now," the eggplant said, looking at the high pile of tapes. The phone rang persistently, and they tried to ignore it as they sipped their Scotch.

"You know who that is?" the eggplant asked.

"Yes. He'll call again.

When it stopped, the eggplant took the instrument, opened it and muffled the ringing device. Then they began to listen to the tapes.

The effect on Fiona was awesome, appalling, beyond belief. To hear that voice, girlish, innocent, despite the bizarre circumstances being related, was as if a ghost had joined them. Fiona had to look around the room to see if Dorothy was present, dreading the possibility of seeing her resurrected. She felt chilled, as if a ghost had touched her. The eggplant's hooded eyes could not hide its effect on him as well. Strange sounds emitted from him, groans, sighs. Dorothy's voice sounded eerie, as if it were emanating from some intangible source. They listened throughout the morning and on into the afternoon.

Martin sat quietly, offering the tapes selectively, so they could get the full picture. It would take days, perhaps weeks, to hear them all. It crossed her mind that perhaps they were faked, preconceived scenarios, but it soon became evident that it wasn't possible.

Occasionally, they heard the muffled sounds of the telephone's ring, but they ignored it and sipped the Scotch slowly. It had little effect. By midafternoon they hadn't stirred. Martin rose from his chair only to change the tapes, sometimes hiding his eyes and sobbing uncontrollably when something in Dorothy's voice struck him. For hours, not a word passed between them. Only once, late in the afternoon, Martin spoke, after the muffled telephone persisted for nearly five minutes.

"He knows I've got tickets on SwissAir tonight at ten."

The eggplant looked at his watch and turned his eyes to the tape recorder again. Listening had, by then, become an addiction to both of them. Dorothy's awesome innocence had set the stage for the public destruction of six men. When she heard Dorothy talking about Senator Hurley, Fiona's stomach tightened. His dancing nude for the benefit of this strange but powerful woman astounded her. This was the man whom both Clint and his wife feared. It was impossible, after all, to live totally without guile.

Her mind whirled with questions. The problem now was to absorb all this information. It stunned her, made her giddy. It both revolted and fascinated. At times, she would look at the eggplant, whose skin shone like a cue ball. What they were hearing was beyond their experience. Perhaps beyond their comprehension. She wondered if even the logic of Martin's explanation could be understood. So why did she die? She shivered and took a deep sip of the Scotch.

It started to grow dark, but no one reached for the lights and the telephone rang again. The eggplant stirred, sighed and reached for another cigarette. The mound of butts had grown and when he crumpled the empty pack, he searched the pile, found a useable butt and lit it, inhaling deeply.

"Answer it," the eggplant ordered.

Martin stood up, wobbly, glass in hand. Apparently, he was the only one of the three on whom the liquor had any effect. He reached for the instrument and suddenly the eggplant jumped up and stayed his hand. When he had placed himself beside Martin, he nodded. Fiona noted that his shirt was bathed in perspiration. Martin picked up the phone and the eggplant positioned himself so that he could also hear.

"Where the hell were you?" Arthur screamed.

Martin cleared his throat and grunted. He was beyond caring now. He glanced at the eggplant and shrugged.

"I tried all day," Arthur Fellows screamed hysterically. "They have nothing. Absolutely nothing. No evidence of anything. That's straight from the mayor."

"What?"

Martin's reasoning was sluggish. In the quiet of the room, Arthur's voice carried as far as Fiona's ears.

"They have nothing." He was screaming into the phone. "Don't you understand? It's over. Over. And the cops who leaned on Tate and you are suspended."

The eggplant pinched Martin's arm, who reacted with a grunt.

"You bring the tapes to Dulles," Arthur said, "I'll meet you."

Martin started to speak. But it was too late. The eggplant had already broken the connection.

Martin looked inexplicably at the mouthpiece, then at the two of them.

She had never before seen such hatred in the eggplant's eyes.

XX

The eggplant's car sped along the Dulles Access Highway. They had repacked the tapes in the envelopes and he had thrown them into the trunk of his car.

After his conversation with Fellows, Martin had collapsed on the couch like a cast-off puppet, his expression empty, his eyes glazed. As they gathered the tapes, they ignored him. And each other. They seemed to be sharing some mutual embarrassment, like being forced to stand naked in a room together.

At first, she thought they would be heading back to headquarters. Then it became apparent that he was on his way to Dulles Airport. She wanted to question that course of action, but held her silence, knowing she was following him into an uncharted wasteland.

Occasionally she glanced at him. He didn't acknowledge her sudden attention, his eyes flickering in the glare of oncoming headlights. Yet she knew that a volcano was seething beside her. A question had nagged at her all day as they listened to the tapes, but somehow she couldn't find the courage to ask it: Who'll punish them?

He was answering it now. "I will," he was saying. His silence could not disguise it.

In the distance, she saw the blaze of light over the trees and soon the white cantilevered marvel of the main airport building, looking like a lit-up cake.

She knew she couldn't stop him now. Hell, she hadn't been able to stop herself. She felt a little like Cates must have felt in the beginning not knowing why, but going along. Maybe Dorothy had found her way into the eggplant's gut as well. Face it squarely, she told herself. She agreed with what he was doing. She was going along because she believed in it.

He swung the car into the winding embarkation road, pulling up to the curb. She followed him blindly, a spectator. The eggplant's bulky figure moved into the building. The hooded eyes were alert now. Predatory.

The large glass-walled building was filled with overseas travelers standing patiently in ticket lines for the evening flights. He strode toward the SwissAir counter, surveyed the crowd, then moved to a deserted area at the end of the bank. Reaching over the counter, he picked up a telephone. His physical actions were surprisingly economical. He knew exactly what he was doing.

"This is Captain Greene, MPD. Would you page . . ." He looked briefly at Fiona, flashing a tight thin smile. "A Mr. Fellows."

A voice crackled over the speaker as his eyes searched the crowd near the SwissAir counter. A man who had been leaning against a window wall moved suddenly, hesitated, looked about him, then furtively approached a counter and picked up the phone. The eggplant moved with the stealth and speed of a leopard. He was next to him in a moment. Fiona followed close behind.

The man was slack-jawed, his eyes burning with fear as they searched for escape. The eggplant flashed his shield. Without a word, he placed his big hand under Fellows's arm, leading him forward. Fellows tried to resist, looked into the eggplant's determined face, then yielded. They moved through the detection counter to a deserted part of the airport. A plane took off in the distance.

"What is it?" Fellows asked. His skin had mottled with anxiety. The eggplant watched, calmly assessing him.

"Arthur Fellows?" the eggplant said softly.

The man nodded.

"What is it?" Fellows asked again. The deliberate suspense was cruel work. She half expected him to read Fellows his rights. But it wasn't an arrest. Again she asked: Where is the crime?

"We know everything," the eggplant said.

Fellows swallowed, desperately trying to gather the shreds of his courage.

"Know what?"

The eggplant emitted a croaking, derisive sound. He's enjoying this, Fiona thought, like holding a butterfly's wings. Fellows turned to her, pleading. She shrugged helplessly, watching the man's dignity disintegrate.

"You have nothing," Fellows said bravely. "I'm the counsel to the President." She sensed the explosion coming, the spew of lava.

"Fuck you. Fuck the President," the eggplant said.

Like battering rams, the curses seemed to push Fellows back against a window wall. Fiona watched, stunned, unable to react. He can't do this, she thought, yet found herself unable to shake the sense of alliance with the eggplant's actions.

"If I've done something, charge me," Fellows said, challenging him.

"Turd," the eggplant said. He looked toward Fiona. "Like the dogs do."

Fellows turned dead white. She thought he was going to faint. The eggplant chuckled. "We heard all about it," he said calmly.

"It's no crime," Fellows mumbled, searching Fiona's face. "Besides, you have nothing." Fellows sat on the ledge of the window wall. "The mayor confirmed it. Nothing."

The eggplant watched, lifted his finger, almost touched the man's nose.

"You're dead in the water, man. And you got three things to do." He continued to hold his finger taut, like the muzzle of a gun.

"You can't," Fellows protested. "I can bust you."

"Three things," the eggplant said, ignoring him. "First, you're gonna call the mayor. You're gonna say it was all a mistake. Dig?"

He seemed to be throwing Fellows a bit of flotsam to hold on to. Fiona felt strangely relieved. "You know what you're gonna tell him?"

Fellows said nothing, lowering his eyes. The eggplant was relishing it.

"Then you're gonna fucking resign."

"Resign?"

"As of immediately."

Fellows's face collapsed into his skull.

"You can't do that. I'm the counsel to the President."

"You were," the eggplant hissed.

"Martin! He was the one. He set us up. What about him?"

What little residual fight was left in the man evaporated. He looked toward both of them with tired eyes. Fiona braced herself. He had said three things. What more was there to extract? Surely, it was over now.

"Now there is the matter of the others," the eggplant said, his words flat and clear. Fellows's body began to tremble.

"The others?"

She could see there was no stopping him now.

"All of them. I want them all to resign. Every last son of a bitch."

"You can't make me do that."

"Yes, I can." He spat the words, mocking him. Enough, Fiona screamed within herself, the guilt rising.

"All of them. Do you understand me?"

In her heart, she wanted to intervene. *We* don't dispense justice. The words tumbled in her head, but she couldn't find her voice. Wasn't he dispensing her justice as well? Briefly, he turned toward her and she wondered if he was seeking validation. Was there something he knew that she had missed? Or was his pain deeper than hers, the product of a thousand lifetimes in a black skin? Without thinking, she nodded consent.

"We didn't kill her," Fellows gasped.

"Didn't you?" the eggplant said slowly. "She died for you, my friend. A sweet Jesus lady."

It came to her like the distant trill of a black spiritual rising from the agony of stifled pain. Was he avenging a race as she had sought to avenge her gender? Everyone seemed to cry out from the depths of their own terror.

"You do it, man," the eggplant said softly.

He walked off and Fiona followed again. Then he stopped and strode back to the broken man.

"The money."

Fellows shrugged and looked at the dispatch case that lay flat on the floor. Picking it up, he walked off again. This time Fiona caught up with him.

"Not that," she said. "You can't do that."

"I can do anything I fucking well please," he said.

For money? Her mind screamed in protest. All this for money?

Her stomach turned. So he was just another greedy little bastard.

That night she couldn't sleep, twisting and turning until her sheet became a shroud around her. Unwinding herself, she got up, removed her sweat-matted pajamas and sat naked by the window, watching dawn cast its amber light over the city.

The eggplant had dropped her off at her apartment, grunting a perfunctory goodbye. Not a word had passed between them. It was the bottled up response that was keeping her up now, the jumble of confused thoughts. And the guilt. Hadn't she put the match to the first batch of dry tinder?

It was always her secret pride that although her job forced her to step down to the source of human degradation, when she stepped out of it at the end of the day she was as clean as when she had entered. There were times when it had taken longer for her to rid herself of the stench, but the self-cleansing talent always performed and, miraculously, she always became clean and whole again. Now she wasn't sure the stench would ever go away.

For one glorious moment, the eggplant, her nemesis, the very epitome of cowardice and chicanery, had emerged from the swamp of his own self-pity and egocentricity and had become . . . she groped for the term . . . a man. She shuddered at the thought. Would this experience forever inhibit her view of men? Males. What she had

observed of them in the last week had been a catalogue of infamy.
She ticked off their sins on her fingers.

Hypocritical. Vain. Deceptive. Ambitious. Frightened. Violent.
Lecherous. Manipulative. Cowardly. Undisciplined. Cruel. Needing
more digits, she curled her toes, then stopped. It was too depressing.
Better her mother's world, she told herself, like a horse with blind-
ers, trained only to run around the accepted track. Perhaps it had
been a mistake to intrude on their world. Evolution had simply conditioned them differently. Her sex was meant for other work. Home
and hearth and children.

She felt chilled and got up to put on her robe. But in the hanging
closet mirror, she paused and observed her naked form in the soft
light. She cupped her breasts in her hands, squeezing their fullness,
affirming her body's difference. Her hands roamed downward over
her hips, rounded by nature, the skin smooth, softer than theirs. Her
eyes lingered over the dark-haired triangle, the harbinger of their
sexual difference, which stirred their blood mysteriously. The curse
of Eve, she thought, an image plumbed from somewhere in the
depths of her Catholic childhood. The eggplant had called Dorothy
the sweet Jesus lady and she had thought then, as if by rote, that
maybe Dorothy did die for their sins. If Christ was a man, then
where, indeed, was the daughter of God? Were they unlike Mary,
doomed to sin because man had defiled them? She trembled.
Religion was created for men by men. Stop it, Fiona, she begged herself. Yet, it was against nature to irrevocably hate them.

She put on her robe and went into the kitchen, happy to tinker
with life's more mundane duties, She made herself a cup of coffee and
began to let the real world back into her mind. If she was to walk
among them, she had better learn their ways, she told herself firmly. Or get the hell out.

The sound of the buzzer interrupted her thoughts. She looked at
the clock. It was 6 A.M. on the minute, as if her caller had waited for
that exact hour.

"Who is it?" she asked.

She waited, fearing that it would be Clint.

"Ann Chase," the voice answered.

Her hand reached for the thumblock, hesitated, then turned it. She removed the chain lock and opened the door. Ann's form was silhouetted against the corridor's light. She couldn't see her face until she moved into the dim light of the apartment. Then it dawned on her. This was the enemy. Her rival. The image had been far more formidable then the reality. She was simply a rather vulnerable looking, frightened woman on the wrong side of forty.

"I'm sorry," Ann said.

"No. It's all right."

She flicked the switch of a lamp, and the room was bathed in a soft yellow light. Often in its glare she had seen Clint's face. Is this the way it ended? she thought. A tacky little triangle.

"I was up. Would you like a cup of coffee?"

"That would be kind."

Kind? Was Ann mocking her?

She left her standing in the center of the room. Pouring out another cup of coffee, her hands shook. She spilled some in the saucer, but in handing the cup to Ann, her hand was quite steady. It was Ann's hand that trembled as the cup clattered in the saucer. She had to put it down on one of the end tables.

"Please," Fiona said, pointing to the couch.

Ann sat down, stiff-backed, her knees pressed primly together. She was somewhat shorter than Fiona, her hair blonde, trimmed short with a sweeping wave across her forehead. Her even features were carefully made up, her high rounded cheeks lightly rouged, her small eyes highlighted with mascara. Fiona was surprised at the details of her observation. She was inspecting the woman, comparing. She wore a blue suit with a white-bowed crisp shirtwaist. Fiona tightened her robe around her. Compared to Ann's clothes, it seemed tawdry. Worse, it still smelled of Clint. She wished she could shower, change, dress carefully. The disadvantage annoyed her.

"I was waiting downstairs in my car for nearly an hour," Ann said, again reaching for the coffee cup, but the trembling inhibited her taking it.

"I wasn't sleeping. You could have come up."

"Maybe I needed the time to gather my courage," Ann said, folding her hands in her lap to keep them steady.

"I could have used the time myself," Fiona said.

"I'm sorry."

The long wait, Fiona could see, had not done its work. How could it? If she had been here at five, she must have been up the entire night. It was a policeman's observation and it steadied her for the moment. She wanted to say something to put the woman at ease but she couldn't think of anything.

"This isn't easy," the woman began. Fiona felt her searching look. So she, too, was comparing. Would she pass muster? Fiona wondered, feeling helpless under her gaze.

"I know," Fiona said softly.

"It started out very well," Ann said, her eyes looking downward, the words contrived, as if she had decided earlier that this was the way to begin. "We met in college. The University of Michigan. Clint was majoring in journalism. I wanted to be a sociologist. In those days, sociology seemed important. The sixties. Everything we did seemed important . . ." Her throat choked for a moment and she coughed it clear. "So it was good for a long time. We had two kids. He adores them. Real nice kids. Sometimes we wonder why we deserve them . . ."

"Please . . ." Fiona interrupted, feeling the woman's embarrassment.

"You get caught up in it," Ann continued. "This town. The striving is terrible. I grew up in Traverse City. Do you know it?" She didn't wait for an answer, nor did Fiona feel it appropriate to break her chain of thought. The words had to come as she had arranged them earlier. "We're all from somewhere else here. I know you're from New York. Brooklyn." So Clint told her that as well, told her everything. She was suddenly resentful, but she remained silent. The woman's pain was certainly more than hers. "It's the pressure. Ambition. It's the great American virtue, you know. But they don't tell you about the people that have to get hurt." She smiled, but it was without real warmth. "They don't tell you about the steamroller. Get in the way of that. Splat. So you're always thinking about how to get out of the way of the steamroller and you begin to rationalize. You tell yourself it's all public service, assign greater virtues, mouth platitudes about great goals. At the bottom of it, we're all scared."

She seemed to be drifting now and Fiona was losing her.

"We get dependent on other people. Most of us owe our livelihood, our future to a single individual, to a single man's ego. We're like satellites."

What was she driving at, Fiona wondered.

"He's not an evil man," Ann continued. "They overwork themselves. They get caught up, carried away. Their drives become distorted, magnified. They mean no harm. They have good instincts. It's the value system. We all know it's hypocritical. But it's the standard of the country."

"What the devil are you talking about?" Fiona asked, unable to listen to her rambling any longer. Up to then, she had been patient and polite, thinking she was referring to Clint.

"Senator Hurley," Ann said.

"I thought you came about Clint."

"I did."

Fiona got up and looked out the window. The rising sun was hidden by a pall of dark clouds that hung low over the city, promising more rain.

"I work for him," Ann said, her voice taking on an edge of panic. "Clint owes his appointment to him. Don't you understand? If the senator goes, we go."

Fiona watched, observing Ann's agony. Some of her mascara had run.

"It was only a silly little diversion. It didn't mean a thing to him. The girl was just a toy. Things like that have been going on forever. He meant no harm. He was used by that journalist, set up to be deliberately destroyed. It's just not fair." She covered her face with her hands and when she removed them her makeup was smeared even more. "You can't let that happen. Not to Clint."

"Clint? Now it's Clint again?"

"I'm sorry. You don't understand what it means. None of them can stand and fight it. It's too big, too involved. Too out of kilter with the prevailing standard . . . and the girl was a whore, sleeping with six men. My God."

Ann reached for the coffee and drank it quickly, ignoring her trembling.

"And I'm a whore as well," Fiona said angrily. "Hell, I slept with a married man. Your man. That makes me a whore, doesn't it? But not him. Not dear old Clint. Or wonderful Senator Hurley and the rest of them. They're not whores."

"Please," Ann said, her fingers running nervously through her hair. "I'm doing this badly. Don't you see what I'm getting at? You *can* do it. I know you can do it. Spare him. Spare the senator. Woman to woman, I'm begging you . . ."

"Woman to woman?"

"And I'm prepared to give you Clint. He loves you. He wants you. I know he does. It was false pride on my part. I know it was partly my fault. Please, Fiona. I know you love him. You can do it. You can save him. And have Clint."

So it had come full circle, back to her.

"You'd do that?"

"Yes," Ann said firmly. "Things move fast. He would just hang on. Then it would pass. If the tapes remain secret, who would know. You can do it, Fiona. Please."

"The senator? He knows you're here?"

Ann nodded, watching her. She hesitated, then stood up, coming close to Fiona. In the clear light, Fiona could see her imperfections, the masked blemishes, the pleading helpless look in her eyes. "If you need more . . . I'm not the perfect innocent that Clint thinks . . ."

"The senator?"

"It was only a game. I went along. Accepted the rewards." She bowed her head. "I'm also a whore," she whispered. When she looked at Fiona again, she was sobbing. Tears streamed down her cheeks. Fiona took a tissue from the pocket of her robe and gave it to her. "Can you . . ." she began.

Fiona took her in her arms. The woman clung to her.

"I'm so sorry, Fiona."

"So am I."

"I'm frightened."

"Who isn't?"

When she calmed, Fiona released her. "It's not the end of the world, Ann," Fiona said. "Even if I wanted to, I couldn't. And wouldn't. I think it's time to start fresh. You and Clint. Maybe it was a game for me as well."

"He said you loved him . . ." Ann said, struggling to regain her dignity.

"What's that got to do with the price of peanuts?" Fiona said. "He's yours."

Before Dorothy, she might have been tempted. Not now.

"You're lucky, Ann," Fiona said.

"Lucky?"

"You have Clint—and your sons."

After Ann left, Fiona took a long, hot bubble bath, resting her head against the porcelain rim of the tub, her eyes closed. The telephone rang, but she ignored it. The soft warmth soothed her, but she still didn't feel cleansed. She sighed. It was impossible to exorcise the early years, eternities in hell, the holy spirits, heaven, saints, the

will of God, and, of course, the sins of the flesh. What exactly were
the sins of the flesh? she asked herself, opening her eyes to the misty
steam, the disappearing bubbles, revealing her nakedness again
beneath the slick water's surface. What was the real guilt here? They
had no right to convict those men, to be both judge and jury. It was
wrong. Immoral. They were merely police, not society's avengers.

The bath water grew tepid and she rose quickly, feeling suddenly
dizzy, slightly nauseous. Standing before the misty mirror, seeing the
outlines of her vague form, she moved to wipe away the moisture.
Then she hesitated, afraid to confront herself. What would she see?

Wiping away the mist, she saw that it was still only herself.
Nothing had changed. There was Fiona. But was it frightened, vulnerable little Fiona? Or evil, mischievous, selfish little Fiona who
had maliciously, capriciously, removed a single domino from the pile
and watched as the structure collapsed? She had to be punished, she
decided. She could not get off scot free. She had no right to be society's avenging angel. Nor could she be silent in the face of the eggplant's corruption. She had to resign from the police.

Before she had rubbed herself completely dry, the telephone rang
again. It was persistent and relentless, as if the caller knew she was
there. Finally, she answered it.

"Have you heard?" Cates said with excitement. She muttered a
vague response.

"On the radio. Justice Strauss resigned, citing ill health." He
chuckled. "And Congressman O'Haire. He's announced he's not running again."

Her knees felt rubbery and she sat down, acknowledging the news
with a faint response. Cates continued, his agitation rising.

"But the big one is this: are you ready?" He paused. "The Czech
ambassador has defected. The ambassador. It was the ambassador.
Can you believe it, Fiona? We did it." Nothing more? she wondered.
Fellows would resign quietly, as would the general. The military had
its own form of professional suicide. And Hurley? He had little

choice now. She felt chilled to the bone, although the telephone sweated in her palms.

"I have a confession, Fiona."

"Confession?"

"I rousted him. The son of a bitch. I told him what we had. It's obvious. Whatever it was, he was in it." He waited now for some complimentary response. When it didn't come, he went on, but his voice carried a hint of disappointment. "We did it, Fi. You and me."

But where is the crime, she wanted to say again? They had no right.

"And you know what? The suspension has been lifted. The eggplant called. He said he called you, too, but you were out."

"Did he say anything else?" She held her breath.

"Like you said. It just blew over. But a lot faster than expected. He said it's all fixed, if we just shut up. And since there's obviously no evidence that makes any sense, what the hell? It's over. But we got the bastards."

"And Martin?" She was operating by rote now.

"I think he's had it. All he needed was one hard push. They tried to fuck us over, Fi."

When she didn't respond, he said, "Well? What do you think?"

"I think it's . . ." She wrestled with herself. "Great. Just great."

He was disappointed.

"I thought you'd be ecstatic. I thought you liked poetic justice." After a long pause, he bucked himself up. "One other thing. The captain wants us to be at this Catholic chapel on Michigan Avenue, the one near the cemetery. At four."

The request puzzled her.

"Apparently somebody's funeral," he said, detecting her confusion. "He said it's orders."

"Orders?"

So it was business as usual. It wasn't uncommon for homicide officers to attend the funeral of a victim.

"A murder victim?"

"I hope so. Maybe he's putting us on real work for a change."

She debated whether or not to go. She was going to resign any-way. Yes, she decided, I'll be there. She would do it by the book. But quietly. No fanfare. No parties at the F.O.P. A simple, professional death, like the rest.

"I'll pick you up in a couple of hours," Cates said.

"No," she said abruptly. "I'll go myself."

Again, there was a long pause.

"I thought you'd be pleased," he said before hanging up.

She timed herself to arrive precisely at four. Oddly, there were no mourners. Cates, the eggplant and Dr. Benton sat in the front row. Organ music drowned the appropriate dirges. On the dais in front of them was a large, expensive looking coffin with four gold handles. As she came forward, her high heels made tapping sounds on the stone floor and the three turned to look at her, then turned away. She gen-uflected and slid into the pew beside Dr. Benton, who patted her arm.

"Dorothy," he whispered.

"Dorothy?"

She was stunned. The eggplant and Cates stared straight ahead as a young priest walked to the pulpit and began the Requiem Mass. The voice of a small, unseen choir began to sing.

As the ritual progressed, her fury increased. How dare he? Paying for this out of the money he had stolen. An obvious salve to his conscience. She glanced at the eggplant's impassive profile, the lips tight, the hooded eyes glazed and indifferent. Yet, despite the anger growing in her, she found herself responding to the spir-it of the Mass, imagining the bruised, much abused body laid out in the dark coffin, once more being subjected to men's need of her, men's hypocrisy.

The service was quickly over and the men rose. They stepped to the dais, each grabbing one of the gold handles. Dr. Benton motioned her forward and she moved to join them. Despite the years away from the Church, she found it too powerful to resist and made the sign of the cross, as she had done a thousand times before.

Lifting the coffin she felt the pull of its weight and needed two arms to keep it balanced. She moved ahead cautiously as they followed the priest down the center aisle. It had finally begun to rain and the childish image of God crying, which was her mother's early explanation of rain, jumped into her mind. She felt sick and powerless and ashamed.

They hefted the coffin into the hearse and the driver closed the door before he jumped into the driver's seat. The hearse drove slowly toward the adjacent cemetery.

"It's not far," Dr. Benton said, motioning them into his car. The eggplant got in beside him and Cates and Fiona got into the back seat.

"Somebody apparently cared enough," Cates said. "At least she didn't have to get burned."

When there was no response, he shrugged and brooded silently. In the rearview mirror, she suddenly saw the eggplant's eyes. She wondered if behind their stoic emptiness, he was smiling.

After a short drive they arrived at the opened grave. Cemetery workers quickly placed the coffin on a mechanical device and lowered it into the gaping hole. The priest said a prayer and sprinkled holy water into the grave. Fiona crossed herself. One of the cemetery workers yawned.

Dr. Benton was the first to grab a handful of dirt and throw it into the grave. It made a hollow drumbeat on the coffin's lid. Cates did the same. Then both men turned and started back to the car, leaving the eggplant and Fiona alone. She watched him staring into the grave as the cemetery workers, shovels poised, waited for them to leave.

"Make you feel good?" Fiona whispered bitterly.

"What the hell." He shrugged, still staring into the grave.

"I suppose she deserved a good send-off. She worked hard for it." The indignation began to seep out of her. She bent down and grabbed a handful of dirt.

"Let he who is without sin cast the first stone," he said, watching her carefully.

"Self-righteous son of a bitch."

She tossed the dirt into the grave, started to walk away, then came back. "You think I'm blind. The money, the tapes. What you did to those men . . . I can't live with that. I'm getting out."

"They were all guilty," he said.

"Of what?"

"Murder."

"That's a legal definition. We had nothing. You just got even. That's all." She paused, the anger building. "A nigger's revenge."

She waited for him to react. It was the ultimate insult and she knew it. She saw the flash of anger, the knee jerk reaction, then the fight for control.

"Men like that . . ." he said calmly. "They make us all niggers."

His answer confused her. He was playing with her now, as he had played with the men. Wanting to get it over with quickly, she opened her purse and pulled out her badge in its black leather case. But before she could fling it into the grave, he wisked it out of her hand.

"She's got enough in there now," he said quietly.

"Enough?"

He smiled. "The tapes."

He tossed the leather badge case back into her purse and snapped it shut.

"Only the dead get buried," he said, throwing a handful of dirt into the grave and striding off to join the others.

The workmen dipped their shovels into the mound and began to shovel it onto the coffin. She watched them for a moment, listening to the eerie drumbeat of the falling earth, then turned and walked back to the car.

In a lifetime, Fiona supposed, it happened at least once to everyone. The sense of life seemed suspended, without forward movement. Feeling vanquished, judgment disappeared, the senses closed. The mind floated in a vacuum.

Déjà vu, she heard Cates say as he looked upward at the high arches of the Ellington Bridge, its concrete skin a burnished orange in the early morning light.

She followed him across the parkway onto the marshy grass to the edge of the creek, unable to shake the eerie emptiness inside of her. She was steadier than her last visit here, as if she had got the hang of it.

"Naturals again," Cates had muttered, ignoring her silence. "He's being a shit."

There had been another teenage girl murdered and the eggplant had been up all night. They had caught the briefest glimpse of him that morning, barely visible in the clouds of smoke that filled his office.

"Sorry," the lieutenant said, handing them the assignment. "You're the jumper squad."

The ground was especially soft from the long week of rain. This time it was Cates who slipped and Fiona who had to help him up. When they got to the body, the officers gave way to give them a better look.

"My God," Cates said, turning away.

The body of Jason Martin lay broken and sprawled obscenely on the creek's edge.

"They always do it the hard way," one of the uniformed men said. She scanned the body perfunctorily and waved to the medics peering down at them from the parkway.

Cates leaned against a tree. He looked like he was about to be sick. After the technicians bagged the body, they carried it back to the ambulance.

"I don't believe it," Cates said, when they got back into their car. He was in no condition to drive. She headed back toward the office, but seeing his condition, she stopped at Sherry's instead.

Near the counter was a newspaper vending machine, filled with copies of the *Washington Post*. She put a quarter in the slot, took out a paper and brought it to a booth. Sherry, sweaty and fat in her dirty apron, came by and poured out two cups of coffee.

" 'nother one," Sherry said, nodding to the banner headline about the new murder. "Some crazy," she sighed, moving on.

Fiona's eyes drifted to other headlines. Orson Strauss's resignation, Tate O'Haire's declining to run again, the Czech ambassador's defection.

"We seem to have made all the news today," she said wryly. His brooding look was impenetrable. "Drink your coffee."

"I don't know how I can live with this," he said, shaking his head.

"Don't," she snapped. She felt a sudden jolt as feeling came to life inside of her again.

"Don't what?" He looked at her helplessly. "I pushed him hard. I drove him to it."

"Bullshit," she shouted banging the table. A few of the other customers turned to look at them.

"I feel . . ."

"Feel?" She glared at him. "You're a cop." She pointed a finger at him. "Once you start identifying with the victim or feeling guilty about him, turn in your goddamned badge."

He was startled by her vehemence, but it had helped calm him.

"I feel like I murdered him."

She reached over and grabbed a handful of his shirt.

"You ever give me that again, I'm going to ask for a divorce. I want a partner, not a crier. He was a jumper. Case closed. A jumper. A damned fool jumper."

Cates lowered his eyes in acknowledgment and she released him. Picking up her coffee cup, she scanned the paper. There was a box in the center of the story on the new murders.

"Son of a bitch."

The curse seemed to shake him out of his brooding and he looked down at the paper, turning it to see. A drop of coffee had splattered on the box. He read the headline aloud.

"Anonymous Donor Gives Victim Fund $115,000." He looked up at her. "Is that it?" he asked, confused.

"That self-righteous bastard."

"Who?"

"The captain."

"Captain?"

She smiled. She had never called him captain before.